Wetherton

A novel by

Laurie Griffith Walker

ISBN 9780615402598

To my parents, Dave and Judy Griffith, who taught me the value of hard work and perseverance.

Acknowledgments

To my husband Jeff, who endures our creative chaos,

To my daughters, Finley and Gwenan, who inspire me with their imagination and talent.

To Beverly, who braved the task of reading and editing.

To Meegan, who formatted, styled and guided through the world of technology.

To everyone who works and volunteers at places like the New Canaan Historical Society and Colonial Williamsburg; who are dedicated to the preservation of history so that future generations will always know, question and respect the past.

Cover photo taken in the Historic Area of Colonial Williamsburg.

CHAPTER ONE

"I am not content to sit idle while fate has its way with me, but rather I will fight to make my mark upon this world." C.W.B. 1771.

Jillian Garrett tapped her brass-buckled toe impatiently on the floor. For no apparent reason, other than the fact that her computer was old enough to vote, her Internet connection was slower than usual this morning. She scratched absently at the heavy petticoat that gripped her waist. To the outsider looking in, Jillian was an odd juxtaposition of time and place. Her colonial dress contrasted sharply with the blank computer screen that stared back at her.

"Come on," she coaxed. "We talked about this yesterday. I know you can do this." An indistinguishable buzz came forth from the boxy hardware master that sat upon her desk. Jillian squinted back at it, cocking her head and trying to determine if this was a positive sign. She raised her eyebrows into the sort of encouraging gaze a new parent gives a toddler who wants to eat peas for the first time.

Bzzzzz. Creckity. Bonk. The computer groaned its herculean effort. Jillian pushed back into the Windsor chair, her face tight-lipped and filled with concentration. She straightened her 18th-century mob cap and crossed her fingers in respectful silence. Yet, nothing. Nothing at all. She leaned forward, still hopeful. Still, nothing. Silence, until finally, "Welcome. You've got mail."

"Yes!" Jillian shouted, jostling her cat, Patriot, who sat up in her lap. "Sorry, fat cat," Jillian said, smoothing her fur and dumping her onto the floor. Patriot flicked her fluffy tail at the insult and sought out greater comfort in the sunbeam by the hearth.

Certainly, it was in Jillian's long-term plan to budget for an upgrade in her computer system. In the world of Wetherton, Connecticut, however, long-term was a relative term.

It was nearly ten years since Jillian landed her job at the Wetherton Historical Foundation. Fresh from her graduation at Yale, B.A. in History hot in her hand, she had marched into town with the spirit of a yesteryear patriot. As the new Director of Marketing and Special Promotions, she instantly found herself with an almost unlimited supply of responsibilities and opportunities. She couldn't even begin to imagine how luck would have landed her such a plum role. Sure, the staff was almost entirely comprised of well-meaning volunteers with no particular expertise or training. Yes, it was true that fundraising, a skill curiously absent from the history curriculum at Yale, was her most important ally. Surprisingly, there was almost no marketing or special promotions budget available, save her meager salary that lay somewhere between starving artist and passionate zealot. And yes, the period costumes she was frequently obliged to wear did little to flatter her ego or cajole her non-existent social life.

On certain days, truthfully, there were quiet moments of despair. The kind of moments that make a girl wonder what she was thinking when she chose that history major in the first place. The thought of being an attorney in Manhattan, and making tons of money with a closet full of beautiful clothes and a state-of-the-art laptop beckoned. Perhaps a career in advertising, like her best friend Taylor, with a closet full of even better clothes, parties with celebrities, photo shoots and great looking guys. Regret and fear of the road not taken was often overwhelming.

Then again, there were the days when she would catch a glimpse of the sunlight glinting off the eighteenth-century window glass where Elizabeth Benson had etched her name using her diamond engagement ring from Thomas Miller. Or the days when a volunteer docent, rooting around in one of the many gardens, would unearth a long forgotten treasure of life 200 years earlier. In particular, there were the days when eager visitors would gather around her and she would share stories of the great patriot, Catherine Brownley, and tour the tavern and the home where she lived her married life, raised her children and drew her dying breath in 1791. Those were the days when Jillian remembered why her passion for things long past compelled her to push forward.

"Some people like new, I like old," her Grandfather had told her as he polished his 1955 Ford Thunderbird. "There's a story in things that are old. Just like me," he added with a wink. She instantly understood what he meant. While other children sought out science fiction, Jillian lingered in the biographies. While others asked for ski vacations or trips to Barbados, Jillian preferred Plymouth, Salem, Sturbridge and Williamsburg. Her most prized possession was a spinning wheel, circa 1790, purchased by her mother at a tag sale in Vermont when she was just twelve years old. It now sat by the fireplace in the living room of her 18th-century home. The lure of America's colonial history and the people who lived it was intoxicating to her. Jillian's passion was to recover, revive and preserve the stories of lives and days gone by.

Now, however, she tapped at the keyboard, excited by the global possibilities at her fingertips. She scanned the list of new messages, eyes darting left to right and back again. Delete, delete, Jillian clicked, her hand skillfully scrolling downward. A pout curled her bottom lip and she slumped back in her chair. Junk mail on the Internet, although environmentally-friendly, was particularly disappointing, and on her salary, even 20% off with free shipping held little cause for excitement. Not to mention, if she had to open one more photo of Maggie Paul's cats she thought she would scream. How nice it would have been to receive an e-mail of substance. Even a joke forwarded from a friend of a friend would have been pleasant, although she was grateful to be spared from the chain letter e-mail she would be obligated to forward to ten other friends.

Above all, she had been eager for a response from Lady Jane Rochester. It was hard to be patient in this matter. Lady Jane must be at least 85 years old, Jillian reasoned, and time was wasting to enlist her much needed help in solving the mystery of Catherine Wentworth Brownley's arrival in the colonies.

She flicked at a piece of lint on the face of her 18th-century stomacher and glanced at the watch that dangled from a long gold chain around her neck. It was nearly time to go, she thought, pushing back her chair and straightening the folds of her gown. She was never particularly sorry to leave 21st-century America, with its crime, pollution, climate change, poverty, hurried indifference and general state of decline. Life in today's world was spinning out of control most of the time. Business leaders indicted for embezzling, political leaders resigning amid sex scandals, oil spilling into the oceans and teachers running off with their teenage students. Honor, decency and character were all but extinct in the world today.

Wetherton, however, was a world apart, and only ten minutes down the road. In the Wetherton of colonial America, honor not only meant something, it meant everything. A man without honor had nothing, regardless of affluence. He was not respected. He was not admired. And his company, no matter how jovial, was not sought by the gentlemen of the day. Jillian couldn't help but admire such simple and profound standards.

"Here we go," she muttered with an unusual nervous flutter, rising to her full height and glimpsing herself in the mirror for a quick check. She took in her reflection, brown eyes and suntanned cheeks peering out from under a ruffle of white. Not bad, she reasoned, given the limits of the Foundation's ever-shrinking costume budget. She inhaled loudly, smiling back at her own face, and headed for the door.

Today would be difficult. Short-handed on volunteers and expecting a busload of school children, she would be obliged to spend most of the day corralling and coercing her charges. The expression "herding cats" leaped to mind. By day's end she would be exhausted, but that would be just the beginning. Tonight, at 6:30 sharp, the Foundation would meet to determine if the funds were available to keep their not-for-profit town afloat for another year. The historic town of Wetherton was forever on the perilous brink of going broke.

The air outside was stifling. Historically, Indian summers in New England could be brutal and today would be a monument to history. Jillian pushed through the gate in the white picket fence that surrounded her house and headed north on King Street. The swooshing petticoats twirled around her legs as she walked, and she could already feel beads of sweat rise on her neck in the morning sun. She made a mental note to check the air conditioning unit at the Robbins house and moved on in the early morning humidity.

The town of Wetherton had been lovingly restored to its pre-Revolutionary War existence some 30 years before Jillian Garrett was born. Lifelong residents, concerned historians and a healthy handful of local politicians, created the Wetherton Historical Foundation when it became clear that the town was recklessly driving down the road to ruin.

Strip malls crowded in on all sides and residents fled in droves for a better economy in Boston or New York. Many of the town's original buildings, most of them residential, trembled in such a state of disrepair they begged the wrecking ball to come in and put them out of their misery.

It was around that time that a local businessman, named Nelson Pugg, made a pitch to the town government for historical protection and restoration. Mr. Pugg was a 12th-generation Wethertonian and confessed to feeling a certain fondness for the town. Indeed, the sort of fondness that only 200 or so years might produce in a New England Yankee. He wore his best Sunday suit and hat, although it was a Tuesday, and made his arguments to the most influential men of the day. He cited the success that John D. Rockefeller had achieved in Williamsburg and challenged the local government to wonder if a few good Yankees couldn't do what it had taken hundreds of southerners to achieve.

In mere moments, the room was enrapt with the notion. Surely Wetherton, with its significant connections to colonial trade between Boston and New York should be saved for the benefit of posterity. It wasn't every town, after all, that could claim shoe-making and onion farming as its ancestral heritage. The die was unanimously cast, and tiny Wetherton, Connecticut, began to seek its' rightful place in preservation history.

Jillian turned right onto Parish Street and glimpsed the peak of Mable's Hill in the distance, the execution site for eleven sad souls of Wetherton who lost their lives to the fervor of witchcraft trials in 1665. She passed through the gate in front of the Becker house, recreated from a lone surviving daguerreotype circa 1855. Elizabeth Becker was a stunning young widow who had traveled from New York to settle in the cooler New England climate. It was not long at all before she began carrying on a passionate affair with the town's very handsome, and very married cobbler, Henry Thurston. Details were hearsay, but most believe Henry's wife secretly called upon Elizabeth one night, beat her senseless then burned down the house around her. The scandal was fierce, but the cobbler defended his wife with unfailing loyalty. If it was murder, sadly, it would not be the first or last to go unpunished.

Smith Lane, the first street Jillian reached within the official historic district, was named after Captain Josiah Smith, a blockade runner during the Revolution. His house was built in 1766 and featured many architectural features distinctive to the Connecticut River Valley. Josiah had only two toes on his left foot, the result of a cannon misfire in the midst of a dangerous engagement with the British fleet. Centuries-old legend dictated that Captain Smith kept his three unattached digits in a box near his bed, although no proof of the claim had ever been discovered.

From Smith Lane, Jillian turned right and waved a cheerful hello to the gentleman at 75 Park Street who offered only a grumpy head nod in return. He was immersed, as always, in the seemingly unending business of clipping his lawn to manicured perfection. It was not the heat that annoyed him, but rather the grass itself which always grew too fast or too thin to suit his needs. He pestered away at it day and night. Yet, come November, he would pack his lawn tools neatly into his shed and emerge with an army of snow shovels. Thus, he would spend the winter months, cursing each flake in pursuit of snow removal perfection for both his driveway and front walk. In spring, the lawn tools would reappear and the business of grass growing would start all over.

She dabbed at the back of her neck with a cloth. "Good Lord it's going to be hot today," she thought, silently reflecting on the merits of a commute within the confines of an air-conditioned automobile.

An abundance of ghost stories were available to the interested listener in Wetherton. The most frightening of all, would be the legend of Noah Hubbard.

Noah Hubbard was a hardworking tanner and saddler, a well-known and well-liked resident of Wetherton. He was also a brilliant horseman, which was why his accident was so shocking to the local folks. While fitting a saddle to Richard Abbott's horse he was violently kicked, twice in the head. All form of medical aid available at the time was administered, but, in truth, no one expected Noah to live through morning.

Incredibly, within just a few weeks, Noah appeared remarkably recovered. Surely it was a miracle at hand. His friends rejoiced and marveled at the apparent blessing from God. It wasn't long, however, before everyone noticed a marked change in Noah's personality. He would sometimes strap dead sparrows to his belt, a bizarre practice even for 18th-century America, and was often seen wandering the streets of Wetherton late at night speaking to himself in unintelligible gibberish. It was late fall in 1798 when the fire started. Jonathon Cooke was the first to reach Noah's house, already nearly engulfed in flame.

Later that day, Noah's body was pulled from the cinders and rubble, his blackened gaze still fixed in a horrifying stare.

The townspeople buried him on graveyard hill, once again thankful to God for sparing him the further pain of his obvious insanity. It was not long, however, before Noah began reappearing in the oddest of places. Once, he was seen in the tavern, as if in a brief attempt to rejoin his long lost friends. In another instance, he was spotted in the onion fields surrounding the town, simply sitting among the onions, staring off into the distance toward the

Connecticut River. At each sighting, the same horrible gaze crossed his face, making him a shocking and unwelcome apparition.

He was last seen in 1954, by a restoration worker who found himself alone late at night near the spot where old Noah's house once stood. The workman had just finished some carpentry and was in the midst of packing his tools when a noise from behind gave him a start. He whirled around to stare into the fixed gaze of Noah Hubbard, the stench of burning flesh infiltrating his nostrils. The workman never again returned to Wetherton.

Jillian shivered a bit, even in the oppressive heat, at the thought of Noah Hubbard. He was one ghost she would not like to see, although she doubted that even old Noah could keep her from returning to Wetherton.

Now it was a right turn onto Robbins Street and quick glance at the hazy, early morning sky and searing New England sun. Robbins Street was home to The Erastus Robbins House, where the man himself and his thirteen children once lived. Not at all surprisingly, it was behind the Robbins house that Jillian found the Wetherton Historical Foundation handyman, and her very good friend, Duke Parker. Duke was tinkering with the sensitive HVAC system, whacking it with a wrench every minute or so to keep everything awake and functioning. In a sleepy little town like Wetherton, a ubiquitous wallop now and then was requisite.

"Hello," Duke called to her, a smile of sunshine beaming from his face. He was, without exception, one of the craziest people Jillian had ever met.

He was born Duke Parker, in 1946. His father, an army veteran from WWII, had declared that his son should be named for greatness and pinned every hope for the future on his tiny newborn.

"Can you imagine how disappointed they were?" Duke once said to Jillian in his usual, ironic way. "Here they were, expecting "The Duke" and they ended up with me." His meaning was clear. Duke was the original hippie. He was educated at Berkeley. He was a conscientious-objector to the war in Viet Nam. He fought for Title IX and women's rights. If there was a cause, there was Duke, in newspapers, magazines and on television. He was larger than life, and then, he was gone. His fifteen minutes of fame ebbed away and he was replaced by a younger generation of ideas and idealists. Who needed hippies when there was disco? Who needed disco when there was Wall Street?

He and his wife, Dahlia, found a place in the tiny town of Wetherton and made it home. Dahlia, a former-attorney-turned artist, earned a living painting charming New England scenes on anything that a tourist might buy. In wintertime, there were little wooden sleds painted with winter-white scenes of a Connecticut Christmas. In the summertime, there were little glass jars and bottles with ships and onions and flowers.

They embraced the people and the history and Duke found a new passion, historic preservation. It wasn't sexy, but someone had to save all those moments in history when one step in the opposite direction could have sent fate careening down an entirely different road. There was no 10-gallon hat or proud stallion for Duke, only crazy, fly-away, wispy curls tucked under a bandana headband and a mo-ped parked in the employee lot. He turned himself into an indispensable, one-man, historic institution, fixing clogged sinks and broken wagon wheels. No one in Wetherton dared to do anything without first consulting Duke. Except for Jillian.

"How is it?" Jillian called in the direction of the ornery AC, crossing her fingers behind her back. Duke reached over to his radio and turned down the volume on his classic rock station.

"Well, you know how it is with Hevy," Duke said, his pet name for the HVAC system. Jillian's heart sank.

"Honestly," Jillian said with a tight smile, "I don't think anyone really knows how it is with Hevy. All we ask is that he'll make it through the day." Jillian raised her eyebrows in a show of optimism. "I have a bus-load of summer-campers coming this morning," she added imploringly, trying not to break her smile. Duke winked and nodded in his usual placid way, as if she just asked if he'd like a cappuccino. Jillian stared at him with controlled alarm.

"You can never be completely sure of what will happen," he said, smiling in a crazy, maniacal way, "but I think all will be well today." He reached for his half-eaten, glazed cruller and munched a giant, gooey bite. Jillian crossed her arms in front of her chest and exhaled loudly.

"Those things will kill you, you know," she offered, silently wishing for a glazed cruller of her own. "I thought hippies were supposed to eat alfalfa sprouts and kale."

"Hah!" Duke retorted, smiling even brighter. "What do you know about hippies?" He licked the sugary glaze from his fingers, in a mocking display of defiance. She had to admit, he was right. Hippie was some weird concept she had grown up with that meant people with long hair and peace-sign necklaces from the sixties. Could anyone be a hippie with the right outfit? Jillian wondered. Duke swallowed the last of the donut and turned to face her, adjusting his bandana headband and wiping the sugar from his face.

"Had any word from the Lady?" Duke inquired, eyeing Jillian for a reaction.

"No," Jillian sighed, fumbling with the gold watch chain around her neck. "Have you heard anything from the Board?" Duke shook his head. "I suppose I'll be looking for a new job tomorrow," she added. Duke smiled. He leaned his head to the left, assessing her mood.

He had liked Jillian from the moment they met. She had a fiery, almost crazy, passion that reminded him of himself in younger days. It had been a long time since he met anyone so dedicated to a cause that most people didn't give a rat's ass about. A person willing to walk through fire to save a spinning wheel or a musket ball embedded in an 18th-century corner post. He called her Diabolita.

"Lady Jane is probably too busy having tea with the Queen," he offered at last, pushing himself up off of the ground and stretching his back into a reverse warrior yoga pose. "It ain't easy being Lady Jane," he said, stretching right, then left, then straight down to the floor. Jillian rolled her eyes.

"It ain't easy being anybody," she said. "Especially a hippie on junk food."

"With a serious Hevy problem," Duke fired back with a wink. Jillian couldn't help but laugh.

"No pun intended I'm sure," she offered, kicking the crumpled bakery bag at his feet.

"And the Board," Duke went on, "will find a way to cover our puny paychecks for at least another year. They always do." Jillian shook her head and frowned.

"Not this year," she shrugged. "People can't pay for gas to drive to work, they certainly can't afford to support this place." Duke nodded agreement.

"I know," he said, "but you'll see. Bit by bit it'll happen." Jillian rolled her eyes. Why did it always have to be bit by bit? Why did it always have to be so difficult? Visitors loved coming to Wetherton. Schools loved bringing their classes here. Grandmas and Grandpas poured off buses to learn about their colonial heritage. It just wasn't fair that it was so hard to find money all the time.

"Bit by bit sucks," she said with annoyance. "How come it's never big and bigger?" Duke shrugged.

"Because bit by bit is the way we change the world." Jillian rolled her eyes.

"Whatever, Mr. Hippie." Jillian answered. "One way or the other we'll find out soon enough. See you tonight. I'm off to the tavern," she added with a swish of her weighty petticoats. "Have a lovely day." Heading back down the narrow street, she turned to look at Duke who offered her a two-fingered peace sign in return.

Mercifully, it was only two quick turns to the right to reach the tavern. The air conditioning unit there was brand new, thanks to last summer's Christmas in July fundraiser, and could be relied upon without fail due to a five-year warranty. Jillian glanced up at the wooden sign that hung suspended from reproduction ironwork over the front door. Brownley Tavern, built in 1764. She quickly scanned the building, almost completely original, and soaked in the familiar details. It was one of the most beautiful and comforting places she had ever known.

The clapboards were painted crisp white, a clean and welcoming treat for the eyes that cut through the heavy, damp air all around. The paneled shutters were black, as was the front door that had for centuries opened gladly to the weary, the curious, the rebellious and those simply hungry for a good meal and some lively company. Jillian smiled to herself, wishing she could know even one-tenth of everything that building harbored within its walls. Worn floorboards called out the footsteps of revolutionaries and abolitionists. The ceilings whispered secrets of ages-old conversations, plots and plans.

Jillian wasn't the only Wethertonian absorbed by the power of Brownley Tavern. One volunteer interpreter, Nathaniel Davids, was so captured by his desire to recreate the character of John Brownley he insisted upon bleaching his brown hair into grey in keeping with the only known portrait of the proprietor that now hung in the main dining room. Even Jillian felt such commitment to preservation and restoration to be a decidedly unnecessary concession to the cause.

She drew her chain of keys from one of the pockets her costume provided and clicked the front door open. Inside it was dark, quiet and still. A rush of welcoming cool air brushed her face as she closed the door behind her and locked it tight. One could never be too careful, she had found, as visitors were willing to try almost any door at any time, even those clearly marked "No Admittance". This was well etched upon her mind from an extremely embarrassing incident some years past in the ladies washroom. She pulled the mob cap from her head and soaked in the relief that 20th-century technology now provided.

The morning sun filtered in from the east, casting hazy beams of light across the dining tables and chairs in the Game Room. Gambling had once been a popular pastime in this place, although no longer, and one could only imagine the many poor souls who had left considerably poorer for the sake of the Game Room and its many distractions.

Ale was the most popular drink of the day, although rum drinks ran a close second. The famous Brownley punch was still served even today, strong with rum and a bit of spice and ginger ale, for the hale and hearty. On holidays, and special occasions, an enormous punch bowl would be set up with a special blend of fruit juices, mostly cranberry and apple thanks to the New England bounty, which could be relied upon to send guests on their way with the smile of over 200 years of festivity on their faces.

Jillian tossed her cap and keys on the table and glanced up into the gaze of Catherine Brownley staring down from her place of high-honor above the mantle. The oil-on-canvas portrait was a posthumous likeness, painted in 1791, the year of her death. As with many such paintings, it was assumed that her incredible beauty was more a product of grieving adoration than entirely natural gifts. Nevertheless, it had never been argued, in any documentation ever found, that Catherine had been anything other than a remarkable and captivating woman.

The large, round, soulful blue eyes now surveyed her surroundings in a fixed and placid staree. Her porcelain skin was flawless and charmingly pink on her high cheekbones. The wavy, honey brown hair was swept up, away from her face with tendrils of carefully placed curls falling perfectly on her shoulders. The blue ribbon rosettes shimmered on her green silk gown.

Blue and green had always been Catherine's favorite colors. She once wrote that they were the first colors emblazoned in her mind as she approached her new life in this new world. The bright blue of the sky and the vivid greens of the New England tree line would have been a welcome sight for anyone who had sailed the seas for a month or more.

She arrived in the spring of 1771 as Catherine Wentworth of County Kent. Her marriage had been arranged by her family. At least that was the commonly held belief. In truth, no one knew exactly how it was that Catherine had made her way from the prestigious realm of Broadhurst Hall to the tiny colonial town of Wetherton, Connecticut. It was a mystery to historians on both sides of the Atlantic. So many details were unknown, but it was certain that Catherine arrived on the ship, Windsor Rose, in April of that year. It was also certain that she was married just days later to John Brownley, born in Hartford, Connecticut, 1743, and eight years Catherine's senior.

Their first child, a boy they named Jacob, arrived in 1773. Sadly, the child would not survive to see his first birthday. In her diary, Catherine wrote "A mother must be prepared to lose some of her children, but I simply cannot bear to lose all of my children. I pray God will send me ten more so that I may find peace for the terrible emptiness in my heart."

Less than one year later, in the spring of 1774, God sent a tiny infant daughter named Grace Jane. In the ten years following, Catherine safely delivered eight more children, losing only one to fever in the turmoil of 1777. The large and raucous family fit themselves into the tight upstairs quarters of the tavern, while running a thriving business downstairs. John and Catherine became well known in the region for their fine food, ale and exceptional warmth and generosity.

It was 1791 when Catherine went to bed complaining of a horrible headache. Historians surmise it must have been a stroke or aneurism to take a woman, not in child-bed, at the tender age of 40. In truth, most women, having survived their child-bearing years, lived well on into later life. Poor Catherine would be an exception. Although born in England, her heart would be forever given to America and the cause of freedom she so passionately served.

Very recently, the Wetherton Historical Foundation had taken the remarkable step of earmarking a small fund for further research into the life of their local heroine. It was one of Wetherton's most intriguing centuries-old mysteries. Why had Catherine Wentworth, a beautiful young woman from a wealthy and formidable English family, travelled to the colonies to marry John Brownley? Jillian instantly raised the question that there was little or no information available on Catherine's life prior to her arrival in the colonies, and didn't it make sense to explore her childhood in England? Her question was met with a room full of puzzled stares.

"How is England going to help the summer tourist season in Connecticut?" one board member had asked.

"I don't know too much about that, but I do know that people really like that Catherine Brownley rum punch. Maybe we should be thinking about a cookbook," added another. "We could sell it on the Internet." Jillian bit the insides of her cheeks to keep herself from screaming. She was a detective, a guardian of history, a seeker of truths, in the midst of cookbook peddlers and retired accountants.

"Let's think about this logically," she had started, "Catherine Wentworth Brownley is the centerpiece of our Revolutionary War history in this town. No single person has a greater claim to the acts of patriotism that Wetherton is famous for. And, let's not forget, she's a woman. Very unusual!" From there Jillian launched into a ludicrous speech on the merits of childhood history and cookbook sales, on tourism trends to England and more, until she finally brought it all home with some wild statistics on cranberry juice consumption in Europe and the Pacific Rim.

"I say, let's just do it," said Maggie Paul breathlessly, a seventh-generation Wethertonian and fanatical volunteer docent, joined by a chorus of enthusiastic approval throughout the room. This was an unprecedented victory and Jillian seized the moment to run from the room to begin her research.

The Internet, one of the modern world's most remarkable tools, made easy work of the genealogical research needed to uncover one of Catherine Brownley's only living relatives in Great Britain. A few telephone calls to England had heeded little effect, until a sympathetic servant had suggested that Jillian might try an e-mail message. Her mistress, she explained, had only recently installed Internet access at the house and was very excited to try it out for the first time. Jillian thanked the woman profusely and rifled off a brief yet thoughtful and well-composed message to Lady Jane Rochester dot com.

CHAPTER TWO

"Sadly, I feel it is true that we must all share in life's overwhelming burdens."
C.W. B. 1772

Lady Jane Rochester slipped on her favorite old pair of Wellingtons and headed out on her daily walk. It seemed to take a good deal longer to make the journey than it used to, but she hardly cared about time anymore. It was the walk itself that was important. Dudley, her eight-year-old yellow Labrador trotted faithfully beside her today and every day. Only the very worst of English weather could keep the pair inside.

Lady Jane had been willful and wild from the day she was born 86 years earlier. At that time, it was her father, Richard Wentworth, who kept things running smoothly at Broadhurst Hall. That responsibility, however, had long ago fallen to his eldest daughter, Jane.

Construction on the original building began in 1532 and was completed sometime around 1536. Roger Wentworth, a wealthy aristocrat and somewhat eccentric artist, drew the plans himself and commissioned a team of highly skilled builders to turn his dream to reality. The exceptional Tudor dwelling boasted stately rooms and some of the finest and most elaborate woodcarvings of its time.

Many years after Roger's death, it was his great-grandson, Edgar, who inherited the estate and the wherewithal to tackle a massive expansion project sometime in the mid to late 1600s, making Broadhurst Hall one of the largest privately owned homes in all of England.

Never had there been a time when Broadhurst had fallen from Wentworth hands, a remarkable achievement to be sure. Growing up on the immense estate in the heart of Kent had been privileged and idyllic, but Lady Jane Alexandra Wentworth Rochester never pondered her pedigree when she was young. It was not until she reached her more considerable years that she truly appreciated the responsibility that one carries with such a legacy, and the enormous burden that responsibility may at times bring.

She was born in the blue room, reputedly the room where dozens of Wentworths had arrived on this earth throughout the centuries. Ironically, her mother, Amelia, was determined not to give birth in the house, despite her mother-in-law's stern objections. Arrangements had been made to transport Amelia to hospital on a moment's notice. Moments, however, would be all the warning anyone had to prepare for the arrival of the newest Wentworth. Much to the surprise of everyone, and the pleasure of her mother-in-law, Iris, Amelia found herself being dragged to the blue room without a moment to spare.

Jane Wentworth arrived on a chilly November morning in 1920. Amelia Wentworth could not have been more pleased. Richard Wentworth, the proud father, spent the afternoon celebrating at the local pub, The White Horse. Iris Wentworth, the grandmother, silently wished for grandsons.

To put it plainly, Jane grew up spoiled. Her father doted on her every whim, while her mother made every effort to raise a respectable young lady. In three years time, her little sister Phillipa was born, also in the blue room, because even Amelia could find no harm in testing her luck for the second time. Once again, Iris, who was now getting to be quite an old woman, silently longed for grandsons.

There had always been men in the Wentworth family; old men, young men, little men or incredibly fat men, the size or age of them hardly mattered. From the time of Roger Wentworth, there had never been a generation that had failed to produce a male Wentworth heir. Yes, there had been many charming and influential Wentworth women throughout the centuries, but they had always stood dutifully behind the Wentworth men who came before them, even if they were born after them. Never, not in several centuries, had the Wentworth family faced such decidedly uncharted territory.

As fate would have it, Richard and Amelia would have no more children, leaving Jane and Phillipa to stand as the only two heirs to the vast and formidable Wentworth estate. To see Jane, scraped-kneed and bloody-elbowed begging for a tart, next to her infant sister, sucking on her ring and pinky fingers simultaneously, the great Roger Wentworth must have rolled over in his grave. Could it be that all these centuries of breeding and power had come down to these two? It was almost unthinkable. Yet, Richard and Amelia could not have been more pleased with their beautiful little women, and time would surely tell the tale of their Wentworthiness.

As a young girl, Jane was at ease in the country, never tiring of the diversions such a vast estate could offer. Her parents hired the very best tutors to expose their daughters to a remarkably rich and diverse curriculum.

Jane was something of a mathematical success, if she could be made to sit still long enough to finish her work. Languages were another gift, and she became fluent in both French and Italian at a surprisingly early age. Little "Pippa", on the other hand, showed a remarkable gift for painting, and a love of history, religion and Greek mythology. Despite their differences, the two sisters were extremely loving and close. Jane was the older, wiser and craftier of the two, Phillipa was the quieter, shyer, more earnest and fretful sister.

No matter the subject, it was the confinement of the indoors that drove Jane mad, and she often slipped away in the early morning, much to her parents' consternation, and was not seen again until teatime. Having missed a day's lessons and developing a handful of minor bodily injuries as well, it was not surprising that Jane often found herself eating cold turnips and bread for dinner alone in her room. She would smile wistfully and eat the entire plate. It had long been noted that Jane's character was strong and unwavering, and she would always accept the consequences of her own actions.

There were stories aplenty of Wentworth ladies throughout the ages who were kindred spirits to Jane. There had been Anna Marian Wentworth, born 1699, who was the first girl to jump the garden wall on her pony, Gladiator. She later went on to marry the Earl of Sussex. Who could forget the irrepressible Miss Judith Anne Wentworth, born 1748, to Howard and Anne Wentworth. She was the sixth of seven children, but the only surviving girl, and the absolute apple of her father's eye. Her father was a man of notorious tyrannical displays, yet there was almost nothing Miss Judith could do that would ever inspire his wrath including an affinity for sword fighting.

In the west sitting room, a cozy nook of painted oak panel and lazy summertime sun, there is a commanding portrait of Judith. The same brown curls, piercing blue eyes and square Wentworth jaw that Jane also possessed. She died from smallpox, just weeks before her sixteenth birthday and was buried in the chapel floor next to her paternal grandmother. Howard Wentworth fell into a state of despair beyond measure. So great was his pain, it was said he died of a broken heart just weeks later, leaving Broadhurst Hall to his eldest son, John. His widow, Anne, lived another thirty-two years and died at the remarkable age of 92. Jane couldn't help but nod her respect every time she passed Anne's portrait in the inner hall.

Childhood at Broadhurst passed by slowly for Jane. While the distractions were abundant, the playmates were almost non-existent, and she would spend hours upon hours at play with only imaginary friends to be pirates or buccaneers or wild animals of the African plains.

Phillipa, a far more delicate child who suffered from allergies and asthma, was rarely seen outdoors. Instead she preferred to play dress-up and tea party with her favorite dolls in the comfort of her warm, cozy nursery. She didn't like to get dirty, she didn't like to be damp and she most certainly did not like to play games like explorers or pirates or wild animals of the African plains.

"What's wrong with her?" Jane had whined to her Mother on numerous occasions.

"Whatever do you mean?" her Mother had replied. "We are not all meant to traipse about in the damp and smell of grass and sheep, young lady." Jane hated it when her Mother called her "young lady". It had the distinct ring of an insult.

"Well, she never comes out to play," Jane retorted. "All children like to play. Even the prissy, boring ones," she added with a mutter. Hot tears began to fill her eyes, but Jane willed them back with a fierce determination. There was nothing she detested more than being a cry-baby. Well, perhaps long Sunday sermons were the worst, but cry-baby was a close second. It wasn't that anyone had ever admonished her for crying. In fact, it was quite the contrary. People instantly softened at the sight of her tears. They would do almost anything to stop her crying, and Jane hated that. She hated to be pandered to and coddled. She hated to appear weak or at the disadvantage. Her pride was incredibly stubborn.

Even now, Jane thought to herself absently as she huffed and puffed across a field that she had long ago traversed in mere seconds. Perhaps it was that stubbornness that was the secret to her remarkable 86 years of good health and well-being. She could hardly remember a time when she had been ill. Pippa, on the other hand, had suffered a new ailment almost monthly and it had been a trial to keep her well and her spirits high throughout her youth. Jane missed her. God help her, she missed her more than she could ever have imagined. They were as different as night and day, yet two sisters nonetheless. They were the young Wentworth ladies. Jane smiled at the gray sky above her and blew a kiss from her withered fingertips to the winds of the heavens.

She moved on, with the fortitude of a bloodhound. Although the ground beneath her feet was soft with the mud of a heavy, overnight rain, Jane trudged on in her determined style. She should check the fence on the northern edge of the paddock, she reminded herself, tapping the side of her head for emphasis. The smell of the mud and the dampness of the morning brought back the memory of Phillipa's 16th birthday. It was remarkable, she thought, how the sense of smell should be such an acute catalyst to the brain.

She could see that day as if it were yesterday, literally yesterday, and she smiled the half-smile she had long been famous for. Lady Jane never smiled a broad toothy grin as many would do. She had always, from the time she had been very young, pursed her lips into a left-sided twist of amusement. It was Phillipa who possessed the gracious, lovely white-toothed smile of perfection. She could see it now, just now, as it had always been.

In the spring of 1939, England had yet to grasp the true horror that Hitler and his army would flaunt at the world. It was not until September that Great Britain would enter the war. Presently unaware of the road that fate would take, the promise of spring held peace, and the celebration of Phillipa's 16th birthday was the most important matter of the day at Broadhurst Hall. It had long been a tradition in the Wentworth family to celebrate the 16th birthday of their female members with a party of unrivalled extravagance.

It was generally considered to be the single occasion when Wentworth women were allowed to outshine their male counterparts. Some believed the tradition had begun with Helen Wentworth in the early 1700's when her father married her off to Lord Webster, a man nearly three times her age, on her 16th birthday. The guests were treated to an entire week of festivities and a marvelously good time was reportedly had by all, save one. Helen Wentworth Webster spent the week crying in her bed chamber and, upon being whisked away from her childhood home by her new husband, vowed never to speak to her father again.

Presently, Phillipa's birthday celebration promised to be a far happier occasion for all parties concerned. No detail was too small to be ignored and no sister was too old or important to be relieved from the obligation of party planning. Jane, for her part, detested large parties. A festival of strangers she had declared when her own 16th birthday had drawn near. Phillipa, too frail to be much help, but excited and radiant at the prospect of her own celebration, implored Jane to assist in the affair, "because no one could ever know my true heart more than my own dear sister." Jane sighed in resignation and availed herself to every task, menial and mundane though they seemed, to ensure a perfect day for her only sibling.

If only God, or Mother Nature, had been committed to the task, then the day might well have been perfect. Ah, but the rain. The torrential, incessant downpour of rain that began thirty-six hours prior to the party and lasted a good twenty-four hours beyond. It was, quite possibly, the wettest week in the history of England. Plans for the outdoor garden party were scrapped and the event was hurriedly relocated inside the house, it's massive rooms enveloping the hundreds of guests without the slightest hint of trouble.

Jane combed Phillipa's hair as she sniffled and pouted at her stunning reflection in her dressing table mirror. Nearly an exact copy of their own dear mother, Pippa possessed the porcelain skin, silky blonde hair, doe eyes and swan-like neck of perfection. Jane, on the other hand, favored her father with a head full of soft crazy brown waves, a squared-jaw of determination and light blue eyes that seemed to take in everything in quiet concentration.

"Oh stop your sniveling, Pips," Jane said in exasperation. Phillipa sniffed again and dabbed at her eyes with a white linen handkerchief. Her dress, a hand-stitched design of the palest blue silk shantung, sat perfectly around her shoulders to silhouette her long neck and high cheekbones.

"I just wanted everything to be perfect," Phillipa offered. Jane rolled her eyes. How could two sisters be so completely different?

"Perfect?" Jane answered, pinning a curl behind Phillipa's left ear. "What on earth does that mean? Nothing is ever perfect, Pippa. Everything is what it is, and you find the good in it and move on." Phillipa stared at her sister blankly. Jane leaned forward to whisper closer to her sister's ear. "If you build your hopes high and so completely upon one thing, you're likely to be disappointed. Your dress is lovely, you are lovely, the house is full of guests waiting to see you, including some very handsome young men, and if you don't hurry downstairs I shall be forced to dance with all of them myself." Phillipa giggled.

"Thank you Jane," she sniffed. "You always know just what to say."

Pippa descended the great staircase to the inner hall like a pale blue angel floating on a cloud. Jane followed just behind. A quartet played Bach, while the guests toasted and cheered the guest of honor.

"Oh Jane," Phillipa said turning to her with a stunning smile as she reached the last step, "isn't it just perfect?"

"Of course it is," Jane answered, watching her sister disappear into the sea of well-wishers. Every eye in the room seemed to be on Phillipa, who showed all the grace and warmth of her Mother. She mingled with a natural ease that was remarked upon often. Phillipa, they would say, was much more of a Stamford, her mother's family name. Jane, they would add, was much more of a Wentworth.

It was difficult to be certain which girl was being praised more highly, but Jane had long suspected it was Phillipa who was the chosen one. The Wentworth's had been a shrewd, wealthy, hard-dealing clan for all these centuries and Jane knew all too well those were not the qualities young ladies should profess. There was, however, nothing to be done about it, for she was a woman and she was a Wentworth and that was an end to that.

Jane mingled amid the swarm, deliberately steering herself toward the library where she knew she could find Uncle Clive by the punchbowl. She scarcely knew any of the guests and navigated the crowd almost undetected by anyone. All except one. He stood in the corner of the entrance hall, pretending to enjoy the noise and frivolity all around him. Lord Arthur Rochester was a giant of a man with a fabulous head of wavy blonde hair. He was shy and reserved and walked with a cane and pronounced limp due to a riding accident in his youth. He was nearly 15 years older than Jane, but that didn't stop him from setting his gaze upon her the moment she entered the room.

"Uncle Clive," Jane said beaming, finding him as predicted with a glass of punch sloshing in his hand.

"Darling girl," he answered under his enormous white mustache. "Tell your old uncle all the news, and don't leave anything out." Jane helped herself to a glass of punch and joined him near the window where the rain pelted down in buckets.

"The news? Yes, well let's see. Apparently there's this fellow named Hitler causing quite a bit of trouble. Have you heard of him?" Jane asked mockingly. Her Uncle frowned and dipped in for more punch.

"Yes, well, I had been hoping for some happier news. Tell us princess, what news of you that will make me smile?" Jane sighed.

"What news indeed?" Jane scowled. "I'm afraid my life is sinfully dull."

"No such thing. An oxymoron if ever there was one." Uncle Clive gestured around the room, sloshing his punch on the carpet and his trousers. "Look around you, darling princess, at the handsome young men everywhere. You should be finding yourself a nice romance. It's almost summertime after all," he added with a wink. Jane scoffed.

"Good God, Uncle, you're even worse than I remember."

"Ah," Uncle Clive said, interrupting, "come, young Arthur, and meet my niece." Having summoned the courage to follow her, Lord Rochester had made his way to the library under the guise of requiring some punch. Jane turned to see him walking toward her, his massive hand holding tight to the cane that aided his every step.

"Lord Arthur Rochester, may I present my niece, Jane Wentworth," Uncle Clive said, sloshing his punch on Arthur's shoes, although neither Arthur nor Jane, nor Clive for that matter, seemed to notice.

"Miss Wentworth," Arthur offered.

"How do you do," Jane replied, smiling her twisted left-side smile.

"My goodness," Jane now whispered to herself at the flood of memories that often filled her head. She could remember it all in such clear detail. It was almost as if she could reach out and touch all those long ago moments and all those remarkable people she had loved so dearly.

She placed two fingers against her tongue and whistled for Dudley, scanning the horizon of pristine English countryside that spread before and all around her. The happy yellow dog appeared suddenly from the small stand of oak trees that sprouted from the vast expanse of open fields that ran in every direction. It had been in those trees where Jane spent much of her childhood pretend playing at swords, or Robin Hood or Camelot. Her mother was forever scolding her over scraped knees and muddy clothes, but Jane could not be kept still for long. She remembered days when she would take sticks and branches and build lean-to forts and hide in them all day long, emerging only for food and drink and then back to the fort again.

On one occasion, she tumbled off a rock and landed in a little stream that sometimes sprang up after a heavy rain. Fretting over the mess she had made of her clothes, she almost hadn't noticed the faint gold shimmer in the water next to her. Her father had explained that the small gold band set with six green stones might be very valuable if she would like to sell it, but Jane wouldn't think of parting with such a treasure.

"Such a foolish, stubborn girl," Jane now chuckled to herself, glancing down at the tiny ring she still wore on the littlest finger of her left hand. She noticed the spots of age, the wrinkled pale skin and the protruding blue veins. "Good God," she muttered. "I have gotten to be quite an old thing, haven't I?" She smiled wistfully. It was a long time now since she stopped wondering why it was that everyone she loved had been taken from her, and yet she lived on and on through the years. Clearly, God would take her only when he had a mind to.

"Although, He may have forgotten about me," she mused aloud, glancing to the cloudy sky and hesitatingly offering up a wave of recognition. Lady Jane paused, for the longest moment, gazing to the heavens for a sign of acknowledgement. She clicked her breath to the left and shook her head in bewilderment. She was now a good deal older than almost anyone she knew, or had ever known. How much longer could she expect to go on? How many more mornings of sunshine or overcast skies should she imagine? Who could possibly answer the question?

She turned, with Dudley, and headed home to Broadhurst Hall. Her nephew, James, the only grandson of her sister Phillipa, would be waiting for her in the breakfast room.

"Heaven help us," Jane whispered at the thought of him as she trudged silently through the fields toward the great house in the distance. It wasn't that she disliked James. In truth, she found him to be very good company, especially on cold winter evenings when the days and nights would edge in on one another. She would even concede that she loved him, although she would never admit to it openly. He was tall and thin like his father, but possessed the square Wentworth jaw and the ancestral determination to do things well and properly.

It was just that he was so overwhelmingly boring, as a man anyway, and she worried for his future happiness. After all, she wondered, what woman in her right mind would be willing to spend a lifetime with a bow-tie wearing, train-spotting, bookworm like James? She couldn't even remember the last time she had heard him speak of any social life at all, save his two equally pathetic chums from Cambridge going to the pub after work. For Jane, a woman who took great pride in her uncanny ability to assess the true nature of everyone, James presented an unsettling puzzle.

She had reasoned that James might be gay. Which, of course, she told herself was perfectly within his right. Yet his uncommonly bad taste in clothing, interior design and food left her convinced he was decidedly heterosexual. Had there been any other male heirs to the Wentworth estate, Jane might not have given the matter much thought. James, however, was the only man for the job. Sooner than later, it would fall to James to carry on the legacy of Broadhurst Hall. As it was, the young man could barely carry his groceries without bungling the job.

Still, on this day James had promised to educate her in the new world of Internet access. He had warned her to stay off her "system" until he could arrive this weekend, because of all the "malicious intent that was rife on the Internet".

"The Internet," he had explained to her by telephone, "would be just as if you were speaking with total strangers in Picadilly Circus, or worse." Jane paused for a moment of reflection. She was 86 years old after all, what harm could it do to converse with the devil himself for a moment or two?

She had to admit, however, that she was unusually and completely beyond her realm of experience in this Internet world. Eighty-six long years of living and never once had she even touched a "mouse" or "clicked" anything. Still, she believed in keeping one's mind open to new ideas. She decided to allow caution to take the better of her in this world of computers and looked forward to her first real lesson with her nephew this very morning.

She could see him waving to her from the distance, his peculiar choice of salmon-pink bow tie gleaming like a beacon. Jane waved her approach and continued on, shaking her head in bewilderment and muttering something about being gay after all.

"Hello, Aunt Jane," James said smiling. "We're all set to go." He guided her officiously toward the paneled library across from the inner hall. "Are you excited?"

"Heavens yes," she replied flatly. "I can scarcely control myself." Ignoring her patented brand of sarcasm that he privately referred to as "Janiness", he pressed on.

"I think you'll be excited when you see that you've received two e-mails."

"Two?" answered Jane. "And I thought all my acquaintances were dead." James smirked.

"Hardly," he said quickly. "Now have a seat here, and I'll show you how this is done." He held the chair for her, and gently pushed her forward. He showed her the keyboard, the mouse, and answered her every question with the patience of a saint. It must be said that James truly was a pleasant, charming man, if only he weren't so damned boring.

"Here we are with your message," he said proudly. Lady Jane frowned at the screen for a moment, tipping her head backward to peer through the reading glasses down low on her nose. "This first message is from me." James pointed to the screen with an enormous smile. "Shall we open it so you can read what I've sent you?"

"Just a moment now," Jane interrupted. "What is this other one here?" she asked, pointing to the screen as well.

"This is from a J. Garrett at the Wetherton Historical Foundation. I must caution you most strenuously to never open an e-mail from anyone you do not know." James raised his eyebrows and nodded the importance of this instruction to her. Jane reached for the mouse and moved her cursor to "read".

"Do you know this person, Aunt Jane?" he asked.

"Certainly not," Jane replied as she clicked. "She's an American whose been ringing here for me. I was told she would be sending a message through, let's she what she has to say." James rolled his eyes in disbelief.

"This is exactly what I'm talking about," James ranted. "This person is a total stranger. She could be completely mad. She could be sending you a virus."

"A virus, good God, whatever shall I do?" she replied with mock alarm.

"Aunt Jane, you really must appreciate the worldwide access of the computer," James lectured. Jane paid him no mind whatsoever. She was intrigued by the message. The Wentworth family never considered itself connected to America, puny little upstart nation across the ocean, but there it was for the whole world to see. Jane knew it was true, too. Catherine Wentworth had indeed left

England for the colonies in the 1700's. Jane pursed her lips, oblivious to James' nagging.

"James," she said finally, cutting him off mid-sentence. "I should like to address a response to this young woman. Could you please show me how that might be done?" James sighed defeat.

"Of course," he answered, moving the cursor to "reply" and continuing on with the day's instruction.

CHAPTER THREE

"When I meet the man or woman who can truly say they have done as they pleased in this life, making no concessions to anyone or anything, I will commend that soul most gladly."
C.W.B. 1772

Much to everyone's combined relief and dismay, the Wetherton Historical Foundation had announced that, while revenues continued to slide, the town's operating budget was healthy enough to continue on for at least another six months.

"Six months?" Jillian had asked pleadingly. "What happens at the end of six months?"

"We'll have to take another look at things," answered Burt Payne, sixty-something retired engineer from a state job in Hartford. "But we're not worried," he added with a wink. "Jillian, we just know that you and your people are going to come up with something terrific to help us out of this pickle." He smiled a toothy, crooked grin. The room nodded emphatic agreement.

My people, Jillian thought to herself silently. What people? Do I have a fundraising staff that I'm unaware of? Are there people hiding around town somewhere that I don't know about? She had gone to bed exhausted, confused, and concerned, falling into such a deep sleep that only Patriot's incessant meowing in her ear could roust her awake. She rushed over to the Foundation offices with an enormous cup of ice coffee clutched in her fist to begin what might be the last six months of her career in Wetherton.

Duke Parker admired himself in the mirror of the costuming room. He was not often called upon to dress as a re-enactor, but Ben had gone fishing for the weekend and T.J. was too short for the outfit. He looked very different in the three corner hat that replaced his bandana headband and, had to admit, he was pleased with the change. Jillian emerged from the hallway, toilet plunger in hand.

"Carter house?" Duke offered. Jillian shook her head and stowed her plunger in the closet.

"Don't ask," she sighed. "Hey," she brightened, "you look pretty as a picture."

"You betcha," he said, turning back to his reflection with a wink. "This is far out."

"Wait until you step outside, pretty boy. It's far out when you're in air-conditioning, but it's a hell on earth when you're back in 1775."

"God, I hope my hair doesn't frizz," he said, tugging at the wispy tendrils of gray that shot out at the sides.

"Keep your hat on," she shot back, blowing air kisses at him and settling back in with her paperwork, "and you'll be just fine."

Maggie Paul breezed through the door wearing an indentured servant's plain and unflattering dress. "Does this make me look fat?" Maggie asked, howling at her patented one-liner. At least once a week, Maggie asked that question in her own good-natured, self-deprecating humor. In truth, everything made Maggie look fat. There was no costume of this century or beyond that could hide that fact. Jillian smiled at her warmly.

"You look fabulous," she answered. "You look just like Elizabeth Becker." Maggie spun in the mirror next to Duke to see her reflection. She loved that answer. Everyone knew that Elizabeth Becker was a great beauty of her day, and everyone knew she was every inch the size of Maggie Paul. When had beauty become skin and bones? When had curves and flesh become anything other than womanly and wanton? Today, she did not care. Today, she was in yesterday. Today, she was beautiful and fabulous.

Jillian shuffled her notes on emergency budget preparedness and considered any other non-essential items that could be added to her list of cuts. "OK," Jillian began without looking up at anyone in particular, "here's one that's been bugging me."

"Shoot," Duke called out, not flinching from his reflection next to Maggie's. Jillian raised one eyebrow and continued.

"All summer long the man at 75 Park Street cuts his lawn and blows all the extra grass clippings and leaves and whatever into the street toward his neighbor at number 68 across the way." Duke puzzled a moment then turned to face her.

"Proceed," he said in all seriousness.

"Then the man at 68 Park Street cuts his grass and blows the clippings and sticks and whatever off of his property, back out into the street and back over toward number 75."

"Interesting," Duke said at last, his brilliant mind obviously piqued. Jillian raised her eyebrows, eyes wide with encouragement. She loved a healthy discussion from Duke. It was one of her favorite pastimes. He was a brilliant mind and Jillian challenged herself to keep pace. Duke could spend hours pondering the value of solar energy over hydroelectricity as earnestly as he would compare the quality of plastic shopping bags from various local grocery stores.

"First of all, the question is a legal one," Duke began. "Is it legal to blow your lawn debris into the town-owned public street?"

Maggie shrugged her ample shoulders. "I don't see why not. The wind might just as easily blow it there anyway." Jillian pursed her lips in a sign of reasonable concurrence.

"The next question, of course," Duke continued, "is one of morality. Courtesy. Do unto others as you would have done to you." He tilted his head, left and right, then left again, as if weighing the merit of his argument on some hidden scale inside his head.

"That's exactly what I'm thinking," Jillian chimed in. "It's no different than throwing apple cores into your neighbor's yard. Sure, they're organic and they'll decompose, but it's still garbage. It still isn't right to throw your garbage onto someone else's property."

"Is he lazy?" Duke asked, waving his hand absently in the air.

"I'm not lazy," Maggie chimed in. "I get up at six o'clock every morning, without any alarm clock mind you, and walk two miles rain or shine."

"Good for you," Duke said, genuinely impressed.

"I hit the snooze," Jillian admitted, "but I run around the green sometimes." Maggie nodded her approval.

"Technically, he's not blowing the grass into his neighbor's yard," Duke pressed on, "he's only blowing it into the street. Of course the street belongs to the town, for which he is presumably a taxpayer." Jillian tossed her notes to the side.

"My neighbor has the snow plowed from his driveway right out into the street in front of my house," Maggie said. "He's been doing it for years."

"Have you complained?" Duke asked.

"No," she responded with a shrug, "it's been that way for years."

"Doesn't it bother you?" Jillian implored.

"I guess," Maggie answered, "but it seems silly to make a fuss about it now. It's been that way for years."

"I think it's wrong," Jillian said. "I think it's one of those gray areas."

"A gray area?" Duke asked thoughtfully.

"You know," Jillian said, clipping two papers together and filing them in her bag. "You couldn't sue somebody over it, but it just feels wrong. It feels sneaky and dirty and rude and wrong."

"I agree," Maggie added wholeheartedly. "Let him keep his grass in his own yard. He grows it, let him mulch it."

"You can sue somebody over anything," Duke said rolling his eyes. "Believe me when I tell you." With a glance toward the clock, Jillian rose to her feet.

"Well I wish I could stick around and help you solve this one, but I have to run home and get ready," Jillian said, swigging the last of her coffee.

"Oh right," Duke said, smiling and twirling around. "Mr. Money Mack, I presume."

"The one and only," Jillian smiled dryly. "It's that time of the year, I'm afraid. And this year it's going to be more important than ever."

"Oh honey," Maggie offered in sympathy. "I wish there was some way one of us could help you."

"Really?" Jillian answered, her eyebrows raised. "Because I'd be happy to have one of you come with me. Apparently, you are "my people.""

"Oh no," Duke and Maggie said simultaneously, cutting her off before she could make her argument.

"You know how I hate New York City," Maggie said. "And I couldn't possibly leave my cats for the whole day."

"Don't look at me," Duke said, defensively holding out his arms in a dramatic, perpendicular pose. "I think I'm already doing enough work for the Foundation today, don't you?"

"Charming," Jillian said. "And where in my job description does it say, Director of Marketing, Special Promotions and Occasional Sucking-Up-To-Rich-Old-Men-For-Sponsorships? Hmmm?" Duke and Maggie glanced at each other then shrugged their shoulders back at her.

"Someone has to do it, dear," Maggie added enthusiastically. "Everyone looks forward to the Harvest Party. The town would just be lost without it. And money is getting awfully tight."

"Think of the millions of children who will benefit from what you're about to do," Duke said, with the sincerity of a commander sending troops into battle.

"Millions?" Jillian said with a sneer. "Right. I think it's more like eighty-seven, but who's counting?"

"Exactly," Duke said. "Besides, you'll get out of this moth-eaten town for the weekend and into the action. New York City, baby, it is so far out in the summer." Jillian looked at him, not knowing whether to kick him or kiss him.

"Far out?" she said in response. "Do you know you're the only person on the planet who still uses that term?" Duke raised his eyebrows up and down under the brim of his three-corner hat in a gesture of encouragement. "You're a whacko, you know that?" she said to him, tipping the hat over his face. "Wish me luck," she called over her shoulder as she opened the door and stepped out into the heat.

The record heat had pressed on with its cruel, ironic joke. Just as New Englanders, who adore the diversity of their four-season climate, had grown tired of summer and had begun to look forward to sweaters and crisp, cool evenings, Mother Nature delivered her most oppressive temperatures of the year. Overloaded power grids had crippled portions of the town, making the Foundation's generator one of Jillian's greatest accomplishments during her tenure at Wetherton. The thought of autumn foliage and jack-o-lanterns made turning her attention to the annual Harvest Party a welcome distraction.

Although there was no record of any official Wetherton harvest party prior to 1876, diaries and newspapers alike had long detailed an annual merrymaking event dating back to at least the 1770's. Originally described as "the merriest of ways to celebrate the fruits of a long, hot summer's labors," the Harvest Party was simply a chance for townsfolk of all ages and affluence to join together in fun and camaraderie.

In a purists' interpretation, fun and camaraderie meant food and drink. In 21st century Wetherton, it also meant games and face-painting, pumpkin tossing and bobbing for apples, as well as a healthy portion of food and drink for anyone and everyone with the price of admission to the biggest annual fundraiser Jillian could invent.

Of course, fundraising requires funding, and every year in late summer, Jillian gladly accepted an invitation from the very wealthy Archibald Mack to discuss her plans for the upcoming event. Archibald was most certainly not a Wethertonian. He was, in fact, a Virginian from Richmond whose family money went back as far as tobacco plantations and Thomas Jefferson. While he admitted to a certain condescension for anyone and anything that was not created in the Old Dominion, he also felt a personal obligation to support the cause of preservation and restoration wherever possible. A critical observer might see that by furthering the importance of lineage and historical significance, he was simply improving his own importance and self-worth. With a practical eye, however, Jillian concluded she couldn't care less just as long as that big sponsorship check arrived at the Foundation every autumn.

It had not gone unnoticed that Archibald's interest in the Wetherton Harvest Party had grown substantially since the lovely young Yale graduate had taken over some years ago. He was instantly enraptured, and promised his support as Jillian's faithful servant with a wink and a smile.

So it was settled. Every year Jillian would make her pilgrimage to Manhattan to meet with Archibald Mack and enjoy dinner in one of the city's finest restaurants. He would flirt with her, and she would smile and laugh warmly and graciously. He would invite her to go dancing, and she would decline claiming she could never keep up with him. He would laugh and ask her back to his apartment. She would cover her stifled yawn with her beautiful young hand and plead she was much too tired and wouldn't that be inappropriate after all. He would laugh, a hearty soulful laugh, and admit that it might be considered inappropriate by some, but that he was much too old to be concerned with anything those people might think.

In the end, he would thank her for a lovely evening. He would promise to send his check to the Wetherton Historical Foundation as usual. She would thank him for his generosity and continued support and assure him that she could not imagine a more pleasant evening and looked forward to seeing him again next year. Of course, she would invite him to visit Wetherton, at any time, for a personal tour. He would kiss her hand good night and explain that he was not generally inclined to travel to Connecticut, but he would certainly keep her invitation in mind. He would offer to drive her anywhere in the city in his private car, but she would politely decline and insist on taking a taxi to meet her friend Taylor who lived only a few blocks away. He would bow, in an oddly outdated yet curiously charming gesture, and she would drive away, glancing back at him from the rear window of her yellow taxi.

Jillian had to admit, there was something strangely appealing about Archibald Mack. Maggie claimed that it all came down to money and that any old man could be charming with $80 million in the bank, but Jillian had to disagree. Of course she found his advances absurd, albeit relatively harmless. In fact, there was something altogether absurd about him. He was like a human time capsule from a bygone generation. He was a curious and intriguing glimpse into our country's recent past. He was a modern-day fossil of a man still seen in re-runs from the 1970s.

Yet, at the end of the day, there was something in his manners and protocol that set him apart. Jillian believed he was a harmless, silly flirt, dutifully playing the role of wealthy playboy that had been handed to him at birth, who would probably faint dead away if she ever accepted one of his thinly disguised propositions. Duke said that

Jillian was delusional, but that delusions could have their place of importance in everyone's life.

"You might understand the whole fundraising game, Diabolita," Duke had warned, "but you don't understand men. Believe me when I tell you." He wagged a finger at her for emphasis, and Jillian smirked at the notion that a hippie from Berkeley would attempt to protect her from the evil of a seventy-something Virginian named Archibald.

"I think I can handle myself," she had answered with the confidence of a Yale graduate, and tossed her head back for effect.

Jillian trudged on ahead toward her small house, sweating puddles down her back. "Good God," she thought, "am I in hell?" She pushed through the gate that lead to her front door and turned the key as quickly as possible. Air conditioning hit her in the face like an ice blast in winter. "Aaah. Thank you my little Hevy," she said, and stood almost frozen in the arctic air that surrounded her. Patriot sauntered over to circle around her sweaty ankles.

The message light on her answering machine flashed, and she pressed the button while shaking her hair free from the ponytail she had worn all morning.

"Hey Jillie, it's Taylor," came forth the voice with the decidedly Texas twang, "just wanted to firm up our plans for tonight. I figure you'll probably wrap things up with the Money Mack by 9:00, so just park at my building, go do your thing, and then meet me at my place and we'll go from there. I'm really looking forward to seeing you, honey. I have tons of great guys to introduce you to and a great job I want to talk to you about. See you tonight." Beep.

Jillian cocked her head to the side thoughtfully and gave a deep, heavy sigh. This time, she was determined to have a good time. To meet men younger than her grandfather, who didn't live in suburbia with their mothers and sleep in their childhood bedrooms. Tonight, Jillian Garrett would be wild in Manhattan. Then, another big sigh.

CHAPTER FOUR

"I do miss those loved ones who are now lost to me, but I find comfort in my memories with faces so vivid and life-like I feel I can almost reach out and touch them," C.W.B. 1789

A heavy mist filled the air, and a weighty dampness pressed down upon Jane Wentworth Rochester like a wool blanket. Her feet lumbered through the mud in an unpleasant thumping that was magnifying the throbbing in her head with each aching step. She was irritable and uncomfortable. The night had passed interminably, hour after hour, with no welcome relief of sleep. She had tried reading, she had watched bits of an old movie, she counted sheep, she drank some sherry, she had done everything she could think of and yet the luxury of sleep would not come to her.

It was not the first time she had spent such a sleepless night. In fact, nocturnal slumber seemed to elude her more and more frequently as the years passed on. Thank heavens for those chairs in the east parlor which were so comfortable and warm. It had become a pleasure to enjoy a cat nap in one of them after breakfast on most days.

For now, however, she trudged on in angry silence, huffing and puffing and lamenting the damned rotten weather that pressed in upon her soul. She paused to cough, a long, rattling sound emanating from her chest, and wheezed a moment or two before looking around in a mild confusion. Her heart raced, her mind felt dizzy, she looked left and right for some sign of recognition.

"What?" she heard herself murmur. "Where in bloody hell?" She looked side to side, spinning around too quickly and making herself almost sick with the turn. The buds of panic began to rise within her. Why could she not remember the way?

"Ruff!" came the sound from behind her. Lady Jane spun around to find Dudley, panting and wagging his formidable tail, imploring her to follow. Jane exhaled her relief and smiled with gratitude.

"You darling old dog," she muttered. "Come along then. Help an old girl find her way. I fear I've lost mine."

Dudley trotted ahead, but never too far ahead for Jane to follow. At last, she could make out the shape of Broadhurst through the mist in the distance, and was almost overjoyed to once again regain her bearings.

It was a long walk home that day. Lady Jane could not help but notice it. Each breath seemed to come with greater effort than the one before, and it was only by the grace of God that she found herself shuffling through the kitchen door, with Dudley wagging his tail determinedly by her side. She grasped a chair back with shaky hand and nearly dropped into its seat as Dudley announced her arrival.

"Stop that noise, Dudley," came the voice of Liza from the pantry. It wasn't until she had emerged into the kitchen that Liza realized why the dog had been so uncommonly vocal on this morning.

"My Lady," was all Liza could manage in alarm as she rushed forward, dropping eggs and bacon on the floor.

"Now, now, Liza," said Jane indignantly. "I may have some trifling cold. Please do not alert the media as to my imminent demise. I fear you shall all be terribly disappointed."

"Oh no," Liza said. "I'm ringing the Doctor right this moment. Jane puffed a breath or two.

"Very well," she answered, with uncharacteristic obliging, "if you must." Jane's mind darted wildly, trying to catch her breath and realizing, with unpredicted alarm, that she might indeed be facing her imminent demise. "Bollocks," she muttered softly. "I'll be damned if I'll die in the kitchen," she said, shuffling slowly toward the door and then to the left toward the great entrance hall to the stairs that would take her to her bedroom.

Her mind wandered as she walked. She remembered the day when Arthur had come home from London, sweating with fever and beyond his customary sensibility and calm. For an extremely large man, Arthur was surprisingly frail. Jane was often caught off-guard by his bouts with pneumonia, which seemed to come almost every winter without fail.

"Stop fussing," he scolded her, as she pulled the sheets taut against his chest and remade the bed for the eighteenth time that day.

"It's not fussing Arthur," she had admonished quickly. "It's nursing." With that, he had let out such a laugh, which began such a coughing fit, which required the support of almost the entire staff to contain, that she would never forget his face when he finally regained his composure.

At last quiet, he looked at her with soulful eyes and whispered, "Darling, you are a truly magnificent woman, but a nurse you are not." He coughed on again, stifling the noise of his laughter as much as possible, in the face of his wife's defiant glare.

Of course, he was right. In his quiet, observant way, Arthur was almost always right. She couldn't deny it. From that moment on, Jane's modest attempts at nursing would be forever known to the two of them as "wifing" and with that Jane was free to torment Lord Arthur Rochester with any means or device she deemed necessary to fulfill the role of good wife.

It was like that with the two of them. It had always been like that. From nearly the moment they met they had found a way to complement each other. Their union had been one of uncanny and abundantly pleasant compromise. No one would have believed that anyone could tame or tolerate the stubborn determination of Jane Wentworth, yet those were two words Arthur would never have used to describe his wife. Where others saw stubbornness, Arthur saw conviction, and where others saw a lack of feminine guile, Arthur saw a thin veneer of duty and obligation.

Jane breathed fitfully. The Doctor had arrived quickly and for nearly an hour she had been poked and prodded like a goose being readied for Christmas dinner. She now rested uncomfortably in the bed she had shared with Arthur for all the years of her married life. Those were the days, she thought, when Arthur had been beside her and all had been right with the world.

They had both wanted children, but luck had not been on their side in that endeavor. In those days, of course, either God gave you children or he did not. There were no options, no resources, and no assistance of any particular value other than a kind-hearted wink-wink and some silly nonsense about not trying hard enough or that learning was more than half the fun after all. Jane pulled the quilt up closer to her chin.

"Feeling better, Mum?" Liza inquired with concern as she removed the tray of tea and warm broth that had long gone cold. "The Doctor said you must rest."

"Bloody hell," Jane blustered for effect. "I think I know my own mind in my own house." The doctor re-entered from the hallway and took a chair by the bedside.

"And how are we feeling now, Mrs. Rochester?" the doctor asked.

"Right as rain," Jane responded, submitting to another test of her blood pressure and pulse.

"I shouldn't think you'll need to go to hospital today," the doctor went on. Jane harrumphed her indignation with a cough. She most certainly would not be going to any hospital, today or any other day, and she would like to know how this scrawny little weakling of a doctor would try to make her do anything she did not want to do.

She would never leave Broadhurst Hall, not of her own free will at any rate. She knew that when God finally came for her she would die at Broadhurst Hall, as any respectable Wentworth would have the decency to do, and be buried in the Chapel along with everyone she had ever loved.

"I am tired," Jane conceded after a moment. "I did not sleep well last night. I don't know why."

Jane's mind wandered aimlessly, fixing upon a trip to Barbados with Arthur in 1948. The heat of the sun was burning on her face. She could see Arthur smiling at her from his chair as she dove into the clear water yet again in search of palest pink shells. Dudley yelped softly in his sleep, startling Lady Jane back to consciousness. Another rumbling cough shifted in her chest.

"There now," the doctor said, removing the stethoscope from her ears. Jane eyed her suspiciously through her coughing. Dr. Latrell had been called away on an emergency, so this woman, a Dr. Vanderwheel, had arrived instead. The fact that Dr. Vanderwheel was a woman was actually quite pleasant to Jane, who had grown up in a world where only men were doctors and women were nurses. It was the fact that she was so damnably young that bothered her. She couldn't be more than twenty or so, it seemed to Jane. How on earth could anyone so young know anything about such an old mind and body.

"I will want you to come into the office tomorrow morning for a few tests," Dr. Vanderwheel went on.

"Silly girl," Jane muttered under her breath closing her eyes against everyone in the room. Dr. Vanderwheel smiled back knowingly.

"I will insist upon it, Mrs. Rochester, as I'm sure Dr. Latrell will agree when I phone him to discuss it." Jane opened her eyes to tiny slits, again eyeing her Doctor with caution and suspicion.

"Yes, well," Jane relented, "as it happens I had planned a trip to town tomorrow and I'm sure I could squeeze you into my schedule." She raised her chin imperiously and closed her eyes hard against any further comment.

"Very well then," the Doctor said. "I'll see you in the morning," she added, rising to take her leave. Jane lay silently, pretending to be fast asleep. She heard murmuring. Something about ringing later to check in, but she couldn't quite make it out. Her mind was restless and confused. She saw bombs falling from the sky into open fields in the distance. She saw the stones of ancient castle ruins underfoot as she jumped and played with Phillipa in the grass with the rocky coast just along the narrow path.

She shifted her shoulder and turned slightly, listening for the sounds of voices in the hall. Had they all gone? She opened one eye cautiously, looking around the luxurious bedroom all but empty of life except for herself and Dudley who was snoring away at the foot of her bed.

She smiled the crooked left-sided smile, sipped at the glass of water on the bedside table and smoothed the blankets all around her. With that, Jane finally drifted off, taking note of the surprise in everyone when they realized she was indeed not dying on this day. She chuckled triumphantly, and fell long and fast into a deep sleep.

CHAPTER FIVE

"I have received news from a dear friend who has moved to Boston. She says it is lovely there and I should visit, but my heart is in Wetherton and I think I am content to know that this is where I belong," C.W.B. 1788.

The drive into New York took Jillian about two hours of white-knuckled, teeth-grinding, pure adrenaline agony. The Merritt Parkway through Connecticut was fast and hair-raising, but pleasant enough. Crossing into New York State and getting onto the Hutchinson was another matter. Traffic flowed bumper to bumper at a steady 75 miles per hour. Cars and SUVs jockeyed for position to enter, exit or simply go as fast as possible. The lane-changing skill and sheer nerve required was extraordinary. Edging past a construction-induced bottleneck, where the right lane was closed with no evidence of construction in sight, she flew down the East River Drive and made it to Taylor's building on East 77th Street in reasonably good condition. She extricated her fingers from the steering wheel, wiped the beads of perspiration from her forehead and admitted she had grown pretty soft with her 10-minute pedestrian commute each morning.

She walked out to the corner of 77th and Park decked out in an end-of-season markdown black dress she bought last year specifically for this occasion and hailed a cab.

"Café des Artistes," she told the driver, knowing full well it was considered one of the city's most romantic restaurants. The driver smiled, perfect white teeth gleaming against his dark skin, and looked at her in his rearview.

"You have romantic evening, yes?" he asked with a happy nod.

"Hardly," Jillian replied, pulling out a compact mirror and assessing her hair and make-up.

"But this is most beautiful romance place, yes?" the driver persisted.

"Not always," Jillian shot back. "You'd be surprised."

"Ah, ha, ha, ha," he chuckled in a way that Jillian found to be almost maniacal. "You'll see. I know this thing. Very romantic. I promise you." Jillian shook her head in resignation.

"Well maybe you're right," she offered at last, "but I sincerely doubt it."

Café des Artistes was a beautiful place and an icon of Manhattan's fine dining. Other restaurants would come and go, trends in Pan Asian and minimalist décor, but Café des Artistes, with its cherubs floating on walls and ceilings, was a beacon of constant light in a turbulent sea. Jillian reached the maitre de, refreshed from her air-conditioned cab ride with Muhammed Bal Hali, who had graciously shared stories of his childhood in Pakistan and his family now living in Queens with his wife's brother and their nine children. Jillian had tipped him very well, in spite of her own desperate finances, because she felt that anyone as cheerful as Muhammed deserved a little good fortune on a Friday night.

She was led to a banquette, encircled by cherubs in the upper atmosphere, and greeted by the smiling face of Archibald Mack. He was not an unattractive man. Jillian would even admit that, in his day, he was probably considered quite a catch. In fact, even on this day there were those women who would consider him quite a catch, albeit not for his good looks. Jillian imagined him in his prime, circa 1969 maybe, with ridiculously long side-burns and a mustache. "Ick", she responded silently.

Today, his grooming and Saville Row suit were classic and impeccable. His manners were so elegant and overstated that a woman might allow herself to be taken in by the sheer exaggeration of him. It was almost as if he were a cartoon character of the quintessential multi-millionaire bachelor, embodying all of the good stereotypes mixed in with a concoction of oddball qualities required to inspire a good laugh.

He graciously rose to greet her, kissed her hand in his usual charming manner, and collapsed back into the soft upholstery to drain his martini and call the waiter for another.

"My dear," Archibald said, in his lingering southern drawl, "you are even more stunning than I remembered." Jillian smiled demurely and predictably.

"You're a shameless flatterer Mr. Mack," she said, turning to the waiter to order a glass of their best Chardonnay.

"Please, won't you please call me Archibald? My heavens, how long must I know you before I can hear my own name from your lips? I cannot believe it has been a year since we last met," he said, leering at her over his glass. "You are continually in my thoughts."

"I'm sure that's not true," Jillian replied, silently counting to ten in anticipation of her drink.

"No it is, I swear," he protested, grabbing for her hand and bringing it to his lips. "I think of you working so hard up there in Connecticut, and I say to myself, why don't I go visit that lovely young woman?"

"You should," Jillian smiled, pulling her hand away and gratefully accepting her drink from the waiter. "You know you have a VIP invitation any time. We would truly love to have you. I would truly love to have you," she added, with dramatic emphasis on the I. She sipped her wine while Archibald stared at her for an uncomfortably long time. So long that, for a moment, she wondered if he was asleep with his eyes open, but suddenly he burst to life once more.

"How long are we going to keep meeting like this?" he asked with a wink.

"Forever," Jillian said without missing a beat. The Money Mack roared with laughter.

"You are feisty," he said. "I like feisty women." He paused to drain at least half his glass. "Do you know how old I am, darling?"

"Hmm," she paused, not sure how to respond. "Over 50?" she answered, again to uproarious laughter.

"That's right. That's exactly right. And do you know what an older, over 50, gentleman like myself wants most in his golden years?" Jillian paused again, tempted to answer "world peace" but restraining herself.

"A legacy," she said finally, secretly thrilled with the brilliance of her response. Archibald reared back into the soft cushions, as if a thunderbolt had struck him straight in the heart. Clearly the idea of a legacy had never once seemed important until this very martini-induced moment. His look of bewilderment gave Jillian just the opening she needed to begin her impromptu pitch.

"Just the other day I was thinking of you, Mr. Mack, when I was discussing plans for the Catherine Brownley Visitor's Center we'd like to build someday. I mean, after all, look at the fuss they've made over the Rockefellers down in Williamsburg, and I was thinking, Wetherton needs our own Rockefeller." She paused to sip her wine and let the notion float for a moment. "Of course, I thought of you," she continued, "but you have already been so generous with your patronage, I hate to come to you with anything new unless you're interested in reviewing some of our preliminary plans."

"Rockefellers," he grumbled with a distasteful look crossing his face. "Yes, well they certainly do make a fuss about those Rockefellers down in Williamsburg, don't they? And isn't that odd, really, a few well-heeled Yankees coming down to the South and making a name for themselves."

Jillian struggled to stifle her amusement at the notion that the Rockefellers had to come down to Williamsburg to make a name for themselves. As if no one had ever heard the name prior to the reconstruction that took place there in the 1930s. She went on delicately, sensing that she could be making some extraordinary progress if she proceeded gingerly and with a bit of luck.

"It is funny, isn't it," Jillian began, shaking her head. "Wouldn't it be just as funny if a southerner, like yourself, came north to New England to save our own colonial town from extinction?" She paused again, sipping her wine and glancing around to admire the cherubs who seemed altogether shocked by her shameless ploy.

"I like it!" Archibald pronounced, with a fiery growl, waving for the waiter. "Another martini, my dear?'

"No thank you, but I'd love to look at the menu."

"We have some wonderful specials I would like to tell you about," the waiter interjected. And thus began one of the most exciting and challenging fundraising meetings Jillian had ever commanded. By the end of the evening, she was fairly convinced that Archibald had agreed to set up a substantial endowment for the Wetherton Historical Foundation that would support the creation of a visitor's center. In addition, of course, he would sponsor her Harvest Party, and even threatened to surprise her with his own presence at this year's gala event.

"Wouldn't you like to go dancing with me, darling?" Archibald asked as they emerged into the cooler evening air.

"I could never keep up with you, Mr. Mack," Jillian answered sweetly.

"Can I drive you somewhere?"

"You are too kind," Jillian said, "but I'm staying with my college roommate, Taylor, tonight and she's only a few blocks away. I'll just grab this cab." As the cab approached, she whirled around to say goodbye, only to find herself in the clutch of Archibald's good night kiss.

Remarkably, the old man had found the wherewithal to launch a surprise attack, and Jillian was utterly flabbergasted by his maneuver.

"Until we meet again, darling," he said at last, loosening his grasp around her waist and heading for his private car. She stared at him, weak-kneed and dumbfounded, as he turned to bow before slipping into the sedan.

"I'll be damned," she whispered to herself, as she watched him turn to wave to her through his rear window.

There she stood, alone in front of Café des Artistes, in a fabulous black dress and Archibald Mack had just given her one hell of a kiss good night. Who could have imagined? Other than Muhammed Bal Hali, of course.

She puzzled it over and over in her mind all the way back to Taylor's apartment. It was a mix of enthusiasm and amazement that was simply unaccountable. Ten minutes later, she was sitting in Taylor's tiny one-bedroom co-op recounting every detail.

Taylor was a bubbly blonde from Dallas. She and Jillian had roomed together throughout their four years at Yale. Meeting awkwardly on move-in day freshman year, they had instantly become close friends. Fourteen years later, Taylor, the advertising executive, sat enrapt as her good friend spilled out the early evening's events.

"And then what happened?" Taylor asked, sipping on a Cosmopolitan.

"He kissed me," Jillian announced.

"What?" Taylor shouted in her Texas drawl, a look of horror on her face. "But he's like 800 years old."

"Seventy-five," Jillian answered, nodding for emphasis. Taylor shook her head in disbelief.

"Was it gross?" she asked.

"Actually, I don't know," Jillian muttered. "I was so stunned, I don't think it even registered. But no, I definitely don't think I would say it was gross." Taylor shook her head again, and poured herself another Cosmo from the glass pitcher on her coffee table.

"Jillie, I want you to purge this from your mind, do you hear me?"

"Why?"

"Because making out with old men on the street is not good," Taylor pleaded. Jillian rolled her eyes.

"We weren't making out," Jillian retorted with mild annoyance. "It was just a little goodnight kiss."

"Good Lord," Taylor said, draining half of her glass.

"It was shocking. Just shocking," Jillian went on, clearly unable to wrap her mind around the smooth moves of the Money Mack. "And surprising. Remarkable, really. It's the only way I can think to describe it. He even bowed to me before he got into his car." They sat quietly for a moment, both seemingly without response or explanation. "To be honest," Jillian offered finally, sipping from her own glass, "it's the first kiss I've had in quite some time, and I have to say it really wasn't all that gross."

"Oh my God," Taylor said in horror.

"What?"

"Listen to me," Taylor began, barking like a mind-numbing, brain-washing drill sergeant. "I have one night to show you all the great guys you are missing out on because you have chosen to live up in the woods of New England with plaid flannel and deep-fried clam rolls." Jillian shrugged mildly, but didn't dare to offer a word of objection. "We are going out, you are going to have a great time and I do not want to hear about American history or men over 70 for the rest of the night. Is this understood?" Jillian nodded dutifully. Taylor rose to her full 5'4" in 4" heels, making her one of the tiniest women Jillian had ever known. Still, she commanded like a field general, and Jillian knew better than to start an argument.

"Let's go," Taylor announced, downing the last of her drink, as the two ventured out for another cab ride into the New York City night.

First, there was a private party at Club Bistro, a fun-loving but conservative crowd on the Upper East Side. Jillian was surprised by the number of single men who were eager for an introduction, although they all seemed equally anxious to impress her with stories of their latest Wall Street conquests. She noticed she had not uttered the words "Wetherton Historical Foundation" in over an hour, and had to admit it was not because she was unwilling to discuss her work with the men she was meeting.

"Let's blow this place," Taylor said, sidling up to her at last. "These guys are such a bunch of self-obsessed, Wall Street stiffs. I know a great party in Soho." Before she could wave goodbye, Jillian was whisked into another taxi for a ride downtown.

"You can't waste time with some of these losers," Taylor explained, as the cab veered right and left with lane changes, both she and Jillian swaying to the motion of the ride down Park. "Some of these guys," Taylor went on, "will talk about themselves all night long." She shook her head with disgust. "Self-obsession is so overrated. Personally, I'd like to meet a guy who wants to talk about me for a change." She nodded for emphasis, and Jillian eagerly nodded agreement.

The party in Soho was for a magazine executive that Taylor had known for nearly a decade. Tommy Colavita, of Brooklyn, was moving to Italy, for a newer, fresher, better assignment. Everyone loved him and there wasn't a dry eye in the house, much less a heterosexual eye, and Jillian and Taylor lasted about 30 minutes before wishing their final farewells and heading on to Dive.

Dive was one of the newest, hippest spots in the West Village, and it was definitely on the must-see list for Friday night. Sometimes, Taylor warned, the crowd could be a little "funky", but most of the time it was uptight, Ivy-Leaguers, just like them, searching for something out of the ordinary. One hour later, even Taylor, the venerable cheerleader of fun, was ready to pull the plug.

"Let's just go back to up to Roscoe's," she said with a certain weariness, closing the door of the cab with a mighty tug, as they headed back to the Upper East Side.

Roscoe's was full of college charm, cleverly disguised with a successful-in-my-twenties-is-so-much-better panache. Jillian was instantly surprised to recognize at least ten people, but was equally somewhat alarmed to realize that this was the sort of place where people like her would hang out.

It was a dark, dreary, even dirty bar, with filthy floors and an even filthier "ladies" room. The crowd was drunk, happily drunk but drunk nonetheless, and there was an air of desperation all around. Jillian couldn't decide if it was desperation to hold onto a vanishing past or desperation for a future yet unsecured and uncertain, but it was desperation in its plainest and most earnest form.

"Hey, Jillian, right? Jillian Garrett?" came a voice from behind her. She turned to see Josh Pennington, an absolutely beautiful face she hadn't seen since graduation day.

"Josh?" she said, with a genuine look of surprise. "My gosh, how are you?" They exchanged a brief hug and kiss on the cheek.

"My God," he said, "you look fantastic. Where have you been hiding out all these years?"

"Oh, I'm up in Connecticut, actually."

"No," he answered emphatically, a look of alarm crossing his perfectly chiseled face. "What, you're still at Yale?"

"No, no," she said, smiling casually, "I live up in Wetherton. I work for the Historical Foundation there."

"Really?" he said, circling around her for a less crowded space. "That's great. What do you do for them?"

"Uh, well, I'm the Director of Marketing and Special Promotions, so a little bit of everything, I guess, would be the best way to describe it." She deliberately checked the register of her voice to make sure she sounded casual and confident.

"That's terrific," he said, with unusual enthusiasm. "Wow, good for you. What are you doing in the city? Still hanging out with Taylor?" He gestured to Taylor, who was a tiny, animated dot in the center of three men six feet or taller. Jillian smiled her confirmation.

"So, what about you?" she asked.

"Me? Oh, you know, still working for my father downtown." He fiddled with his tie, and pushed back his gorgeous brown hair. "It's alright for now, you know, the money's really good, but someday, I'd like to go out and do my own thing."

"And what would that be?" Jillian asked with genuine curiosity.

"What?" he asked, suddenly confused. Jillian paused a moment.

"What would be your own thing?" she asked again, trying to speak louder over the incredible noise.

"Oh, well, you know," he stammered, "the same thing, hedge funds, but my own place. You know." Jillian nodded as if she understood.

"So I guess," she ventured cautiously, "hedge funds are your thing." Josh looked at her with a very queer frown.

"Hell no," he answered at last, "but the money's really good, you know?" Jillian smiled, although she most certainly did not know. "Listen," he went on, moving closer to her ear so that he would not have to shout quite so loud, "my place is just a few blocks away. Can I interest you in a nightcap?" Jillian froze with fear. Was it true? Was Josh Pennington actually inviting her to his apartment? Josh Pennington, the cutest, most adorable man who had ever invited her anywhere. "Uh oh," he went on, "I can see by your stunned silence that you think I'm a predator and you don't know what to say."

"No, no," Jillian insisted, shaking her head in a mild panic, "it's just that I only have this one night in the city with Taylor, and I really think I should stick with her."

Jillian glanced over at her friend, who at that moment was holding a lime wedge in her teeth for one of her male admirers to snatch from her lips before shooting his tequila.

"I don't think she'd mind if you had a change of plans," Josh replied quietly, slowly encircling her shoulders with his arm.

"Well hello, Josh," said a high-pitched female voice from behind. Jillian and Josh both turned to see a well-heeled, well-coifed, beautiful blonde tapping her Manolo Blahniks at record speed.

"Kitty," was the feeble, surprised response from Josh's lips. "You're back from L.A.?" Josh dropped his arm to his side in a pathetic attempt to appear calm and casual.

"I am. Who's this?" said Kitty with a tight-lipped smile, eyeing Jillian suspiciously.

"Yes, this is Jillian Garnet, I mean Garrett," he stammered, "we're old friends from Yale."

"Kitty Conran," she said, thrusting her hand toward Jillian. "I went to Sweet Briar," she added.

"How do you do," Jillian said graciously.

"Where do you work?" Kitty attacked instantly.

"Connecticut," Jillian answered vaguely.

"Connecticut? My God, how horrible! How do you survive up there?" Kitty asked, in one of the meanest tones Jillian had heard in quite some time.

"Well," Jillian answered cheerfully, "we do the best we can, you know, we needlepoint and garden and play golf." Kitty pulled herself closer to Jillian for dramatic effect.

"I'm a rep at Valentina," Kitty whispered in a voice that could wake the dead, "and you should know that we loved that knock-off dress you're wearing when it came out last year. I don't know why more people didn't wear it. It was such a great copy." Jillian looked at Josh, who looked at Kitty, who glared at Jillian.

"Thank you," Jillian said mildly, glancing down at the floor to regain her composure. "Josh," she said suddenly looking up, "hey, it was so great to catch up with you, but I think I need to get back to Taylor." Josh nodded pleasantly.

"Good to see you too," Josh said smiling. "Hey, keep in touch. Good luck to you up there in, uh, Rutherford."

"Wetherton," Jillian said.

"Right. Terrific," he replied vaguely.

"It was very nice to meet you. Have a good night," Kitty snarled as she threaded her hand through Josh's elbow. Jillian waved and wound her way through the crowd, pinching Taylor's wrist with the might of a professional wrestler when they finally made contact.

"I'm ready to go," Jillian hissed with a smile.

"Really? Already?" Taylor slurred with surprise. "Did you meet any great guys? Aren't these the greatest guys? I saw you talking to Josh Pennington. Boy, does he still have the greatest ass in the tri-state region, or what?" All the while Taylor gabbed, Jillian pushed her out the front door, then into one more cab, and then back to the tiny one-bedroom Upper East Side Co-op that was Taylor's home.

Jillian stayed awake on the sleeper sofa for a long, long time that night, reflecting on the last several hours of her life. It was funny she thought, but Archibald Mack, the predicted low-point had, in fact, been the highlight of an otherwise shockingly scary evening. Yes, he was utterly absurd, but he was predictably utterly absurd. There was no reinventing him. He never changed from one season to the next or from one year to the next. He was remarkably, refreshingly content to be exactly who he was. There were no tricks. There was no phoniness. Jillian had found it surprisingly pleasant to spend time with someone who enjoyed such a firmly committed sense of self.

It was ironic, she thought, that she should be the object of so much pity and mockery. Was it deserved? Was it really so much better to live in Manhattan? A place where a taxi could take you somewhere exciting any time of the day on any day of the week? Jillian wasn't sure. No one seemed particularly happy, she reasoned, not even Taylor.

Restaurants. There were great restaurants, fabulous five-star-mortgage-the-house restaurants, but she had yet to find a restaurant that served a better apple cider donut than "Tina's" back in Wetherton on Main Street. Bars. Well, yes, New York had more bars than a federal penitentiary, but no bar anywhere in New York could compete with the charm and hospitality of the tavern in Wetherton with its 257 years of hospitality and home-brewed ale. Fashion. Of course, she would have to concede the point on fashion. Wetherton's idea of fashion was casual and comfortable and never ventured beyond practical. Reflecting on a veritable treasure trove of white sneakers and black socks, along with bicycling shorts that were worn by people who hadn't seen a bicycle in at least a decade for the 4th of July festivities, she admitted she could not craft a debate-worthy argument for fashion. Although she made note that bandana headbands were alive and well in New York just as they were at home. Men. Well, clearly Manhattan had the lion's share while Wetherton had ...... hmmm ..... the mouse's share. In the eligible bachelor under forty category, Jillian could think of only one in Wetherton. That would be Jon Printsmouth, who celebrated his recent birthday with his Mother and his four cats, all of whom wore party hats and special necklaces he had personally beaded for the occasion.

"Eew," Jillian murmured aloud, trying to erase the image from her mind. Good or bad, she didn't know if she could really try to build a life here.

Jillian closed her eyes against the all-night glare of the city that never sleeps, listening to the sounds of car horns, police sirens and general chaos of excitement and endless possibilities only three floors below her, and dreamed of the sleepy town in Connecticut where the leaves would soon begin to turn to gold and the morning air would greet her with the crisp smell of autumn.

CHAPTER SIX

"We are often fooled by those who wish to deceive us, but we are never fooled for long," C.W.B. 1774.

She pulled into her driveway long past three o'clock the next afternoon. Taylor insisted that they go out for brunch, although she was so hung over ice water with lemon and a muffin was all she could manage. Jillian had smiled at her over coffee, eggs, bacon, toast and hash browns, and admitted something she had never before dared.

"Wetherton isn't all that bad, you know," she said, adding a head nod for emphasis and assurance. Taylor shifted her head from the cradle of her right hand to her left and sipped Jillian's coffee without invitation. She sighed long and loud through her nostrils.

"I know," Taylor answered finally, "and I'll drink wine that costs ten dollars a bottle, but I'd rather have the good stuff. Wouldn't you?" She eyed Jillian for a long moment. "I know you think you're happy up there, but I'm worried about you Jillie. I'm worried about all of us. Where are you going to find Mr. Right up in po-dunk Connecticut?" Jillian took a deep breath and frowned. It was a question of increasingly monumental importance as the years had begun to tick by with unparalleled speed.

"I don't know," she answered truthfully, with a bit of alarm.

"It's just that there are so many more guys here in New York," Taylor pleaded. "Don't you see? The odds would be so much more in your favor if you would move down here?"

"Do I really want to live my life worried about playing the odds? And I don't like it here," Jillian answered quickly. "People are mean and rude, and I don't think the men are honest or even decent."

"I'm not mean. I'm not rude," Taylor shot back, holding her temples for support. Jillian sighed agreement. Of course Taylor was not mean or rude. Of course she was decent. She had been Jillian's best friend for over a decade and she deserved better.

"I'm sorry," Jillian offered sincerely. "Of course I didn't mean you. I just meant that, oh, I don't know what I meant." She fumbled with her hash browns, not knowing what to say next that would make either of them feel better.

"It's very hard for me to imagine feeling at home here," Jillian said finally. "I don't know if this is where I belong."

"Oh, and I suppose you belong up in Wetherton?" Taylor shot back fiercely. "With horse poo on your shoes? I suppose you're looking for a man in black socks and white tennis shoes who drives a sensible car and works in the newspaper stand?" Jillian gulped.

"OK. Maybe, I'll admit it, maybe Wetherton isn't where I belong either." Taylor pulled at her blonde ponytail and gently rubbed at the remnants of mascara that lined her lower lids.

"Look, I'm just going to say this," Taylor said finally, "I'm worried you're going to end up alone at 40 and wonder what went wrong, or you're going to marry some dumb New England Yankee who carves birds out of wood for a living and you're going to wonder how that happened to you. God damn it Jillie, you're one of the smartest, most fabulous women I know and I do not understand what you're doing up there in that little town." She sipped her ice water sorrowfully, and massaged her temples again with fatigue. Jillian sat purposefully for a moment, letting the words sink in.

It was a monumental question to confront. A question, in fact, played out in a nocturnal symphony by her nightmares many times before. What was she doing up there in that little town? Who really cared about Wetherton, Connecticut? Except for her, and why did she?

"I promise, I will think, seriously, about moving here," Jillian answered at last, looking at her friend with a heart full of love. "I don't know how you live here. Honestly, I don't. But I will give it serious thought. I know you worry about me and I love that about you, and I promise I am listening," she said truthfully. "I know I can always leave. I can always find something bigger and better and more exciting. For a long time now, I guess I believed I was doing something important up there." Jillian sipped her coffee for a moment. "Besides," she added, after a long pause and a wink, "I like woodcarvers."

They sat quietly for a good while longer. Jillian sipped her coffee purposefully. "Can I tell you something?" she said at last, too nervous to look directly at her friend. Taylor cocked her head and frowned.

"Of course you can," she said matter-of-factly. "We're best friends. You can tell me anything." Taylor raised her head slowly and stared at Jillian with bloodshot eyes.

Jillian bit her lip. "And you promise you won't laugh?"

"Sugar, if I laughed right now my head would explode. I can barely breathe."

"I want to marry a man like John Brownley," Jillian blurted.

"John Brownley?" Taylor answered flatly. "Do I know him?"

"No," Jillian smiled. "John Brownley. The husband of Catherine Wentworth Brownley."

"Good Lord," Taylor whispered, but Jillian would not be put off.

"I want to marry a man who is self-assured and reliable, who is honest and trustworthy. I want to marry a man who knows who he is and knows what he wants and he wants me." She paused for emphasis. Taylor's lower lip hung just apart and gaping. "I don't want to marry an Ichabod Snelling."

"Ichabod Snelling," Taylor replied instantly. "And who is he?"

Jillian proceeded to tell the tale of Ichabod Snelling, the Wetherton colonist who married his wife Sarah, had four children, and then left her for a woman of considerable wealth from Boston. People might have believed that Sarah Snelling thought she had found her true love in Ichabod, but letters to her sister in New York documented her doubts from the outset. And still, Sarah pressed ahead with the marriage saying, "I fear the sting of a lonely, solitary life more than I fear any harm Ichabod may cause my gentle spirit."

"Honey," Taylor responded in her Texas twang, "I've met Ichabod Snelling a hundred times in my life. I've never met a John Brownley." Jillian nodded resigned agreement. Taylor reached out for Jillian's hand with her own "at least we know we'll always have each other." They shared a chuckle, although Taylor's was more of a whimper because the pounding in her temples was becoming almost unbearable. "And when we're old and gray and we can't see well or hear well, we'll drink martinis for lunch and talk about how youth is wasted on the young."

"We can walk around the park arm in arm with our support hose sagging around our ankles," Jillian offered.

"We can take daytrips on a bus down to Atlantic City," Taylor shot back.

"And collect snow globes."

"Oh to hell with snow globes," Taylor answered. "I'm going to hang out down at the Yale club and collect lovers."

"I think it's time for you to go back to bed," Jillian said flatly.

"Please help me up," Taylor replied, only about half-joking. "I'm afraid I might pass out on the sidewalk and someone will steal my new boots right off my feet."

The two walked arm in arm back to the lobby of Taylor's building.

"Promise me you'll think about that studio in my building if it comes up," Taylor asked, hugging Jillian with a good, long tight embrace. The kind of hug that says I will really miss you. Jillian began to protest, but Taylor wouldn't have any of it. "Listen to me," she went on, "just keep an open mind, all right? You can always move back to Wetherton. God help us. How many people are lining up for that job of yours? Four? Three? A couple of little old ladies who have baked goods sales and bingo on their resumes?" Jillian couldn't help but laugh.

"OK," she said at last. "I'll think about it." An uncontrollable puff of determined air exhaled loudly from her lips. Then she was in her car and on her way north with the Manhattan skyline at her back. All the way back to Connecticut Jillian felt confused and out-of-sorts. All the way up the Merritt Parkway toward Hartford she had tried to imagine herself living the life that Taylor was living. All the way back to her tiny cottage, with the white picket fence and restored nineteenth-century paneled shutters, she had boiled the last ten years of her life down to a fifth grade book report.

Yes, there had been a promising and exciting beginning to her life in Wetherton, full of attention-grabbing details that would entice any reader to turn the page. She could easily think of three interesting events that defined the ups and downs of her crazy little town and her place in it. No one would deny her that truth. The ending, however, was the tricky part. Would she live in Wetherton forever? Would she die in a mob cap on a hot and sadly unairconditioned day? Was Archibald Mack the only man who would kiss her in the next six months? In the next six years?

She was a mystery. She was a story without an ending. But who could claim to be anything more than that?

The air in Connecticut was surprisingly refreshing and full of the smells of earth and freshly cut grass. A cold front edging down from Canada had brought the welcome relief of a cool September breeze that instantly perked up her spirits. Finally, the much-anticipated New England autumn had begun. She thought of wool sweaters, hot mulled cider, apple picking, pumpkins, the rustle of leaves beneath her feet, the Harvest Party and Archibald Mack.

The message light on her answering machine was blinking feverishly when she entered.

"You have four new messages," said the pleasant computer voice when she pressed the play button.

"Jillian, my little Diabolita," said Duke, "I hope you had a great time with the money Mack. Meeee-yow! But seriously, I need you to call me about a thing that's going on. Bye." Of course, "thing" could mean anything as far as Duke was concerned. "Thing" could mean the threat of nuclear war, a dinner party, or a bunion on his foot that may prevent him from working for the week. Jillian shuddered to imagine anything further.

"Beep."

"Hello, dear, it's Maggie. I hope you enjoyed yourself in New York. A young girl like you deserves to have some fun. I had a very strange call from Burt at the Foundation, and I didn't know what to do except to call you, so could you please call Burt for me? Thank you dear. See you soon." Jillian frowned.

"Beep."

"Hey Jillie, it's me," began Taylor's voice. "I just wanted to say that I think you're terrific, and I think what you're doing is terrific, and I'm sorry if you thought I was judging you. Good God. I mean, wouldn't it be funny if it turned out that you were the one who ended up happier than all the rest of us put together? I mean, uh, well, that's not what I mean. You know what I mean. Oh Lord, I always talk too much. But listen, and I mean it, really, a friend of mine has a job opening at *Historic Home* magazine. They need somebody exactly like you, can you believe it? His name is Ted and he's calling you tomorrow. It would be horrible for me if you didn't meet with him, so please do me a favor and just meet with him. Love you, bye."

"Beep."

"Jillian, this is Burt Payne over at the Foundation office. I'm sorry to bother you on your day off, but a situation has come up and we're having an emergency meeting tonight at six o'clock. I hope you can be there."

"Beep." Jillian's frown twisted into a look of dismay. Emergency meeting? In ten years the only time an emergency meeting had been called was when Jimmy Barker's python escaped and was feared to be somewhere in the Robbins house. Even then, one exterminator, two police officers and a wild animal expert later, the problem had been solved. Jillian couldn't imagine what the latest emergency might be. Maybe the icy-pops had all melted in the freezer, or a pack of wild ferrets had descended upon the town with six-shooters, intent upon taking it over for their own. She shook her head and glanced at the clock. It was almost five. She still had plenty of time for a shower and a quick check of her e-mails, if the gods of e-mail would oblige her, before the meeting would begin.

Much to Jillian's surprise, her computer fired-up without a hitch. She reasoned that everyone and everything must be in a better mood now that the weather had broken, and scanned the list of new messages, sixteen in all, for some word of interest from a familiar screen name. She instantly deleted the messages promising bigger breasts over night, and cellulite-free thighs in only one week, not due to a lack of curiosity but a fear of anything foreign and evil that might negatively affect the fragile life of her delicate computer. Scrolling down quickly, deleting everything as she went and checking the clock for time, she stopped suddenly and breathed in slowly.

There it was. The message she had been secretly hoping for, but hadn't dared to expect. LJRochester, re: your inquiry. Jillian clicked the mouse with extreme caution, not wanting to risk any chance that she might accidentally delete the precious letter inside.

Dear Miss Garrett:
Thank you for your inquiry regarding my distant relation, Catherine Wentworth Brownley, of Wetherton, Connecticut. I'm afraid I know very little of her or her situation, although there may well be much more information in our family library. I shall look into it as time permits and respond in due course.
Sincerely,
Lady Jane Rochester

Jillian read and re-read the message at least a dozen times. She could hardly believe it was real. Here was the woman who now owned the home where Catherine Brownley had been born. There must be some nugget of information buried somewhere in the vastness of that place that could help the Foundation piece together the childhood and the English life Catherine had left behind before journeying to the colonies over two centuries ago. Still, there was a note of aloofness that suggested Lady Jane was only being polite in her response. Could she manage to build a dialogue with this remarkable woman, a woman who clearly had far more interesting and important things to deal with than her piddly little inquiries? Jillian sat still for the longest time before she composed her response.

Dear Lady Rochester:
Thank you for your message regarding my inquiry as to the childhood of Catherine Wentworth Brownley. I am hopeful that you will be able to help us piece together some picture of her life in England. We are looking forward to proceeding with some exciting new plans in honor of her legacy. I will anxiously await any information you may be able to offer.
Sincerely,
Jillian Garrett
Director of Marketing and Special Promotions
The Wetherton Historical Foundation

After a lengthy re-read, Jillian clicked on send and glanced at the clock.

"Holy crap!" was her alarmed response. At 5:52 there would be no time for a shower, drink of water or last-minute trip to the bathroom. She sailed out the front door in the same black skirt and t-shirt she had left Manhattan in only a few hours earlier, and ran down the street toward the Foundation offices.

She crashed through the doors at 6:01, surprised to find a room full of people in a state of some chaos.

"Jillian," said Burt, the Foundation President, somberly greeting her with a handshake, "we're so glad you could make it. This is some kind of pickle, let me tell you, some kind of pickle." Jillian shook her head absently.

"I'm sorry I'm late," she began. "Maybe someone can tell me what this is all about." The room erupted in a raucous discord. Clearly, everyone was upset about something, but Jillian had no idea what or even if everyone was upset about the same thing.

"Come sit with me, Diabolita," Duke said, sidling up quietly behind her and purring in her ear. Jillian turned to him and whispered.

"What's going on? Don't tell me Jimmy Barker lost another snake."

"It's a snake alright," Duke answered, "but not the kind you're thinking of." They seated themselves next to each other at one of the six rectangular tables that had been set up in the shape of a "U" for the occasion. Burt Payne and his Vice-President, Bunny Pritchard, sat at a small table in the center, facing the crowd.

"I'll call this meeting to order," Burt announced, beating a wooden mallet on the table for effect. The room instantly hushed in anticipation. "We all know why we're here," Burt began. Jillian looked around the room full of faces and realized she was, quite possibly, the only person who had absolutely no idea why she was here. "We're here to find a reasonable, cost-efficient way of saving the Beckwith House."

"What?" Jillian shouted, rising to her feet in the middle of everyone. The room broke out into more chaos. Everyone was surprisingly, even shockingly, outraged about something. This was all highly unusual for a group of New England Yankees who could handle the arrival of four feet of snow in May just as easily as the morning newspaper.

"Excuse me," Jillian went on, shouting to be heard over the crowd and turning to everyone in the room, "but I left for New York less than 24 hours ago and at that time, and for 230 years prior to that, there was nothing wrong with the Beckwith House. And now it needs saving? Can someone please tell me what's going on?"

"Oh my goodness," Maggie rambled.

"It's a pickle, a right pickle," said Burt, shaking his head in resignation. The entire room was either wringing its hands in despair or red-faced with anger and frustration. It was Duke Parker who stood amidst the chaos to make sense of the matter at hand.

"If I may," he began, in his quiet, thoughtful way, "let me recap what we have come to learn over the last 24 hours." It must be said, here and now, that Duke had the enviable gift of public speaker extraordinaire. The room hushed to pin-drop silence, and everyone's eyes turned toward the speaker in the tie-dye shirt and leather-fringe vest who instantly engaged each and every one of them. It was Duke, a living monument to the 1960s, who would explain the 18th-century ramifications of their 21st-century predicament.

CHAPTER SEVEN

"My home, as it is situated nicely above our tavern, is often quite chaotic. Yet the strangers I meet are generally so interesting and diverting that I welcome the chaos with my whole heart." C.W.B. 1780

Lady Jane Alexandra Wentworth Rochester had been sentenced to one week of bed rest by the evil and inexperienced Dr. Vanderwheel, a woman Jane was now determined to detest. Upon his return, Jane had pleaded her case to Dr. Latrell, blustering and fidgeting and damning the lot of them, but Dr. Latrell held firm on the orders. The flu was no small matter, after all, especially for a woman of 86. Everyone agreed this was the most prudent course. James insisted that his Aunt follow the Doctor's instructions and had made a deplorable nuisance of himself by driving down almost every day to check on her.

Jane was like a caged tiger, restless and irritable. She glared at everyone who approached with a calculating stare that was so alarming, some feared she might actually try to bite them. Time indoors was interminable for Jane. No matter the weather, she craved the outdoors.

On the sixth day of her imprisonment, when she reluctantly confessed to herself that the medicine seemed to be working and that she did feel much improved, she wandered down to the library in search of something that could distract her.

"Can I get you anything, Mum?" Liza asked at the doorway.

"Heavens yes," Jane fired back. "Some hot needles, if you wouldn't mind. I should like to stick them in my eyes and experience a new torture today." Liza looked down to hide her smile.

"Tea, perhaps?" she offered in response. Jane sighed in boredom.

"Thank you, but no," Jane answered. "I'm simply trying to find something, with dramatic emphasis on the something, to read." She stared up at the walls covered in volumes of every shape, color and subject. Many of them were familiar to her, while others had not been touched in decades, perhaps centuries. She wandered past their rigid, soldier-like spines, staring up and down, waiting for something of interest to jump out at her. Her walk was slow and deliberate, her breathing was a bit difficult, but she refused to sit. One would think that in such a room one might find something of interest, she muttered to herself. Then something did. Something caught her eye.

Perched in the corner, at the table by the window was an object entirely new and interesting. How could she have completely forgotten about it? Now, her eyes lit up and she walked forthright and determined toward it. The new computer stood silently at the ready, waiting for her gracious welcome and her desire to become reacquainted. A renewed glimmer crossed Lady Jane's face. Treasure. Jackpot. A gem among gems. It was like a toy that had been ignored in the chaos of Christmas morning, only to be discovered hidden behind the tree on the next day.

She settled anxiously into the leather desk chair and lightly touched her fingertips to the keyboard, stroking gently as if to refresh her mind. Her right hand moved to the mouse, pushing it in tiny circles of concentration. Then, with a refreshingly deep breath, she touched the "power" button.

The screen lit up before her eyes and Jane sat motionless, entranced like a child in a planetarium. She watched and waited, trying to remember what James had so patiently taught her. She found her mailbox, with a few anxious clicks of the mouse, and opened a new message.

Dear Aunt Jane,
I hope you are enjoying your new computer.

Kindest regards,
James

"Pfft," Jane spouted with disappointment and clicked on the delete. She opened another, this one from that American again. "Hmm," Jane mused, deciding that even Americans were more entertaining than her nephew. She read with grateful interest, her brow wrinkling up and down with every word. "Very persistent," Jane muttered. Dudley entered the room, tip-toeing over to his master and settling in by her feet. "That's a fine friend," Jane smiled, leaning over to scratch at his soft folds of golden fur.

"Let's see if we can't help this young woman," she went on, a low raspy cough tuggng in her chest. Of course, she had no way of knowing Jillian's age, but to Jane everyone was young. Young and foolish and knowing nothing of life or the world.

She carefully slid the mouse toward "write", only momentarily alarmed when it fell off the mouse pad and the cursor mysteriously vanished. She recovered quickly, however, maintaining her composure. An odd frown of concentration twisted on her face.

She would never admit to it, but she was a bit nervous. Touching the wrong button or "clicking", as James had said, on the wrong symbol seemed fraught with computer peril. She worried that she might type the wrong letter or lead her mouse somewhere where a mouse should never be and the entire computer would crash. James had warned her of such a thing. Careful. Careful, she told herself quietly.

Dear Miss Garrett,
I am somewhat certain that your Catherine Wentworth Brownley had a brother who is buried in our chapel. I will

81

investigate this further. Please tell me about yourself and why it is that you have such a keen interest in this subject.
Sincerely,
Jane Rochester

Enormously satisfied with what she had created, Lady Jane clicked "send" and instantly communicated with a stranger 3,000 miles away in Wetherton, Connecticut. She was thrilled, and decidedly hooked. Never, in all her life had she known such global power. It was far better than anything on the television. Slowly and earnestly she tested this and that. She clicked and typed and clicked and typed. How positively wonderful!

Occasionally, her face with light up in surprise and the twisted half-smile of triumph would cross her lips. She might jump, unnerved by the world of the unexpected that would pop up on the screen before her. There would be moments of fascination, intermixed with a great deal of frowning and surprise. It was not easy being the old dog who was trying to learn new tricks, but Jane felt empowered by the challenge. It had been ages since she had found something so new and unknown to be so very much to her liking.

The typing and clicking, the clicking and typing, it went on and on. Before she knew it, three hours had passed and Liza was inquiring about her tea.

"Yes, Liza, thank you," Jane answered without looking up. "Could you bring it here to the little table please?" she asked, absently tapping the air in the general direction of a small table that stood some ways off. "I'm very comfortable at the moment."

Tea was served. Tea was taken away. The sky darkened outside and the room grew chilly. Jane summoned Phillip to build a fire in the great fireplace beside her. The hot flames roared in her ear, but Jane hardly noticed them. She nibbled her sandwich and continued clicking and typing and typing and clicking. "Heavens darling, do you see this?" she would shout to the portrait of Lord Arthur that hung on the wall in front of her. "You'd never hear of this in our day, I'll say," and she smiled and nodded to him for emphasis.

By eleven o'clock the fire had all but completely died down. The embers cast a long shadow against the empty dinner tray that sat next to her. Jane sipped a fine glass of sherry and blinked her eyes against the fatigue and dryness that stung them. She was suddenly aware of the fact that she had spent hours on end in that chair in front of that computer. Like a bear emerging from hibernation, she realized it was time to get up and move. Her old bones ached, especially her neck and back, and she noticed that even her fingers and wrists were stiff with fatigue. Not that she cared. At last, and for the first time in a long, long while, she had found something that excited her mind. If she could not go out into the world, then she would bring the world to her, and great God in heaven, what a world it was. Never could she have imagined the length and breadth of lunacy that existed in the world today. It was the world of the Internet. A new planetary dimension.

She drifted off to sleep that night, with a bizarre collection of images and ideas dancing through her mind. There was political propaganda, discovery of a shark that had been long-presumed extinct, eco-friendly footwear, homeopathic medicines that could cure everything from erectile dysfunction to warts, and so much more. It was the tip of a monolithic iceberg. It was shocking really, and all at the fingertips with the click of a silly little thing called a mouse.

"My, my, my, my, my," Jane whispered to herself in quiet amazement, as she fell asleep dreaming of newly a discovered dinosaur fossil coming to life in Asia and chasing her all the way back to England.

CHAPTER EIGHT

"We will have none of this deception. Let them all be free to say with whom their loyalties lie." C.W.B. 1777

The timing could not have been worse. Jillian would have preferred the wrath of a nor'easter over what now presented itself. A storm, at least, could be forecasted and predicted. Arnold Murton, on the other hand, was a wild card.

Mr. Murton was a self-made millionaire born and raised on the sunny west coast of southern California. Many Wethertonians would contend that this fact alone was explanation for his unsavory ways. Some would say he had earned his fortune the old-fashioned way, from hard work and a relentless determination. Wethertonians would say that greed and ruthlessness should not be disguised as hard work, and relentless determination was just window-dressing for dirty, underhanded dealings. Either way, Arnold Murton was not a man to be taken lightly.

Mr. Murton did not live in Wetherton. He made his home about an hour away in the far more manicured lifestyle of Greenwich. Wetherton and Greenwich were as much alike as Jack Sprat and his wife, and Wethertonians were as unprepared to do battle with Arnold as anyone could possibly be. The mere fact that Mr. Murton kept a curious eye on the tiny little town made everyone uneasy. The sight of his enormous black SUV with "Murton Construction" emblazoned on the doors in gold letters sent people running to the tavern in a panic to report their latest sighting. Paul Revere himself could not have done a better job alerting the common folk of an omnipresent threat. Now, the threat had become an assault and everyone in town had reason to be feeling far worse than uneasy. Arnold Murton had bought the Beckwith house.

No one knew exactly how the transaction had taken place. No one had seen Arnold Murton in town for several months. No one could confirm that Letitia Beckwith had ever even met the man to whom she apparently sold her family home.

Letitia Beckwith had been a sturdy little fixture in the community of Wetherton for all of her life. She lived in the house where she had been born, and where her great-great Grandfather had been born decades before her. She was known as a spinster, a term oddly out of date in the 21st-century, but employed to describe her nonetheless.

During World War II, she led the local Red Cross. During the Korean War she volunteered as a cook at the local VFW. During Viet Nam, she led a group of Wetherton women who marched in Washington to protest the war. It had even been rumored that she was smoking marijuana on that trip, although no one really believed that was anything more than gossip.

Now frail and failing and living on a meager fixed income, Letitia had been receiving her meals on wheels for a good many years. The minister from the Presbyterian Church stopped by twice a week for a visit, as did the ladies from the knitting group she originally founded. Once upon a time, Letitia's nimble fingers could coax skeins of yarn into elegant shawls and blankets with knitting needles almost a blur. Now cursed with arthritis, the bent and swollen knuckles could barely coax a teacup to her lips. Still, Letitia never complained. Her mind was lucid and sharp as a blade. She would sit and talk for hours to anyone kind enough to stop by. Even Jillian had been known to pay an occasional call for stories of Wetherton history and a little gossip.

On Mondays, the little white van would come to take her to the library and again on Sundays to take her to church. In all that time, in all that conversing among all those friends, she never once mentioned to anyone that she intended to sell her home to Arnold Murton.

How then, had the deed been done? No one knew where Letitia had moved or how she had been moved. Although rumors were spreading through the tiny town like head lice, it wasn't until the Town Clerk's office officially opened on Monday morning that anyone knew anything for certain, and the horrible truth of it made Jillian gasp with pain.

"You know Jillian," Deb Grister began, "I'm not supposed to release this information to the public until it has been formally processed and signed by George." George was the Town Clerk, whose famous fall hunting trip to the Adirondacks had inconveniently fallen during this particular week.

"Deb," Jillian said, "if I leave here without some answers, everyone in Wetherton will be barging through that door, and you don't want that, do you?" The attractive young blonde pushed her glasses up the bridge of her nose and gulped.

"No," she whispered. Then, with only a moment's hesitation and a shifty glance to each side, she relinquished the manila file she had been clutching to her slender chest. "You know Arnold Murton himself was in this office last week," Deb went on. "He had his son and some other guy here, some really big guy, and we all thought, oh please, are we supposed to be scared of you or something? But George wouldn't let anybody see the file. He said that protocol must be observed," she added, raising her nose in the air as if a bad smell had entered the room.

The paperwork was neat, organized, and minimal, yet it left no doubt what had transacted. The seller and her new address, the buyer, the purchase price, the lack of any easements protecting the property, it was all there in black and white and all seemingly legal.

Letitia Beckwith had been relocated to an assisted living facility. The decision had been made by her nephew, Roger Beckwith, whom she had named as executor of her estate. By all accounts, Letitia was very fond of Roger, as was Roger of her. No one would have the gall to presume that he had not struggled with his options before his Aunt Lettie was taken from the home she had loved for a lifetime. Logically, compounding the agony of this decision was the financial burden of paying for that choice. It was here that all became clear.

Letitia would now reside in the surprisingly posh surroundings of River Haven, a beautiful new assisted living facility just up the road a bit in Rocky Knoll, CT. The River Haven facility was built and owned by Murton Construction.

"Of course," Jillian said aloud upon reading the documents and digesting the circumstantial evidence. It all made perfect sense. Roger only wanted what was best for his Aunt. His concern for her was far outweighed by any feeling of sentimentality over an old house. Aunt Lettie was now receiving the best possible care money could buy, which was something he could never have afforded without the generosity bestowed upon him by Arnold Murton. How much, after all, was that old house really worth? With only a meager struggle, Roger had happily signed the papers that would hand over the Beckwith house. But why did a huge developer like Arnold Murton care about a tiny old colonial house?

The Beckwith property fell within, but at the very edge of, the Wetherton Historic District on 1½ acres of "prime" Wetherton real estate. The property straddled Treat's Creek, a tiny tributary of the Connecticut River. On the east side of the creek, directly abutting the "business" zone of Wetherton sat the Beckwith house and its' two outbuildings on just over 1 acre. On the west side of the creek was the remaining half acre of land which had long ago been cultivated as vegetable and flower gardens. Decades of neglect had allowed this land to retreat to an expanse of nothing more than wildflowers.

Abutting the Beckwith property on the business zone side was a rundown Laundromat and a little restaurant which was often vacant. On the other side of these commercial properties, just to the east, were two houses built in the early 1900's of little or no historical significance. All of these properties yielded a combined acreage in the business district of just about four acres. All of these properties were owned by Arnold Murton.

Yet, the town of Wetherton required a minimum parcel of 5 acres within the business district for development of multiple family housing. This point must be made very clear. Two years earlier, Mr. Murton had used the Affordable Housing Appeals Procedure to challenge the town's zoning regulations in what he claimed represented a "blatant attempt perpetrated by the suburbanites of Wetherton to keep affordable housing out of their neighborhood." The town had been outraged. Never before had the question of their collective character been so severely attacked. Especially by an outsider. A Californian no less. Not since the dreadful arrival of Brennan Parris in 1832, had the quiet community endured such a shocking surprise attack.

Mr. Parris had arrived in Wetherton during the summer of 1831. Though he claimed to hail from Savannah, several reports had placed him as a native of Kentucky. Wethertonians, being limited in their experience with anyone or anything that was not New England, believed all southerners to be pretty much the same regardless of their birthplace, and were content to accept Mr. Parris as an outsider. Mr. Parris set up his law practice, for he claimed to be a graduate of the William and Mary College of Law, in the bottom floor of the tiny house he rented from Mrs. Eudora Mills. A widow for some 12 years, Mrs. Mills had an impressive estate of landholdings in the Connecticut River Valley, courtesy of her husband, Benjamin Franklin Mills, who made his fortune importing fine linens and silks.

Eudora Mills was instantly enchanted with her newest tenant. He was polite and attentive and a marvelous conversationalist. Although he claimed to be very busy handling the delicate matters of his wealthy clients back home in Georgia, he was never too distracted to accept an invitation for breakfast, lunch or dinner with any family who would offer their hospitality. His stories of world travel were remarkable. Mr. Parris had been to nearly every country in Europe. All this in the span of his young life, which he counted to be no more than 38 years.

Throughout the winter of 1831 and into the spring of 1832 the town of Wetherton grew to enjoy their token outsider more and more. He attended church every Sunday. He was never too busy to offer a hand of help or a lighthearted joke to a downhearted fellow. Then in April of that year, very much to everyone's surprise, Mr. Brennan Parris disappeared. On Monday he had been busy in his office with his papers as usual and on Tuesday he was, quite simply, gone. There was no sign of his person or his whereabouts. No one had seen him leave and no one had word from him as to where he had arrived. Then the truth of him began to unravel.

Mrs. Mills, believing him to be an honest attorney of good character, had agreed to lend Mr. Parris nearly $500 for a business enterprise he claimed would yield exceptional profits for everyone involved. He had drawn up the necessary legal papers and she had willingly signed them. Tucker Foley, just up the street from Mrs. Mills, had also loaned money to Mr. Parris believing that he was about to become rich beyond his wildest dreams. Once again, Mr. Parris had drawn up the legal papers and once again they had been signed freely and gladly.

The list of Wethertonians had gone on and on. All totaled, some 30 families had "loaned" or "invested" their money in varying sums with Mr. Parris. It was now clear to all of them that they had been deceived most cruelly. They were fools, every one of them. There would be no profit. There would be no return on investment. There would be no justice, for he was never seen again, although Ezra Davids kept a noose strung and at the ready in his undying hope that he would someday have the pleasure of placing it around Brennan Parris' neck.

It was on that day that the good people of Wetherton had a lesson that would last through the decades. Never trust an outsider, especially a southerner who sings at church every Sunday in a surprisingly pleasant tenor voice. Now it was Arnold Murton, the outsider, intruding into their community with the notion that the people of Wetherton were gentle-hearted fools.

"You rotten bastard," Jillian muttered again aloud, realizing what was about to hit them all full in the face.

Clearly, Arnold Murton was not a man to accept defeat. Yes, two years ago the State of Connecticut had handed down a ruling favoring the town, but that was only a setback to Mr. Murton. He wasn't finished. He wasn't beaten. Not by a long shot.

He had simply grimaced at the annoyance the little town had caused him, and laughed off the ruling as a joke. The people of Wetherton, believing themselves to be safe from harm had celebrated victory, but that could not be further from the truth. As long as there were Arnold Murtons there would be no safety for towns like Wetherton, or homes like the Beckwith House.

It would be destroyed, Jillian imagined. Knocked-down. Scrapped. Whatever term one might choose to describe the complete destruction of more than 250 years of history. She presumed that Mr. Murton would once again use the Affordable Housing Appeals Procedure to challenge the town's regulations. This time it would be the historic district. Everything that Wetherton had put down on paper to protect their homes, their heritage and the very nature of their community would be challenged. He would mire them down in legal fees. Their meager resources would be siphoned away from the running of the Historical Foundation to the defense of the Beckwith House.

Was Arnold Murton truly an advocate of affordable housing and the working class poor? Was he really just a great guy, out to fix wrongs and make the world a better place? One could only wonder. It certainly seemed unlikely. The potential profit he would reap from this investment would leave anyone with a head for numbers highly skeptical. Yet again, there were those who would argue that if Mr. Murton could turn a healthy profit and better the lives of others all at the same time, what was wrong in that? America was born and bred on capitalism after all.

Jillian cupped her temples in the warmth of her palms, and sat motionless.

"Rotten bastard is pretty nice talk for this guy," she heard whispered in her left ear. Jillian turned, startled, to see Duke standing next to her with his wife, Dahlia, resplendent in tie-dyed skirt and headband.

"You scared me," Jillian startled. She looked up at the two with an expression of utter despair. "I don't know what to do," she offered mildly. "He's coming at us loaded for bear and I don't know what to do. And I'm ashamed because," she hesitated, "I never saw it coming." Duke merely smiled in response. She had seen that smile so many times, and had almost always found comfort in it, but today even Duke's amazing powers of calm could not help her.

"Diabolita," Duke said reproachfully, "no one saw it coming. You have to play for the other team to see something like this." He smiled and shrugged his shoulders. "But we don't have to play their game to win." Jillian tasted the bitterness of her throat close inside her.

It was humiliating. They hadn't even realized the game was still on. Wetherton had won, hadn't they? The issue was decided. It was supposed to be over, but it wasn't. What fools they all were. Simpletons with simple goals and pure hearts. Believers in justice and hard work and playing by the rules. How could they do battle with an Arnold Murton? How could they ever beat him?

"Murton filed for his intent to demolish based on his professional assessment that the house is uninhabitable and beyond saving. We filed for the construction delay," Dahlia told her matter-of-factly. "We have 90 days to save that house." Jillian stared up blankly at the two of them.

How could two people, so brilliant and well-educated, be standing before her with such house-hugging optimism? They had weathered this storm before. Just after Jillian's arrival, ten years earlier, the Brian house had been lost to demolition. Some had argued that the Brian house, 102 years old and of no particular architectural or historical significance, was a hazard, an eyesore and decades beyond saving.

In fact, some applauded the young couple who came to town with a vision for a "new" old house on the quiet street and the lovely lot that boasted a river view and an elementary school within walking distance. In truth, the new home that they built was charming, and was very much in keeping with the character of the town. The design, the style and proportion were all well suited to the site, the community and the history within which it was created. Yet, it lacked the one thing it could never have and could only hope to rebuild, and that was, of course, a history.

Wethertonians were nearly unglued by the notion that anything in their town could simply be knocked-down and sent to the landfill like so much unwanted garbage. There were chestnut floorboards 18 inches wide. There were custom moldings and hand-stencils and two little closets in the basement used to store homemade preserves and homegrown pickle relish. It seemed entirely un-New England, at the very least, to tear down anything that could in some way be reused and repurposed with some good old-fashioned Yankee ingenuity. Waste not, want not. It was the first time the townspeople realized how fragile the centuries-old existence of their community might be.

The lesson had been clear. Privately owned property could be developed and re-developed as the owner saw fit, as long as that vision complied with local planning and zoning ordinances and building codes. Property within the historic district would only be protected from demolition if "historical significance of note" could be proven with well-documented evidence. All of this, of course, was subject to hearings at Town Hall and court rulings which were funny and unpredictable things at best.

Martin Harkenberry in 1853 had once said, "Let me rather die than subject myself to the scrutiny and peculiarity of the courts." Six weeks later, in a court-ordered settlement handed down by Justice William Fitzgibbon, the title to Mr. Harkenberry's home on Treat Street was handed over to Mr. Charles Slifton.

"Save the house," Jillian responded after a long pause. "OK. How do we save it?" Her eyes became wild and maniacal. "You can't possibly think that we could raise enough money to buy it from Murton. This is obviously the cash cow he's been cultivating for the last six years." Jillian's voice rose half an octave higher. "What do you think? Should we ask Jimmy Barker and all the other kids in town to empty their piggy banks? No! No!" she said with dramatic emphasis. "I've got a great idea. We'll have a raffle, and a baked goods sale and a "Save the Beckwith House" Tag Sale. Right? Yes. Absolutely. That is exactly what we'll do. That is exactly what we always do. And guess what?" Jillian turned to face them, sputtering and flushed with exasperation. "It isn't good enough. OK? It isn't. We could never, in a million years of Money Mack dinners, come up with the kind of money that we need to fix this in 90 days!"

Duke and Dahlia smiled at her, embraced by some form of other-worldly peace. Jillian glared back at them in disgust.

"What?" she said finally. "What are you smiling about?" Duke put his hand gently to her head.

"I don't like your aura," he pronounced. Jillian snorted a retort.

"There is a way," Dahlia stated, squatting down next to Jillian's chair.

"But everyone needs to stay calm and stay focused," Duke said, pressing his palm into her forehead and snapping her neck back simultaneously.

"Ow," Jillian whimpered, swishing her head approvingly left and right.

"You do understand that we have several things working in our favor here, don't you?" Duke asked, pushing her head left, as it wanted to go right, and back again the other way.

"Uh, hmmm, sorry," Jillian answered. "Not really getting that."

"We have the previous ruling against Murton," Duke offered convincingly. Jillian raised her eyebrows in consideration of the point. "We have the fact that his 5 ½ combined acres sit partly within the historic district," he added enticingly. "And we have historic significance of note," he said at last, triumphantly.

"What historic significance of note?" Jillian asked. Duke grabbed her ears and shook her head back and forth.

"No one knows exactly, do they?" Duke answered with his mad professor grin. "That's what you have to find."

"That's what I have to find?" Jillian howled, with emphasis on the I. "How am I supposed to do that?" She muttered something under her breath about calling Taylor for a job in New York. "I don't see how that's going to happen."

"Oh, but you must," Dahlia interrupted. "You must see it."

"You're the one," Duke whispered. "You are the one who can find the link."

"What link?" Jillian asked, Duke swishing her head left and right, then to and fro.

"Our link to the past," Duke said, breathing in her left ear and twisting her head to the right.

"Ow," Jillian said again, this time really meaning it. She glared at him with a hand to her neck. Duke smiled back in his all-knowing way. He knelt down next to her and looked her straight in the eye.

"That house has over 250 years of history," he began. "That house was here when British soldiers came through this town on their way to Massachusetts. British troops slept in that house on their way back through town before the Battle of Trenton. We're talking George Washington crossing the Delaware. We're talking the American Revolution. We're talking the beginning of this great nation, baby. All you have to do is find and prove that a person or event of historical significance is linked to that house and it will be protected from demolition forever." Jillian paused for a star-struck moment.

"Well that should be easy to do," she answered at last with a smile. "After all, Letitia is tucked away in Murton's nursing home and nobody else seems to know a damned thing about that house for the last 250 years, but let me just consult my magic, crystal ring which I keep right here," she said, waving her hand wildly in their faces, "because I'm sure that will give me all the answers."

Duke and Dahlia exchanged forlorn glances. Jillian was clearly at odds with her karma.

"I can see you're going to need a little help with this one," Duke said. "I'll start with Roger Beckwith and Dahlia will head over to the library." Jillian sat stubbornly immobile. She was in no mood to do research on this particular day. In fact, she was in no mood to do anything other than wander over to the tavern for some Brownley punch. Duke and Dahlia, however, quietly turned to leave with an ardent sense of purpose.

"Wait," she stammered after them angrily. The pair turned back patiently. "What do you want me to do?" Duke shrugged his shoulders absently and proceeded out the door, leaving Jillian alone in the cramped dusty Town Clerk's office. She scratched at her scalp with both hands and fluffed up her hair into a wild, brunette mess. She wished for a tall glass of Brownley punch to drop from the heavens. She stared up at the rows of shelves lined with rows of dusty brown and grey ledgers and books.

"What a bunch of crap," she muttered, shaking her head in despair. "Find the link," she said mockingly. "Pigs will be flying around Wetherton before anyone finds any kind of link in this place." Jillian fiddled with a curl at the right side of her head. "It's a needle in a freaking, crazy haystack."

She rose to her feet and perused the tattered bindings all around her. At other times in her life this would be a feast for the eyes and a seductive invitation to an afternoon of intrigue. Today, it was simply rows of filthy old junk that could not be more repulsive. Jillian glared at the strips of leather that filled the room with dingy gray-blue light.

"I'm so sick of this town," she said to no one, begrudgingly glancing at this title or that. The room spun around her with light and life and possibilities, but she snubbed the invitation. She stifled the urge to run her finger along the spine of each book and twisted away from them in revulsion. "I should pack my stuff and go back to New York," she muttered angrily, biting her bottom lip. "It wasn't that bad," she went on. "Plenty of great guys and parties." Her mouth turned uncontrollably down at the corners as she remembered her most recent evening in Manhattan. "Well," she offered in defense, "Taylor is there and she's my best friend in the whole world. What could be better than that?" An image of Taylor shooting tequila scanned through her mind, causing a giant wrinkle in Jillian's forehead. She exhaled loudly in exasperation.

Her eyes fell on an 18th-century map of the town that hung on the wall before her. She edged closer to take a half-hearted look. Of course she knew the map. Every name, property, stream and pasture were as familiar to her as the back of her own hand. Treat, Samuel, Goodsmith, Brownley, and Robbins, were the names that spun from her mind without thought or provocation. She felt she knew them as friends, or at least acquaintances, for she had read their most private journals and their last wills and testaments. What did she know of the Beckwith house? Had there been something, anything, long overlooked by the sleuths of history? Her mind raced through the tattered fragments that were documented and well-known. But what of the gaps in history? What of the years and decades undocumented?

The house had been built around 1740 on land that had been purchased by Charles Treat in 1738. At that time, Mr. Treat had already buried two wives back in England, and was presently moving to the colonies with his new wife, Abigail whom he had married just weeks before they set sail for their new life. The house, a modest two-room wood-frame structure must have been completed by the time of Charles' untimely death in 1743, because his last will and testament clearly gave the home "and two fine oxen" to his widow. It was believed that Abigail died not long after, sometime before 1750, but this could not be confirmed. It was known that at some time between 1769 and 1771, Horatio Beckwith became the owner of the property.

Horatio was an elusive character, often presumed to be a privateer, as no known occupation or family connection to money could be found. He was married to a woman named Margaret, yet no family name was known of her. It was not until the year 1843 that the historical foundation could begin to piece together an impressive paper trail of ownership and ancestry. Of course the Beckwith family had lost nine family members while serving their country, from the Civil War right through Viet Nam. This was well-known and well-documented. Sadly, this would not satisfy their needs. Dying for one's country simply wasn't historically significant enough to save the Beckwith house.

CHAPTER NINE

"Many men hide great secrets in their hearts during these difficult days."
C.W.B. 1777

Jane had always loved the library. When she was very young her father used to sit at the enormous oak desk in his well-worn leather chair and read his newspaper. Jane and Phillipa would play on the carpet near his feet. Of course, all too often, some squabble would break out between the two of them, usually a sniveling complaint from Pippa about Jane being too rough with her dolls or not wanting to pretend to be dragons, and Richard Wentworth would shoo them from the room with his booming voice.

"Pinhead," young Jane would sneer at her little sister who would stick out her tongue in return.

"It's your fault Jane," Phillipa would rifle back. "You're such a bossy boss."

"And you're a prissy little baboon," Jane would bluster.

"I'm telling," Phillipa would shout, running down the hall.

Jane smiled her crooked half-smile as she walked down the same hall in the opposite direction. In her mind, she could see Pippa running past her, all red in the face with determination. It had always been easy to get a rise out of her.

On this day, unusually bright rays of morning sunshine were dancing through the east windows spraying every inch of the room with a lovely warm glow. Heavens, Jane thought to herself as she entered the room, taken aback by the number of volumes that lined the shelves from ceiling to floor. It was impressive. Funny, she thought, how one can see something for nearly a century, but never really see it. Today, for no particular reason, she saw the library with a fresh pair of eyes and it was marvelous.

Settling in behind her little mahogany desk in the corner, she touched the power button on her computer and waited for life to spring forth. It was only a few seconds before the worldwide web lay at her fingertips. She chuckled softly and began to maneuver her mouse with weathered hands that, just weeks earlier, had never known such a task as "clicking".

"What do you think of this darling?" she said, glancing up at the portrait of Lord Arthur Rochester that hung just before her to the right. "Did you ever think an old girl like me would be surfing the Web?" She chuckled again and tapped at the keys in a gingerly hunt-and-peck method. "Watch this darling," she exclaimed, looking up again into Arthur's serious gaze.

"Welcome. You've got mail," shouted out at her. Jane laughed with pride.

"You see? All I do is type away at this and that and, in an instant, the whole world comes to me. Bloody hell! Can you imagine such a thing?" she asked, smiling at her husband. He seemed unimpressed, but she was not daunted.

"Honestly darling, if you were here you would love this!" She pressed a kiss to her withered fingertips and waved it at Lord Arthur. My goodness, he was such a handsome man, Jane thought quietly. How she missed him. How much she had been cheated in this life without him.

"Did you call for me, Mum?" Liza asked at the doorway, wringing her hands into one giant meaty fist. Jane looked up with confusion.

"No Liza, I did not."

"I thought I heard you speaking to someone," Liza offered. Jane continued to tap away at her keys without looking back.

"Speaking to someone," she answered, "really? Certainly not. Do you think I'm mad?" Liza gulped hard.

"No Mum," she offered with a forced laugh. "Of course not. Can I bring you some tea?"

"Tea," Jane said, contemplating the offer as if someone had said 'tea or door number two'. What would she do if I asked for gin? Probably ring my nephew and the damned doctor. A devilish gamble. "Yes," Jane answered. "I'll take the tea. Thank you Liza."

"I won't be a moment." Liza turned her ample figure sideways, looking back at Jane who stared at the computer screen and muttered something indiscernible under her breath. Liza breathed in loudly and hurried down the hall back toward the kitchen muttering her own indiscernible thoughts. A house of madness and muttering.

"You see darling," Jane went on. "They think I've positively lost my mind. Why they should think that I do not know. Nor do I care." She smiled up at him again. "And I neglected to tell you of my new American friend," she paused and raised her eyebrows for effect. "I know what you're thinking darling, but she's a lovely young girl. All full of passion and ideas, it's very silly but very exciting." Her mouth turned down at the corners. "She does seem a bit high-strung, but I do enjoy her company. To be honest darling, it's often lonely here." Jane typed and clicked away, staring at Lord Arthur with a surprisingly misty pair of eyes. "We had such fun, didn't we darling?" she said to him. "Ah yes, those were the days." Jane shook her head full of memories and squinted down her nose through her glasses at the computer.

"Bollocks," Jane muttered absently, typing and clicking, a frown of frustration crossing her forehead. It was not easy, after all. Had she learned this as a child, or even as a woman in her seventies, this business of computers would be second nature. Now edging in on 87, Jane found learning anything new required extraordinary concentration and determination. As luck would have it, Jane Alexandra Wentworth Rochester was the dictionary definition of determination, and she was unrelenting at this age or any other.

"Here we are then," Liza announced with a silver tray of tea and toast. She carefully placed it on the little table just to Jane's left, leaning over as far as she could to try to read what was on the computer. Jane turned to glare over the top of her periwinkle reading glasses.

"Thank you Liza," she said. "That will be all." Liza cast her eyes downward to the carpet.

"Certainly. Please let me know if you need anything else. Anything at all."

"Yes," Jane said, without wavering her glare. Liza forced a fleeting smile. Jane sipped at her tea and sat back in her chair. A twinge inside her toyed with the idea of going outside, but she had promised the evil doctors who cared for her that she would not go out until after her appointment. Oddly, in this warm chair, in this lovely room with this hot cup of tea, she quickly dismissed the notion.

"You see darling," she said, again addressing the portrait, "Old dogs can learn new tricks." She smiled and sipped again at the deliciously soothing cup. "I know, I know," she said settling the delicate cup back onto the tray, "you think I'm getting soft." She knew she could not keep secrets from him. She smiled again, the crooked half-smile, and sat back in her chair. She was a small figure within the enormous room and yet she felt cozy and secure. It was a solitary life at Broadhurst Hall and it had been that way for many years. Ever since Arthur died in 1961 and her life changed forever.

She retired from society and retreated to the sanctuary of her home. Of course, friends and family had tried to get her to date, to come to London, to meet new men, but she refused every attempt. Pippa would come out often and stay for a day or two, sometimes joined by her nieces, Pippa's daughters, Gwenan and Finley. She loved them as though they were her own children and they would have such fun traipsing around the fields together while their mother awaited their return at the house. But time would go by quickly and commitments in London would call them all back again. Though they begged Auntie Jane to join them, she rarely accepted.

When James was born, Finley's only son, she was pleased to be named his Godmother and stayed in London for an entire week for the christening. That was now over thirty years ago. "Heavens," Jane thought to herself, remembering the tiny baby she had held in her arms. It certainly didn't seem that long ago, and yet it was. Where had the time gone?

Her social calendar was now limited to those few occasions, such as hosting the Horticultural Society each spring, that were Wentworth obligations. She did attend church every Sunday, but stayed only long enough to say good morning to the Vicar and then she was home again. Yes, it had been a solitary life for decades. How funny that after all this time she should suddenly be "meeting" new people nearly every day.

This Jillian Garrett, for example, seemed like such a lovely young girl. Hard-working, determined, a little silly perhaps, but she liked her nonetheless. Her questions challenged Jane's lucid mind to snap to attention and it was a pleasure to have someone "listen" to her other than Dudley.

In the sitting room, just adjacent to the library, the telephone rang. Liza, who was on her hands and knees picking up bits of a dog bone and muttering insults at Dudley, raised her portly body to answer it. It was James.

"Yes sir," Liza said to him, "I'll just get her for you." She hesitated. "Sir," she added, "I think I hear her talking to herself lately." James frowned, the telephone held loosely by his chin.

"What do you mean, Liza?"

"Well sir, just now, for example. I think she was talking to the painting."

"What painting Liza?" James asked, a little exasperated.

"Lord Rochester's painting, sir."

"Ah yes, well, she does that sometimes. May I speak with her please?"

"Certainly, sir. Just a moment." She ambled out into the hallway and cleared her throat at the entrance to the library.

"Your nephew is on the telephone for you," Liza said. "Would you like to speak with him?" Jane nodded her assent and waited for Liza to bring her the telephone.

"Yes James," she said with Janiness.

"Hello Aunt Jane, how are you?"

"I'm well, thank you," she said, clicking her way onto her e-mail as they spoke. "How are you?"

"Excellent," James said. "Are you ready for your Doctor's visit today?" Distracted by her computer, Jane took a moment to answer.

"Uh yes," she offered finally, "yes."

"Aunt Jane, are you alright? You seem distracted."

"Hmmm?" she said. "Oh, no, no, I'm fine. I'm just sending an e-mail."

"An e-mail? Really? To whom?" James asked, his concern at a pique.

"Well, not that it's any of your business, but I'm responding to the American woman, Jillian Garrett."

"Again? That's odd, isn't it? Is she bothering you?"

"Heaven's no," she shot back irritably. "She's bright and inquisitive." Jane hunted and pecked a few more words.

"If she becomes a nuisance, you must let me know," he persisted.

"Hmmm," Jane muttered. "Be careful now James. All that worry will make your hair fall out." James offered a half-hearted chuckle, but worry crossed his brow nonetheless.

"You're sure you're feeling better?"

"Right as rain," she announced. "Now, I'm sorry, but I really should be readying myself to go."

"Of course," he offered. Jane continued to type and click, trying to juggle the phone under her chin, but having little success. "Will Geoffrey be driving you?" James added.

"Hmmm?" Jane answered vaguely. James frowned at his phone, this was not at all like his Aunt to be acting this way.

"Geoffrey," he pressed, "will he be driving you?"

"Oh bollocks," Jane muttered, fidgeting with the keys and deleting. "Sorry James, I really must run. What's that you asked? Uh, Geoffrey? Uh, yes, uh, IDK. Talk to you soon," she added cheerily, juggling the phone and absently hanging up. James stared at the receiver that had just clicked in his ear.

"IDK?" He sat motionless, his eyes wild and filled with a crazy look that could only be called panic. Slowly, he reached for his laptop and, with nimble fingers, quickly typed his command. He hadn't wanted to do this. He hadn't wanted to spy on her. He had only set up her email account with modest supervisory provisions, he told himself, only in the event that she should require his assistance. It wasn't spying, really, it was merely his duty to protect Aunt Jane from dangers she couldn't be expected to understand. He was, after all, the person responsible for setting up her computer. His eyes darted across the screen, scanning her correspondence.

"Bloody hell," he murmured, astounded by the seventeen emails she had sent and the eighteen she had received. All from this mysterious J. Garrett of Wetherton, Connecticut. James rubbed two shaky fingers across his dry lips and stared at the screen. What to do?

What to do? Well, clearly it was time for action, but what?

He wheeled his chair closer to his desk, straightened his posture and typed.

Dear Ms. Garrett,
My name is James Cavington, I am the nephew of Lady Rochester. My aunt has relayed her communications with you to me, as she does all Internet correspondence she receives, and has indicated that she is eager to help. I am concerned however, that my aunt, who is quite frail, will be unable to help too much. If possible, I hope that I may be of assistance to you if you require any additional information from our family library.

Please do not mention this communication to my aunt, as I fear it would be embarrassing to her.
Sincerely,
James Cavington

He sat back and gave it a lengthy re-read before sending. That should do the trick, he thought with satisfaction. If this J. Garrett was up to no good, believing his Aunt to be alone and unprotected, she would now realize she had been sorely mistaken. He nodded his head with conviction.

"First they want a little information, next thing you know they're asking for money," James muttered. "God, how do people live with themselves." He glared at the email address on his screen and sneered with disgust.

CHAPTER TEN

"Just when I am most deeply in despair, it seems God always sends an angel to show me the way," C.W.B. 1777

The annual Harvest Party was now only weeks away, the Beckwith House was slated for demolition sometime right before Christmas, and Duke, as usual, was late for the weekly staff meeting at the Historical Foundation offices in the Goodrich House.

Built in 1805, it was not one of Wetherton's oldest or most prestigious properties, yet the simple two-story clapboard structure held a position of prominence on the eastern side of the Presbyterian Church. Most notably, the legend of the Charter Oak Tree, was attached to the house. It seemed the Goodrich family may have played a role in this mischievous bit of colonial Connecticut history.

Believed to have roots in the 12th century, the Charter Oak was a massive white oak tree growing in an area now known as Hartford, just north of Wetherton. Native Americans claimed that the tree had been planted as a ceremonial symbol of peace and persuaded English colonists, ever in need of firewood and farmland, to spare it from the felling axe. And so it was.

In 1662, King Charles II had granted the Connecticut colony certain autonomy by issuance of a charter. Upon inheriting the throne, his successor James II, decided to tighten the reins on the New England colonies, including Connecticut. He was therefore understandably anxious to retrieve the charter to avoid any confusion as to the real or assumed power that the colonies might wield.

Sir Edmund Andros, the newly appointed Governor-General was dispatched to the colonies in 1687 to collect the document. His arrival was not a welcome one.

A meeting was planned, whereby after much pomp and circumstance the charter would be surrendered to Andros. The day wore on and light grew dim. Suddenly, at some seemingly uncanny moment every candle in the room was mysteriously blown out. When light was restored, the room collectively gasped. The charter was missing.

The legend of the Charter Oak Tree dictates that a gentleman named Joseph Wadsworth was handed the charter through an open window and that he secretly stashed the document within a hidden cavity of the massive oak tree. The truth and the ultimate disclosure of the charter has never been determined.

In 1856, a violent lightning storm rocked the central region of the state and the Charter Oak Tree thundered to the ground, taking with it centuries of strength and magnificence. Several local museums boast collections of furniture purportedly hewn from the monstrous supply of wood it left behind. Two such pieces, a cradle and a tea caddy, were presently the prestigious property of the Wetherton Historical Foundation.

Jillian Garrett, who now sat where the Goodrich dining table once stood, sipped a long, steaming hot gulp of coffee and pressed her fingers to her temples. She fidgeted with the 18th-century costume she had been forced to put on this morning when Sally Logan called to say her son was ill and she wouldn't be able to make it over to town today. At least she had been lucky enough to merit the chocolate brown silk gown with rosebud embroidery. Jillian always liked to wear that costume, but could only justify donning the extravagant attire when she was re-enacting one of Wetherton's wealthiest ladies. Today she would be Abigail Webster, wife of Joseph Webster, who was one of the town's most successful attorneys and political figures of his time.

The morning had begun with a tour of the Webster house, an original circa 1770 home where it was a point of fact that George Washington had slept on two separate occasions. Jillian had gone on and on in her most passionate manner to describe the furnishings, the food, the surprisingly cramped bedchambers. Visitors were generally easily engaged by the presentation. Until today.

On this day she was challenged by a curious group of only eight guests. There was a couple from upstate New York, somewhere just east of Rochester, who were entirely put out by the lack of chairs available for visitors. Let us not speak of the moment when the husband actually attempted to seat himself in the chair believed to have been used by General Washington himself and Jillian had nearly wrestled him to the ground.

Then there was a lovely gentleman from Boston who asked more questions, God save her, than anyone she had ever met. He was sweet, he really was, with a chubby face and a Santa-like beard, but he was so annoying. Just as Jillian would resume her dialogue, after suffering another interruption, the man would raise his hand again and again. And the questions were so absurd! Did she know if they kept pigs on the property? How many pairs of shoes would Mrs. Webster have owned? Did anyone know if they had planted kale?

At last, there were the five Pennsylvania ladies on their annual road trip. All widows and all lifelong friends who banded together each fall to travel the back roads of America. Jillian smiled at the thought of them crossing the George Washington Bridge in their minivan during rush-hour and making their way up to New England, but she was grateful to have them on the tour. Who wouldn't love a bunch of spunky old ladies, especially the woman in the lavender pantsuit with matching vest whose primary goal was to sample some Brownley punch.

It was an odd group. An odd group on an odd day that had begun with a phone call from Taylor about that job in New York and an email from a man claiming to be the nephew of Lady Jane Rochester. Taylor had bullied her into agreeing to send her resume to *Historic Home* magazine. It was an advertising sales job, which was not exactly Jillian's cup of tea, but the potential to make a lot of money held huge appeal. She was tired of living like a pauper.

Then there was this email. She recognized the name James from several emails she had received from Lady Jane, but she thought his tone was strange. Pompous and strange. Jillian imagined a chubby, red-faced, spoiled British aristocrat, squeezing himself into riding pants and a tweed jacket and trotting around the countryside on his thoroughbred. What a jerk! Poor Lady Rochester. Saddled with a nephew like that.

She glanced at her watch and realized they had waited more than fifteen minutes for Duke, which was far longer than ever before and far more inexcusable given the strained limits of everyone's patience. She made a mental note to ask Sarah about the cute new guy who was working on the roof at the Treat house this morning. Although she felt she looked fabulous in her costume, she still couldn't muster the nerve to stop and say hello. She offered only a wimpy little wave and kept walking. Loser, she berated herself silently. Spinsters aren't a thing of the past. They're still out there, all around me. Now we call them "career-minded." She chewed absentmindedly on her fingernail.

"Let's begin," Jillian announced abruptly, shuffling papers and glancing at the door.

"Oh dear, don't you think we should wait a few more minutes?" Maggie asked, nervously looking to the door in hope that Duke would appear.

"Duke's a big boy, he owns a watch, so let's begin," Jillian continued crossly. Maggie exchanged a worried glance with the group.

"Let's start with the Harvest Party," Jillian began. "Let's have updates from everyone. Henry, why don't you go first." Henry Robbins, a retired engineer from the Department of Public Works, looked around the room with eyes as wide as a frightened child.

"Me?" he offered meekly.

"Yes," Jillian smiled gladly. "Tell us about your plans for lighting the trees, setting up the bandstand, you know, go ahead." She smiled even more encouragingly, hoping for some sign of life.

"Well," Henry began again, slowly. "Duke said he'd help out with the lights as usual. Of course, I don't know where he put those lights from last year, but I'm sure they're around here somewhere." Henry smiled at Jillian. "Uh," he paused, "and, uh, the bandstand, well that'll go up after the lights, same as always, just as soon as Duke finishes the lights." Jillian slurped another swig of coffee and pondered the merits of taking up a really bad and distracting habit like smoking before finding the composure to go on.

"Sounds great Henry," she began, "but why don't we go ahead and find out where those lights are located and maybe you could be in charge of storing them in the shed out back for next year?"

"Huh?" was Henry's only reply. "Duke's not gonna like that, he's real particular about where those lights go."

"Yes, well, I'm sure he is, but it puts the rest of us in a real bind sitting around waiting for Duke all the time, doesn't it?" Jillian shot back with a tight-lipped smile. Maggie's mouth opened in shock, and glanced at all the faces around the table.

"Next," Jillian shouted, like a woman selling sandwiches at the local deli. "Carol, could you please give us an update on special events merchandise?" Carol Leonard, a fifty-something divorcee who moved to Wetherton five years earlier from Maine, looked up from her clipboard with an officious pose. Her highlighted bangs curled into a shape that reminded Jillian of a croissant pressed against her forehead.

"Thank you, Jillian," she began impressively. "We are very excited this year to be able to add candied-apple flashlights to our list of merchandise." Maggie Paul nodded her approval. "There will also be the expected assortment of t-shirts, baseball caps and pumpkin crowns." Maggie broke into approving applause.

"My kids just love those pumpkin crowns," added Beverly Burch, hardworking, overachieving-mother-of-four.

"Everybody does," added Maggie enthusiastically.

"Pumpkin crowns for the kids and Brownley punch for the grown-ups," Henry said with a smile that seemed to be missing a tooth on the left side.

"Amen," Beverly said with a wink, as the door to the conference room burst open with characteristic drama.

"Sorry," Duke offered loudly, "oh, oh, oh, so sorry I am late." He smiled at the group and grabbed a chair across from Jillian. "Diabolita," he added with a nod in her direction. Everyone, other than Jillian, seemed to breathe a collective sigh of relief. Jillian simply took another long, hard sip of her coffee and turned back to her agenda.

"Thanks Carol, that sounds really great. I'm sure you have everything under control." Carol nodded her agreement, and Jillian moved on to the next item on the list.

"You look fabulous," Duke whispered to Maggie. "Is that new?" he asked, admiring the otherwise remarkably dull, forest green jumper and matching turtleneck ensemble. Maggie giggled. Jillian sighed loudly.

"I had it taken in," Maggie whispered back proudly. "I've lost two sizes since I wore this last."

"Far out," Duke said encouragingly. Jillian glared silently in dismay.

Could it be possible that she was expected, day in and day out, to plunge toilets, coddle crying toddlers and save history with this bumbling pack of fools? Candied apple flashlights? Brownley punch? Pumpkin crowns? She thought her head would explode. She wanted to run, run screaming from the room and from the town and from the entire New England region.

The Beckwith House could be saved how? By a bunch of well-meaning, volunteer do-gooders who would throw their bodies on the floor boards as the wrecking ball pummeled each and every one of them? Much good may it do them. Much good may it do anyone. Who could fight the well-oiled, well-connected, well-financed machine of Murton Construction? Arnold Murton had friends in Hartford. Arnold Murton had friends in Washington. Arnold Murton probably had friends in places that would scare the living daylights out of decent, hardworking people everywhere.

For the Wetherton Historical Foundation, and all of its contributors who wrote checks for five or ten dollars every year, and all of its many volunteers who devoted tireless hours serving as docents or re-enactors or ticket-takers, it was about something beyond priceless. It was about discovery and rediscovery. It was about stories and memories. It was about allowing the future to stand in the actual footsteps of the past, and not simply read about it in a textbook. It was about something beyond dollars and cents, and the Arnold Murtons of the world would never concede the point. They would never apologize. They would never relent. They would never go away. For every Arnold Murton in Wetherton, there would be ten more lined up to step in and pillage and prosper at the loss of everyone other than themselves, and then walk away.

The thoughts sickened Jillian, and yet, as she glanced around the room the inevitability of their situation grew darker and more oppressive. She felt the urge to run home, pack her bags and get out before it all fell apart. She watched Carol modeling this year's version of the pumpkin crown, while Duke smiled approvingly. She heard Henry mutter something about the leaves turning more red than yellow this year and what a wonderful sight it was down at the cove. She sat listening to their mindless, childish banter, lost in thought and despair until the room grew silent and all eyes fell expectantly upon their fearless young leader.

"Dear?" said Maggie quietly. "Jillian, dear, are you all right?" Jillian startled to attention.

"What?" she said, flustered and looking into the collective stare of everyone at the table. How long had she been sitting there in silence? "Oh, right, sorry," she babbled. "I was just, um, thinking." She scratched her head and shuffled her papers. "Uh, hmm, uh, where were we?" Duke eyed her curiously. The room exchanged silent, but concerned, glances. For some reason which escaped her, Jillian couldn't regain her thought. She was lost in a sea of confusion, of pumpkin crowns and apple games, and if this wasn't bad enough, at that precise moment the door flew open yet again.

"Good morning everyone," came the familiar, slurry southern drawl. "I hope I'm not intruding." Jillian snapped to alarmed attention. There he was, the Money Mack, in the flesh. After all the countless times she had invited him to come for a visit, Archibald Mack had chosen this day, of all days, to take her up on the offer. More bad timing and more bad luck. Jillian couldn't believe it. Fighting off a visceral reaction to slide under the table and hide, she mustered every ounce of strength left in her body and smiled her prettiest smile.

"Mr. Mack," she said anxiously, rising to her feet, scattering her papers and extending her hand which he grabbed firmly and blessed with his most gallant kiss. "What a nice surprise," she offered meekly. He winked at her and exhaled loudly, flaring his nostrils in yet another curious gesture that Jillian imagined he often practiced in his bathroom mirror.

"I find myself attending to some business in Boston this evening, and I thought I would stop in for one of those tavern lunches you've been promising me," he replied politely. Again, Jillian was struck by how oddly charming and appealing he was, almost in spite of himself. Who could deny that there was a certain appeal in the manners and breeding that Archibald Mack had pinned down to a science? "Although I wouldn't dream of intruding upon your time, my dear," he added.

"Nonsense," Jillian answered emphatically. "This is the nicest surprise I could imagine." Duke smiled. He had to concede that she was very good, remarkably good in fact, at handling the old man. It was almost as if she was actually happy to see him. Jillian fumbled with the corseted bodice that constricted her breathing.

"If you'll give me just a moment to change, I'll be happy to give you a quick tour on the way over to the tavern," she said.

"Nonsense," Mr. Mack growled quickly. "I love a woman in 18th-century attire. I find it very exciting." Maggie Paul squeaked an audible gasp, while the rest of the room exchanged knowing and concerned glances. Duke smiled his most devilish smile.

"Well then," Jillian offered quickly, biting the insides of her cheeks to maintain her composure, "shall we?" Money Mack offered his arm, within which she encircled her hand, and the pair glided through the doorway like a scene in a 1940s comedy. All that seemed to be missing was a few measures of mood music to set them on their way. With the swinging of the door behind them, Duke began to whistle the first bars of Yankee Doodle.

Maggie Paul's jaw remained open for a good minute or two longer before uttering, "I had no idea he was like that." A few of the men in the room exchanged some hearty guffaws at the comment. Carol rolled her eyes under her pumpkin crown and shook her head disapprovingly, muttering something about men and pigs.

"Ladies and gentlemen," Duke said, "there goes our own little patriot off to battle." The room nodded their collective agreement. A motion was passed to continue the meeting in Jillian's absence. It seemed the least they could do. They would stay and iron out the details of the Harvest Party while Jillian led the Money Mack, arm in arm, through the streets of Wetherton.

The autumn air was bright and crisp. Wetherton was postcard perfect. As they approached the Brownley Tavern, Jillian conducted a mental review of the rest of the day's commitments, fully realizing that Archibald Mack might be drinking his lunch leisurely before drinking dinner in Boston. It was possible, she imagined, that lunch could last a very long time.

"Oh, to hell with it," she thought silently, glancing over at Archibald with a satisfied smile of resignation. He was Wetherton's single, largest donor, and he was, after all, here for today and today alone. She reasoned that this was justification for a liquid lunch in the tavern and hoped that she could hold her own in the face of his remarkably bad habit.

"And just up there is our crown jewel, the Brownley Tavern," Jillian announced proudly, gesturing toward the original building that had been so perfectly restored. An almost irrational smile beamed across her face as they neared the place that Catherine Wentworth Brownley had called home.

"My dear, it is as lovely as any tavern in Virginia, I swear it to be true," Archibald replied sincerely. "I'm so pleased I can finally see it in person. I can tell by the look in your eyes that this is a very special place indeed." Jillian looked up in pleasant surprise. He really was such a charming man, she thought to herself, and he always seemed to say just the right things. Jillian smiled adoringly as they entered.

It only took a moment before Jillian had arranged for the table for four to be changed into a table for two in the corner, by the window, with a view of the Catherine Wentworth Brownley portrait. The midday autumn sunshine was bright, but deflected through the centuries-old panes, casting long and happy shadows on the weathered floorboards that had known the footsteps of Generals, Presidents and presently, a Money Mack. The ladies from Pennsylvania sat across the way and offered waves of recognition and raised glasses of Brownley punch in their direction. Archibald held her chair politely, before seating himself and ordering a double-martini with three olives. Jillian ordered gin and tonic and hoped she could pace herself through the meal.

"Jillian, you look absolutely exquisite in that gown," he started, offering a predictable but effective first blush of flattery. Jillian smiled sweetly.

"Mr. Mack, you are always such a flatterer," she replied.

"I know," he answered honestly. "It's what wealthy old gentlemen do. We socialize in all the best circles and we have lunch with the loveliest young ladies." He raised his glass to her at the suggestion of "loveliest young ladies" and tipped it back to nearly drain its contents.

"Mr. Mack," Jillian began thoughtfully.

"Won't you please call me Archibald?" he said exasperatedly. "For the love of God won't you? My banker calls me Mr. Mack. My driver calls me Mr. Mack, but you, my dear, must call me Archibald." Jillian smiled back in a strangely enchanted way.

"All right, Archibald," she began slowly, "after so many invitations, what gives us the pleasure of your visit today?" The Money Mack raised his eyebrows suggestively and finished off his drink, waving for another as he set the glass down.

"The truth is I am not particularly interested in Connecticut, or Yankees or leaf-peepin' or any other damned thing about New England," he said matter-of-factly, "but I like you and I like this little town. There is a feistiness about you that I can't seem to get off my mind." Jillian pursed her lips into a suspicious, but appreciative smile.

"I can see by your face that you don't believe me," he answered imperiously, rising up to press his back against his chair and accepting his second martini with a charming wink. Jillian looked down and sipped her drink. There was a weariness in her eyes. Archibald frowned.

"My dear, what is it that makes you so sad? I must say I've never seen you looking so lovely and so sad all at the same time." Jillian looked up anxiously in her beautiful chocolate brown silk bodice, with the rosebud embroidery that had been lovingly copied from a 1772 portrait that now hung in the Webster house, and attempted a reassuring smile. Could it be that he really noticed these things? Was he truly a man who took an interest in the feelings and sensitivities of others? Or did he simply notice these things so that he could use them to his advantage? Was Archibald Mack just a cheap playboy? Or was he a kind-hearted, sensitive gentleman in cheap playboy veneer? It was very difficult to decide.

"I'm not sad," Jillian protested, scoffing at the suggestion and fiddling with her paper cocktail napkin. Archibald Mack eyed her with an unblinking stare.

"My dear, I have spent a lifetime as a student of the human spirit," he answered authoritatively, "and I must say you are most definitely sad. Tell me why." Jillian looked down at her gin and tonic and took another sip.

"Actually," she said, "things are pretty tough around here right now. There's a man named Arnold Murton who recently bought the Beckwith house and he's filed for demolition. We think he wants to use the land for condos or apartments." It was now Archibald Mack who pursed his lips into a smile, or perhaps a frown, of suspicion and intrigue. It was the look of a man who knew money, who knew business and seemed to know the human spirit.

"Jillian, dear, why don't you tell me what's going on here in Wetherton. I'm very interested in hearing this story."

CHAPTER ELEVEN

"Must one always subvert one's own passion for the charade of protocol?" C.W.B. 1779

Lady Jane Rochester stared at her computer screen like a junkie on crack. Her white hair was wild and wispy, her delicate, blue-veined fingers were poised nervously at the ready and a good pot of tea steeped silently by her side. She was a sight to behold, one that she would scoff at had she the opportunity to behold herself at that moment. It was true. God knows, it was true and she must admit to it. Other than the remote possibility of gin, she had never encountered an addiction so appealing as her apparent love for … the chat-room.

Who could have imagined the bizarre and twisted world that lay before her? Who could have known the depths to which society might lower itself? Where on God's earth did these people come from?

For a time, she didn't believe they were real. She reasoned that someone in the entertainment industry had dreamed up the chat-room, filling it with paid actors, for an occasional evening of fun. After days of chatting, however, she was convinced that this was something far more sinister. No one, she decided, could dream up the length and breadth of hysteria going on in her computer night after night. The world was, quite simply, going to hell.

She had happened upon it all innocently enough. There had been something on the television a few weeks before about blogs or chat rooms that had stuck in her mind like a germ waiting in the sinuses to take its full affect. Nothing had come of it at first, but the longer it stayed there the more of a nuisance it seemed.

Consequently, a few days later she searched for and found a chat room that she read about in a newspaper article. As God would be her witness, so help her or may she be struck dead by lightning, her initial excitement was entirely due to the fact that she had successfully navigated her computer to the chat room. There was never any intent on her part to do any chatting of any kind.

"Ah, James," she had chuckled delightedly to herself. "You've no idea what a monster you may have created."

Little did she understand how prophetic those words would be. Within a few short days, she had fallen from the joyful exuberance of independence to the pathetic addiction of the Internet.

Jane had spent hours on end "listening" to the most shocking and ridiculous conversations she could ever have imagined possible. Still, she would find herself reasoning that just two more minutes wouldn't hurt. Or, perhaps she should check in on that other site to see how things were progressing. Her nagging curiosity to hear more from this dark world was surprisingly overpowering. The entertainment was extraordinary. She had recently read that keeping one's mind active and engaged was a key to staving off the debilitating affects of Alzheimer's, and rationalized that it was a very good thing to keep surfing the Web.

So Lady Jane Rochester did what she clearly had to do … she listened and she learned. She listened to "PIGGLYWIGGLY" drone on and on about her diet disasters, and she learned what WTF meant. She listened to "LONELYBOY" whine away each night for lack of a mate … the sex of which he desired left her still very much undecided, and she learned what OMG meant. She learned that when one "speaks" in capital letters, they are shouting. She listened to "TOEJAM" talk about how badly she hated her parents and her friends and her teachers and everyone in her life except her pet tarantula, Larry, and how she didn't think she could stand it any longer. Finally, it was Jane who could stand it no longer, and with an uncontrollable will she began to write back.

She chose the screen name "WOC", which stood for wise old cow, although it had been suggested by "64GEEZ" that it stood for "work of crap". Jane was not put off. It was not difficult. In fact, it was surprisingly easy and it was merely an hour or two before she was accepted into a loyal band of correspondents who gladly welcomed her comments. They might write "let's hear what the WOC has to say about this," or "I could use some help from solid as a WOC." Jane was pleased to oblige.

She had written, "Get a hold of yourself woman," to "PIXPOX" who professed a need to shoplift. Then there was, "Stop moaning and, for the love of God, stop eating," to "PIGGLYWIGGLY" when she complained that her latest diet had failed her yet again.

One writer suggested that "WOC" was probably some Star Wars addict having a mid-life crisis, to which Jane howled with laughter. Imagine, she thought, having a mid-life crisis at 86.

She puzzled at the basic lack of common sense. Where was their restraint and dignity? Where was their courtesy or sense of duty? How could she possibly die happy, knowing that this mob of dysfunctional idiots would be running the show? Even more curious was the hysteria and drama that overwhelmed their daily lives. Never had she experienced such utter nonsensical panic, not even in the midst of bombs falling from the sky onto her dearly beloved England.

Would climate change kill the earth? Quite possibly, Jane thought with patent dignity. Perhaps we may want to do something about it before it does. Would the rain forest disappear? Well yes, Jane reasoned, unless one stops cutting it down. Will terrorism be defeated? Of course, Jane frowned silently, as all evil is defeated in the end.

Her mind quickly wandered back to 1943. It had been one of the loneliest and most uncertain times in Jane's life.

Before the war there had always been those things that could be relied upon, but during the war Jane could see that nothing in life could ever be relied upon. She never again made the mistake of believing that it could. Life was an up and down, twist and turn, road of possibilities, she reasoned, and those who kept their eyes blindly focused on anything other than what lay directly at their feet would miss a great deal on that journey.

Could there be a war to end all wars? "Rubbish," Jane snickered. There would always be someone intent upon taking what someone else had. There would always be envy, there would always be fear, there would always be greed and there would always be war. Man was simply too selfish to understand a greater destiny. Man's greatest and most frightening ability, Jane reasoned, was his power to rationalize anything.

She shook her head to clear her mind, remembering that day in 1944 when Arthur had returned home to her. He arrived at 12:43 pm in a shirt with a coffee stain on his right cuff. In the excitement of the morning, he had spilled his coffee while trying to manage his cane and simultaneously shake hands with his best mate Charles who would be leaving for Scotland that day. It was remarkable, she mused, what the mind recalled. Wrapping her arms around Arthur's neck, the smell of coffee in his kiss, the bristle of his hair against her face which she always felt was cut far too short.

She glanced at her screen and took in a quick exchange between "RAZORCLAM" and "PINKY". As usual, the two were shamelessly flirting, although Jane worried that "PINKY" was obviously much too young for "RAZORCLAM" and believed she would soon be forced to intercede if this ridiculous display continued much longer.

It was 1:16 am, and Jane suddenly realized she was exhausted. Thankfully, there had been no conversation from "BARNEYBOY" this evening whose sexual exploits were most shocking and unwelcome. No one, she rationalized, could sleep with ten people in one hour and survive to tell the tale to the Internet world at large. Although, she must confess that her mind had wandered into a bizarre state of sub-conscious one night, and imagined a type of half-goat, half-human creature, yet to be discovered by respectable scientists, residing on some distant mountaintop plateau with a willing herd of partners and an Internet connection by his side.

One shining light in this sea of idiocy was "THECOLONEL" who appeared a reasonable and respectable sort of person. Brimming with knowledge of world history and often quoting Socrates or Sir Isaac Newton, Jane reasoned that he must be an English gentleman with an enviable education and a fine head planted squarely on his shoulders. "Well said," she often muttered after reading any of his posts.

It was long past two o'clock when Lady Jane finally settled into sleep, wrestling for a long while with the thoughts and images that danced through her head. She twisted the ring on her pinky finger and drifted off to sleep.

James arrived on the 6:48 train from Paddington Station the next morning. It was not a long walk to Broadhurst Hall and he enjoyed the morning air. He walked the two kilometers a little slower than usual, arriving at the rear kitchen door no later than half-past seven. He imagined Aunt Jane would be waiting for him, although she would pretend she was not. Surprisingly, all was quiet when he entered his great ancestral home.

"Good morning, Liza," he offered to the maid with his usual cheerful exuberance.

"Good morning, sir," was her dower, customary response.

"And how is our Aunt Jane this day?" came his hopeful reply. Liza gave him a worried glance.

"Right awful sir," she burst into gloomy discord.

James was instantly alarmed. "Have you telephoned the Doctor?" he asked in shock.

"No, no sir, forgive me," Liza explained. "She is quite well. With the flu and all. It's not that at all sir. It's that computer of hers," she glanced again at James for emphasis, her bushy eyebrows raised in concern. James paused, his own eyebrows descending in an opposite frown.

"Sorry?" he said, wondering her exact meaning. Liza edged forward a bit, as if she were discussing something of an extremely personal and confidential nature.

"You know, sir," she said quietly, glancing over her shoulders for discretion. "It's that Internet you've given her. It's ever so troubling to us here." She stared at him with a fixed gaze while James attempted to comprehend her meaning.

"The Internet that I've given her?" he said at last, just a tiny bit defensively. "What exactly has our Aunt Jane been doing on the Internet?" With that, Liza quickly looked to the floor, unwilling to speak another word for fear of some sort of retribution from either her employer or her employer's nephew.

"Liza," James persisted, mustering his most imperious tone, "please tell me what our Aunt has been doing on the Internet." His mind raced in palpable fear. Had she mortgaged the Broadhurst estate in a pyramid scheme? Had she gone crazy on e-bay, buying untold millions in useless merchandise? Had she met an Italian lover who promised to wine and dine her in Venice next week? The endless possibilities of peril spread out before him like a global spider web. "Liza," he said again, more encouragingly.

The poor frightened and exhausted woman tensed for just a moment with fingers twined together in beefy fists, then spilled her soul like the waters of Niagara Falls, leaving no detail undone until she had purged herself of everything she knew. James stood quietly, dumbfounded with silence, and attempted to digest the enormity of what he had just heard. At last, in a voice raspy and dry-mouthed he whispered, "Chat-rooms?"

"I'm afraid so, sir," Liza answered sympathetically, wringing her hands on her apron and then resting them on her ample waist. "And blogs! She's a blogger sir," Liza whined, instantly slapping her hand over her mouth as if she had just used a dirty word in front of the Queen. James stared dumbfounded, in complete and utter shock. Liza paused briefly to regain herself.

"I've brewed pot after pot of tea for her, night after night," she continued, "and still she goes back to it again and again. It's madness I tell you!"

James was beyond stunned. "Huh," was the only response that he could muster, and he staggered for a chair at the small table that stood between them. Now seated and resting comfortably, he fidgeted with the navy blue bow-tie at his neck and rustled the brown curls on his head over and over again. This was a highly unusual predicament, he reasoned. What, after all, should one do when his completely lucid Aunt Jane of 86 years decides to break out of her quiet world in the English countryside and converse with the world at large on the Internet? He fidgeted again with his tie.

He could cut her off, he supposed, but the repercussions of vengeance that may be heaped upon him as a result of such action hardly warranted such drastic measures. He could monitor her conversations, he imagined, utilizing the sort of parental controls and spyware that were routinely employed with teenagers attempting to use chat-rooms, but would that be fair and just given the fact that he was essentially the teenager and Aunt Jane the parent? E-mails were one thing, but chat rooms were quite another. Was it this damnable J. Garrett of Wetherton, Connecticut who had put his Aunt Jane up to such antics?

He sat at that table for a long, great while, mumbling incoherently about the situation. Suddenly, Liza rushed back into the kitchen full of alarm.

"She's here, sir, in the dining room," she said, pulling him from his chair and pushing him out into the hall. "Go on now sir, hurry yourself, she's waiting for you," she added with an enormous shove in the right direction. "And please don't say anything to her about the," she cocked her head in an awkward horizontal pose, "you know what." James muttered his agreement and meandered dutifully down the hall, not at all certain what would happen in the next ten minutes, but understanding full well the enormity that lay before him.

"Don't ever anger your Aunt," were the words once uttered to him by his dear Grandmother. "She is the greatest Lady you will ever know, far greater than I could ever be, and I love her most dearly." His Gran had smiled at him. "You must know," she added, "she has the iron will of a tiger protecting her young. You can never win against Jane because she is always on your side. You can only learn how to be stronger." He had never truly understood what Gran meant, but he always maintained a healthy respect for the woman in spite of all her mystery.

Jane took breakfast in her favorite chair in the corner of the dining room by the window, seated at a table for two draped in fresh white linen with a lovely spread of toast, jam, sausages and eggs laid out before her. She was exhausted, yet she perused the folded newspaper at her side in earnest while enjoying her tea and awaiting her nephew. She quickly stifled a yawn and pretended not to notice him as he entered. It was always such fun to fluster him.

"Good morning Aunt Jane," James offered cheerfully as he entered, acting suspiciously casual as if nothing at all new had been happening at Broadhurst Hall since his last visit. Jane paused for effect before raising her gaze to him.

"Ah," she said flatly, "James." He smiled and took the place laid out for him directly opposite her. He noticed that everything was there to his liking, even the horrible American maple syrup with imitation butter for his sausages, although Jane would never admit to orchestrating any special concessions for the little bow-tied bore.

"And how is my Aunt this morning?" he asked, attempting to be exceedingly cheerful and innocent. "Feeling better, I trust?"

"Hmmm," Jane answered vaguely, staring with unbroken interest at some newsworthy article she seemed desperate to read. "Did you know that women in Kuwait cannot vote?" James shook his head absently, confused by the question and attempting to appear nonchalant as he smothered his sausages in the maple syrup.

"I did not," he said chewing behind his hand.

"I don't like it," Jane replied crossly. "Does our family hold anything of interest with any connection to Kuwait?" James sipped at his glass of water, rinsing quickly to respond with authority.

"I do not believe so, but I can certainly check on that if you'd like," he smiled pleasingly, grateful for the distraction of Kuwait.

"I would indeed," Jane replied tersely. "I want nothing to do with Kuwait from this moment on." James shrugged his agreement absently.

"Very well," he said smiling, hoping to catch some measure of gratitude in return. Jane simply returned to her newspaper. James returned to his sausages.

"Aunt Jane," he said at last, cautiously and deliberately, "are you enjoying your computer?"

"What?" Jane asked suddenly and with obvious alarm. James paused.

"Your computer," he said at last, biting the insides of his cheeks to suppress his own alarm at the sign of Aunt's, "are you enjoying the computer? Perhaps you've had another e-mail from that American woman?" Jane paused herself for a moment.

"Yes," she answered at last, recovering her composure. "Yes indeed. I told you, she seems to be a lovely young girl who is interested in one of our ancestors."

"Really," James responded with pretended interest, "and who might that be?"

"Catherine Wentworth Brownley," Jane said quickly, "18th-century little tart who went to the colonies and turned her back on our King."

"Fascinating," James said, slicing and syruping more sausages, "I'd be happy to help you correspond with her in the future if you require any assistance."

"Yes, well that is very kind of you, but I think there is little I can do to help her," Jane said, attempting to be as vague and disinterested as possible. "She does seem to be a lovely girl, very bright and determined. Perhaps a little aggressive, but she is American after all. I'll do my best." Both continued to enjoy their breakfast with unparalleled precision, not at all certain what the other might say but venturing nothing of their own to the conversation.

"Have you had any other correspondence on your computer," James asked finally, unable to think of a more delicate way of opening the can of worms that lay at his feet.

"Hmmm?" Jane answered again, as if someone had just asked for directions to Cairo.

"Any other e-mails or correspondence of any kind on the Internet?" James asked pointedly, quickly looking down, unable to bear the firestorm that might hit him full in the face. Jane fidgeted with her napkin at the corners of her mouth.

"Actually James," she began, pausing for time to think, "I have been trying with little luck to help this Jillian Garrett with her query." James looked up in surprise. "Perhaps you might be able to help me do a bit of research to settle the matter. She's very determined to find some information on this Catherine, and you are far better at these sorts of things than your old Aunt. I'd like to help her, really I would, but I don't seem to have the knack for it. Would you be willing?" James wiped his own mouth, determined to follow the path of least resistance in order to access his Aunt's computer.

"I would be only too happy," he said smiling his most overeager smile.

"Heavens," Jane thought to herself silently, eyeing the smile that was oddly crooked to the left. Such a silly boy with such a silly smile, she thought. And such a silly bow-tie. On a Saturday, no less. Where will he find himself a wife who isn't just as silly and boorish as he is?

It was decided at that moment that she must begin her work on him in considerable earnest. After all, it would fall to James someday to carry on the Wentworth legacy. Centuries of Wentworth history would, sooner than later, fall to James as the next rightful heir. The care and keeping of Broadhurst Hall would rest upon those narrow, bow-tied shoulders.

"Aunt Jane?" James persisted, looking up with great anticipation. "Where shall we begin?" She peered at him with her piercing blue Wentworth eyes.

"Where indeed," came her flat reply.

CHAPTER TWELVE

"History may well tell the tale of this time and place, but truth will be lost to the ages," C.W.B. 1778.

Jillian rolled over and slapped at the snooze button on her alarm clock. A deep low growl resonated from the back of her throat and out through her nose. She pushed the tangle of brown hair away from her face and forced her eyes open. A puff of breath escaped from her lips and she twisted her body into a fetal position.

Just twelve hours earlier, she was in Manhattan, sitting in the offices of *Historic Home* magazine interviewing with the Director of Sales, a nice enough guy named Ted. She could hardly believe it. Ted was a year younger than her. She knew this because he wasted no time in mentioning that he was the youngest person to ever hold the Director of Sales position, and took every opportunity to encourage her to guess his age. A golden wedding band twinkled on his ring finger and a black and white photo of his stunning bride beamed at her from the credenza behind his desk. Yup. Ted was the quintessential snapshot of success.

Of course Ted's knowledge of history, homes or otherwise, paled in comparison to Jillian's, but that was no matter. Ted could sell ice to the Eskimos, he told her, and he didn't need to know what kind of ice it was. Jillian smiled nervously. The interview lasted all of twenty minutes, most of that time focusing on base salary, commissions and incentives. It was here that Jillian's eyes lit up. A base salary that was more than double what she currently earned, with an almost unlimited upside. Most of the sales staff easily earned six figures, Ted boasted. Jillian gulped. Right she thought. She could sell advertising space in *Historic Home* magazine. She could sell like hell, a slogan heavily promoted by Ted from the comfort of his window office.

She dreamed fitfully all night of parties in New York and real Valentina dresses in her closet. Now, in the early morning light of the morning after, she felt cheap and nervous like a wife who had gone on a drunken spree of infidelity. She thought of Maggie graciously covering the Kiwanis dinner event at the tavern because Jillian claimed her friend had an emergency in New York. Her eyes opened again to the charmingly pale blue walls of her own historic home. She was a liar. It felt awful.

A few minutes later she was down in her tiny kitchen, painted top to bottom in Wentworth Green, an official paint color of Historic Wetherton sold exclusively at Smithridge hardware down on Main Street. She measured the coffee in great mounds, preferring a good strong cup in the morning, and fixed her oatmeal in the microwave. It was a far cry from the breakfast preparation of Wetherton women before her, which probably consisted of leftover bread from days before and some cider or milk if she had her own cow. Jillian had worked at the dairy barn a few years earlier for an exhibition event and was evermore disinterested in milk as a beverage.

She scavenged through the refrigerator for margarine and some orange juice, then picked up the phone to dial Taylor.

"Hey sugar," came the familiar twang on the other end of the line. "What's up?"

"I'm heading down to Yale today and wanted to know if you need anything," Jillian replied while she nibbled a triangle of toast. Taylor was forever in need of Yale memorabilia for her nieces and nephews.

"Uh no, I don't think so, but thanks. Why are you going down there today?"

"Lecture," Jillian replied, pouring steaming coffee into a travel mug. "Dr. David Webster, history professor from North Carolina, giving a lecture on revisionist history."

"Wow," Taylor offered, "sounds like a day of fun to me. Why don't I see if I can catch the train and we'll go together."

"Seriously?" Jillian asked in surprise.

"Uh, no honey, I was joking. But you have yourself a great time. Maybe you'll meet somebody. Try to look pretty, OK? For me? Wear that new black jacket with the tweed skirt that I bought you." Jillian nodded dutifully.

"What shoes?" she asked with true concern. "The little black flats with the buckle or the chunky little heel ones?"

"Hmmm," Taylor pondered. "Probably chunky little heel, but if those are your only choices in black then you are long overdue for some shoe shopping darling. Why didn't we shop when you were in the city yesterday?" Jillian rolled her eyes.

"Yes, well, it's funny, but they aren't giving out shoe shopping raises right now, so I think I'll have to rely on your hand me downs."

"I wish I would have known," Taylor implored, "I could have loaned you a pair."

"Too late," Jillian smirked. "Besides, my size eight feet in your size six shoes would not be pretty. I'll just have to go ahead and make a fashion fool of myself."

"Honey, you are not a freshman anymore. You can't get away with the sloppy college look." Jillian glanced down at her stained sweatshirt, her faded flannel pajama pants and the slouchy wool socks with holes that exposed her big toe on the left foot.

"You're definitely right about that," she answered with an honest nod of her head. "I'll work on it."

"Come into the city this weekend. We can shop."

"Can't," Jillian quipped. "Big emergencies looming left and right up here. Earth shattering business of pumpkin crowns and what not."

"Good Lord," Taylor answered, "thank God you're almost free from that little town." Jillian pursed her lips and bit the insides of her cheeks. "Did you hear from Ted? He said he was going to e-mail you."

"Taylor, it's 7:00 am and I just woke up," Jillian mumbled, "It will take many, many long painful minutes to fire up my computer." She jostled her orange juice and splashed on her pajama top.

"Well fire it up already," Taylor nagged. "This city doesn't sleep darling. You're going to have to step up your game when you move here." It was true. She certainly would have to step up her game. She'd have to get tough. Really tough.

"Yes, drill sergeant," Jillian shot back. "I'll get on it right away. Relax."

"I'll relax when you're out of that pokey little town."

"Gotta go or I'll be late," Jillian interrupted.

"Love you honey. Call me later."

"OK," Jillian answered with a smile. "Love you too."

She hung up the phone, sipped her coffee and frowned. Tough she thought. How tough could she really be? She was tough enough to chase down runaway ferrets and patch plaster walls, but that was a different kind of tough. Was she New York City tough? That was the question. The other question, of course, was where were those black shoes with the chunky heel? She headed back upstairs to scout them out.

Her 18th-century house afforded much in the way of charm and very little in the way of closet space. Even a girl with Jillian's meager wardrobe found it necessary to stuff clothes, shoes and accessories into every nook and cranny.

The chunky black shoes were found in an under-the-bed plastic storage box that was covered in dust bunnies. Emblazoned with a sticker that read "good shoes" she knew this meant shoes that had cost more than a day's pay and could therefore only be worn on special occasions. Inside, she found five pairs and not a single

133

one showed any signs of contact with horse manure. Ah, she thought, the sign of truly good shoes.

Before long she had brushed out her brown hair into silky perfection. She had even dabbed on a little more make-up than her standard dose of lip gloss, startling at her reflection in the mirror. The black jacket was perfect with the tweed skirt, and yes, even the chunky black shoes were working for her. She thought she looked pretty damned good, if she did say so herself, and smiled at the prospect of heading down to her alma mater for the morning.

It wasn't more than a 40 minute ride to New Haven and traffic was light on the southbound side. Parking wasn't easy, but she remembered her way around the tangle of little side streets well enough to find a spot by a 2-hour meter. She was in a surprisingly terrific mood, propelled by the prospect of intellectual stimulation that had nothing whatsoever to do with candied apple flashlights.

The lecture hall was about three quarters full, half of the attendees being students and the other half a mish-mosh collection of ages and attire right on up through eighty-something Jillian imagined. There was no reason to feel uncomfortable. Somewhere in the middle, she seemed to fit right in. She settled into her seat, fidgeting with a pen and pad of paper. American history lectures were just about her favorite thing in the whole world, and she couldn't wait to learn something new. Dr. David Webster sauntered in down at the front and the room instantly quieted.

"Good morning ladies and gentleman," Dr. Webster began in a pleasant southern drawl that betrayed his New Bern, North Carolina upbringing. "I'm so pleased to see so many bright faces on this cloudy day." Jillian exhaled with anticipation and perched her pen on top of her notepad.

"Many of you," Dr. Webster went on, "are here because you are students of American History. I, myself, even after all these many years of teaching history, still consider myself to be a student of history." He paused, gesturing with his hands to make his introduction. "That is what we do. We learn something. And then we learn a little bit more about it. And over the course of time, the new things that we learn may cause us to go back and reconsider our understanding of things we thought we already knew. We might even change our ideas or opinions." Jillian cocked her head to one side and frowned just a bit.

"The academic world sometimes calls this "revisionist" or "revisionism". I call this common sense." The room chuckled softly.

"Let's take, for example, one of our most beloved founding fathers. Mr. Thomas Jefferson." There were a few knowing head nods. "Thomas Jefferson, author of the Declaration of Independence, lover of freedom and liberty, was a slave-owner. How do we resolve that discrepancy in his legacy?"

It was a formidable point of debate. Jillian had long been familiar with the writings of Jefferson which acknowledged that while he believed that slaves should eventually be emancipated, he also believed that black skin and white skin were not inherently equal and that the races should be kept separate. Of course, how did that explain Sally Hemmings? He was a troubling mix of contradiction between political rhetoric and living reality.

"Today's Republicans will tell you that Jefferson was a great believer in GOP ideals," Dr. Webster said. "Now, today's Democrats will tell you just the opposite. In truth, Jefferson's political party was known as the Democratic Republicans." The room laughed loudly. Jillian smiled.

Dr. Webster went on, and Jillian followed his logic with great interest. After an hour, however, she felt herself beginning to daydream and had to fight her mind's urge to wander. It wasn't until she heard the name Catherine Wentworth Brownley, that Jillian snapped back to attention.

"Let's take a moment to talk about one of Connecticut's great heros, or heroines as the case may be. Catherine Wentworth Brownley. She is the patriot who saved both General George Washington and Lt. General Rochambeau from assassination just up the road here in Wetherton." Jillian's mouth went dry. "Or is she?" No one in the room, other than Jillian, seemed particularly offended by the question.

"Some historians, revisionists if you will, now believe that she wasn't even at the tavern on that day. Others have gone so far as to suggest that if she was at the tavern, she might have somehow been involved in the assassination plot herself. Some have even suggested that the entire reason Mrs. Brownley was here in the colonies in the first place is because her wealthy father sold her service as a spy to gain favor with the King. Why else, they ask, would a young aristocratic woman travel to the new world on her own?"

"What?" Jillian shouted, unable to control herself, and causing every head in the room to turn in her direction. She slapped her hand over her mouth.

"I believe we have a question?" Dr. Webster said, looking up at her from his position of power at the center of the room.

"Forgive me," Jillian began. "I do apologize for shouting out like that. It's just that I happen to have done a great deal of research on Catherine Brownley. I'm even now researching her childhood in England. And I have never come across a single scrap of evidence to suggest that she is anything other than the patriot we have long known her to be."

"Long believed her to be," Dr. Webster shot back. "Your belief is shaped by your interpretation of the information you have been given. Others have looked at that same information and have found themselves believing something very different."

"That's because they don't know what they're talking about," Jillian muttered under her breath.

"Excuse me?" Dr. Webster went on. "I couldn't hear that."

"I just think that people shouldn't be allowed to go around denigrating the legacy of a great woman because they did a little research and want to make a name for themselves," Jillian shot back. Dr. Webster chuckled.

"I think you're missing the point," he said.

"I think you're missing the point," Jillian fired back hotly. "Catherine Wentworth Brownley devoted her entire life to the cause of freedom and independence. Revisionists are marching around with opinions, not facts, and opinions shouldn't rewrite history." Dr. Webster pulled off his glasses and rubbed his nose.

"Miss," he began politely. "I appreciate a good debate. I really do. But this is a lecture, not a debate." Jillian gulped.

"I'm sorry," she whispered, looking down at her chunky black shoes.

"Let's go back to Jefferson, for a moment. He doesn't seem to rile anybody up too badly." The room laughed out loud. Jillian knew they were laughing at her and felt her cheeks flush. She kept her eyes cast downward and tried to become invisible.

After what seemed interminable hours, although it was only twenty-five minutes, the lecture was at end and everyone was collecting their belongings. Several members of the audience waited patiently to speak with Dr. Webster, but it was Jillian's arm he caught despite her attempt to escape undetected.

"I appreciate your passion," he said with a smile. "You obviously have a love of this work." Jillian bit the side of her lower lip.

"I'm sorry I interrupted you," she offered. "I truly enjoyed and appreciated everything you had to say." Dr. Webster nodded acceptance of the compliment and the apology.

"But you don't agree?" he asked. Jillian eyed him cautiously before answering.

"I understand that history is a moving target," she began thoughtfully, "and that you can dress it up in different clothes and parade it around to different people and each time it will take on a different life." Dr. Webster crossed his arms in a gesture that implied his interest was not lost. "I'm not entirely sure that is revisionism as much as it is spin," she said. Dr. Webster chuckled.

"Well, I've never heard that one before, but I take your point," he offered generously. Jillian searched his eyes for sincerity. She felt it was there.

"Catherine Wentworth Brownley lived in Wetherton. She was at the tavern when General Washington and Rochambeau were meeting. That is undisputed. That is fact." Jillian took a deep breath to control her emotion. "Did she foil an assassination attempt? I believe she did. Can I prove it? No, but the evidence points directly at that conclusion. There is no evidence whatsoever to suggest that she herself was an assassin. Catherine Wentworth Brownley was a patriot, not an assassin, in a town full of patriots who risked their lives for freedom. Why would anyone want to tear that down over 200 years later?"

Dr. Webster thanked her for her thoughts and promised her he would bear them in mind, but she left with the decidedly firm feeling that she was the fool of the morning. She was the one everyone would be talking about over coffee later in the day. "What was up with that crazy woman in the chunky shoes?" they would say. Jillian shook her head and wandered down to her favorite pizza place alone. She had been looking forward to a slice of the delectably thin crust pizza that New Haven was famous for, but even this could not lift her spirits. Anger turned to embarrassment, that ebbed into dismay, that now malingered in exhaustion.

She slumped back to her car, completely zapped of all the earlier energy and enthusiasm she possessed. She couldn't believe it. There were actually people out there, probably troll-like creatures hiding behind stacks of books in the basements of libraries, spending their time trying to rewrite Catherine Brownley's place in history. Get a life people! The woman had been dead for over 200 years and still her legacy was not safe. "What's a woman got to do to get a little respect?" she mumbled.

Had Dr. Webster actually implied that the mystery of Catherine's journey to the colonies was that she had been sold as a spy to the King? Could he be serious? She could hardly wait to e-mail Lady Jane about that one. Silly Americans, she would say. Always in the midst of a drama.

Jillian could hardly even remember driving home. She was like a zombie, gripping the steering wheel with both hands, her foot mechanically stopping and starting in the northbound traffic. Her mind tried to wrap around the idea that Catherine Wentworth Brownley could plummet from passionate patriot to conniving assassin in one afternoon. It was too hard. Too depressing. Had Jillian Garrett spent the last ten years of her life building a historical foundation, with painstaking baby steps, only to find the cherry on top of the cake was rotten? She stabbed at the off button on her stereo and brushed a tear from her cheek.

CHAPTER THIRTEEN

"Deception is a decidedly tricky business, requiring at least one part evil for every two parts earnest endeavor," C.W.B. *1776*

Lady Jane and her nephew James had each spent the better part of the day attempting to give the impression they were hard at work on the task at hand. An American woman named Jillian Garrett, known to them only through the Internet, had requested some information regarding their distant relation, Catherine Wentworth Brownley, and the two were spending their Saturday afternoon positively engrossed in pursuit of an answer to that request. Obviously, there was nothing odd in that.

Lady Jane parked herself solidly to the left of her computer, while James was seated further away near the window. He would make an occasional, meager advance, in the direction of the computer, followed by a swift and strategic retreat. Jane eyed him most suspiciously.

"Perhaps I could call up that last e-mail for clarification, Aunt Jane?" he offered casually.

"Nonsense," she replied gruffly, "I've told you exactly what needs to be found. Do you think I don't know my own mind?" Jane had no idea what James may or may not be able to find by accessing her computer, but she had no intention of finding out. Nor did she have any interest in listening to his lectures on Internet safety. She glanced up at the portrait of Arthur. "He thinks I don't know my own mind. Am I a child darling? Certainly not."

"Of course not, Aunt Jane," James offered mildly, "I only wondered if ..."

"Well stop the damned wondering, will you?" she shot back irritably, "I'm already sorry I've asked for your help. Perhaps we should forget the whole thing."

"No, no," James protested, entirely too earnestly, "I do apologize. I'm only trying to do my best. As always," he added, with emphasis. Jane surveyed him with a cautious glare.

The library housed a wealth of Wentworth family history. Anyone willing to scour ledgers, family bibles or personal correspondence for tiny pearls of information would find a treasure trove at their fingertips in that room. All of that, when carefully and prodigiously pieced together in exactly the correct way, could unearth startling revelations of dark secrets, unsolved mysteries or highly diverting gossip.

James had encountered any number of interesting tidbits that stood out in his sharp mind, but he would not allow himself to be baited from the task at hand. Clearly, Aunt Jane knew he would find hours of distraction in the library. Could there be any place more appealing to a man of his quiet nature? Yet, he refused to be taken in. He was on a greater and far more important mission. Damned be the relative who had turned her back on England two centuries ago. What did it matter anyway? What, in God's name, had Aunt Jane been doing on her computer? That was the question of the day. Jillian what's-her-name from sod off, USA could not have been less important. And yet, on this day she was the necessary center of his presumed interest.

He didn't know many Americans. He had been to New York on a handful of occasions and enjoyed himself very much. It was loud and busy, the buildings were enormously tall, the people were rude and pushy but it was still very entertaining. Almost like going to an amusement park. He had also been to Miami, Dallas and Los Angeles. Miami, he thought, was frightfully hot and humid. Dallas, he believed, was quite possibly the most provincial city in the world, and in Los Angeles he had spent so much time in his car driving from one place to the next, he scarcely had a memory of anything other than the smell of his rented Ford and the amusing radio stations he had listened to along the way.

He preferred to spend his time travelling to France and Spain, which he did every summer. The food, the weather and the people were so pleasant, and yet he always looked forward to coming home again. He loved London and his small flat in Sloane Square, and he loved Broadhurst Hall. In truth, he even loved Aunt Jane, although he would never say such a thing to her. Sentimental feelings were not Wentworthy, at least not as declarations between an Aunt and a Nephew. It was assumed that they liked each other well enough for mutual toleration and that was that.

James glanced at his atlas and fingered the tiny dot of Wetherton, Connecticut, just south of Hartford. It had been settled in 1633 by Englishmen. At least they had made a decent start of it. Of course, they were probably all criminals or religious fanatics, but still, they were Englishmen.

Jane, for her part, had spent the last hour pouring over an old ledger which detailed every pence spent upon every horse and bag of grain over the last 800 years, or so it seemed. If boredom had a face, this ledger would be it. Yet, she continued on, diligently surveying every entry and maintaining her position of possession aside the idle computer. She was determined to prevent James from entering the 3-meter perimeter she had artificially imposed by settling herself in such a way. Always a soul of caution. Jane fidgeted with the collar of her blouse and glanced at the clock rolling her eyes in exasperation.

"James?" she began sweetly. "Fancy a lunch down at the pub?"

"The pub?" he answered, wrinkling his eyebrows into curious curves. "You want to go to the pub Aunt Jane?"

"I do," she nodded with certainty.

"But you never go to the pub."

"Well, today I would like to go," she fired back. "So what do you think?" James stumbled to his feet.

"Fine with me," he offered, smoothing a hand through his curly hair. "Would you like me to bring the car around?"

"Yes, thank you."

"Alright then." Absently, they both glanced anxiously at the computer for a millisecond. Jane stared expectantly, willing him to move and free her from this torture. His feet remained rooted to the carpet.

"Right," James nodded, patting the pockets of his pants. "Keys. I'll need keys. I'll get the keys." Jane exhaled a tiny sigh of relief. "Are you sure you're well enough to go out?" he asked, turning back to her from the massive doorway.

"I'll meet you in the front. I won't be a moment." Jane sat motionless, keeping a wary eye on the hallway. Satisfied that James was off on his fool's errand, Jane quickly reached over to tap the keyboard. An e-mail from Jillian about Catherine Wentworth being a spy. "Silly girl," Jane muttered.

I am off to lunch with my nephew James, but will chat upon return. I do not think my ancestor was a spy. I think Americans spend too much time creating drama, don't you? Thank you for the article on peonies. It was very interesting.
Regards,
Jane

The White Horse Inn retained all the expected charms of a 16th-century pub, including a dimly lit dining area and a vibrant crowd of colorful locals. It had been ages since Jane paid a visit, but the time did not matter. Everyone knew Lady Jane Rochester and the room greeted her warmly, even offering a few good-natured bows.

She smiled as the gentleman from behind the bar seated her by one of the few windows in the room.

"Awfully nice to have you Mum," he smiled, his nose and cheeks burning a shade of crimson. "What can we get you?"

"I'll have a schooner of sherry," she replied sweetly. James' eyes widened to twice their normal circumference.

"And for you sir?"

"Uh, a pint for me," James stammered. "Lager. Cheers."

"What fun this is," Jane offered excitedly. "I don't know why I don't come here more often." James leaned forward.

"You don't like pub food Aunt Jane," he whispered.

"Nonsense," she said loudly. "I love a pub lunch." Raised glasses and quiet cheers from the five men at the bar. Jane nodded sweetly.

"Well then, what will you have?"

"Hmm," Jane mused, tipping her head back to read the selections hastily written on the chalkboard. "I think I'll have the sausages, and a jacket potato with cheese." James shrugged his continued amazement. Would Aunt Jane slowly grow more wild and unpredictable? Perhaps he should speak to their attorney about it.

The Wentworth family enjoyed its share of characters through the ages, including a few scoundrels, eccentrics and out and out weirdos. Two Wentworths, one of whom was Aunt Jane's great grandfather, actually challenged each other to a duel of pistols to settle an argument over ale, of all things. A surprising number of guests turned out on the south lawn to witness the affair, and a good deal of quiet wagering was said to be transacted on the terrace. At the end of the day, however, both men were so drunk that neither one hit a single thing, even after two rounds of reloading. Ultimately it was declared a draw and the pair shuffled off to the dining room to share some reconciliatory drinks before parting as gentlemen.

He watched her sip her sherry and smiled. She was a remarkable woman. There were none like her that he had ever met or ever believed he would meet. Lady Jane Alexandra Wentworth Rochester was like a rock on the jagged coast of England. She was solid and unwavering, yet perched precariously and vulnerable. She was 86 years old and no longer the spry woman of her younger days. It could take only a wild mid-winter storm to topple that rock into the sea. He knew it was his duty to ensure that would never happen.

"So, Aunt Jane," James began, peering at her through the haze in the smoke-filled room, "do you think we'll have any success in our quest or are we off on a wild goose chase?" Jane scoffed.

"I'm sure we'll uncover something, large or small, that would prove interesting and helpful," she replied smiling. "This young woman, this Miss Garrett," Jane went on, "she is a bit odd, but I like her."

"Odd in what way?" James asked, hanging on every word.

"Well, I suppose I find it odd that a young woman spends her days tracking down ancestors and dressing up in colonial costumes. She should be out having fun, don't you think?" James shrugged while the barman brought him another lager.

"Cheers." He sipped slowly. Aunt Jane nursed her sherry. "Do you think she's being honest with you? I mean, do you suppose this is a ruse of some sort?" Jane rolled her eyes.

"Heavens yes," she replied with Janieness, "I'm certain she's only using us to discover the true size of Liza's knickers." James frowned.

"Aunt Jane, you are a very wealthy woman. You realize that Jillian Garrett is quite aware of that fact. She may be trying to lure you into some scheme." Jane stared at her nephew in disbelief.

"James," she began, "for how long have you suffered this paranoia?"

"I'm not paranoid," he went on assertively. "You must understand that these things happen on the Internet all the time. You really must be careful." Jane reflected back on her communications with Miss Garrett. They had chatted about America and England, about gardens and pubs, about horses and harvests, but no, not a word about anything that would lead her to believe that James could be right.

"I'm sorry James, but I think you'll have to trust my good instincts," she said finally. "This woman may be a bit crazy, she may be a bit overly passionate about silly things that no one else cares about, but I'm convinced she is genuine in her request." Jane touched her fork to the flaky potato covered in cheddar. "I haven't had such a lovely lunch in ages. We really must come here more often. Perhaps for dinner sometime?" Jane watched him devour his beef pie. "Another lager?"

"Mmm, thank you, no, I'm driving remember?"

"Ah yes of course." A rumble of laughter from the bar turned both their heads. It was good to be out among people Jane thought. Why had she tucked herself away for so long? Arthur always loved the pub and she loved anything he did.

"Aunt Jane," James began tentatively, "I've done a little checking, and this Wetherton Historical Foundation is always short of cash. They always have their hands out looking for donations." Jane shook her head and looked away toward the bar. "Please, I want you to at least be alert. If the subject of money should come up, I want you to phone me immediately."

"Certainly," Jane said primly. "Now, why don't we talk about something else for a change?" James drained his glass.

"Right, but before I forget, I wanted to mention a ledger I discovered belonging to Howard Wentworth, who was in possession of Broadhurst at that time.

Apparently the man was a nutter for detail, he was obsessive in his documentation of day to day expenses."

"Really?" Jane looked up from her plate in surprise. "And how do you know this?"

"I came across some references to him in a few journals and letters, mostly written by his brother William." Jane pursed her lips and shrugged.

"18th-century brothers," she began, dabbing at the corners of her mouth with a white paper napkin, "the eldest inherits the estate, the wealth, the power, and the younger perhaps a horse and a plow. Hardly fair, is it?"

"I suppose not," James said smiling. "It would make for a strained relationship. Although, as I recall, there was some sort of financial arrangement between the two. Perhaps Howard Wentworth felt guilty to have so much and his brother so little."

"Ha!" Jane laughed aloud. "A Wentworth man? Not likely." She smiled at the notion and sipped her sherry, glancing up at James and noticing the crystal blue of his eyes that was so like her sister and her dear Mother. Jane sniffed uncharacteristically. "You know," she continued, "your grandmother did not want Broadhurst Hall." James looked up with surprise.

"Yes," he answered smiling gently, "I do know that. She spoke to me about it on more than one occasion."

"Did she?" Jane remarked. "I'm intrigued."

"She did indeed," he began, "and she was quite clear that there could be no one better suited to care for Broadhurst than you, Aunt Jane."

"Really," Jane answered mildly, fiddling with a crumb that had fallen from her plate. "I imagine she told you that I was a tough old nut, while she was far too delicate and beautiful for the job." James stared at her fondly, realizing how mistaken she may have long been.

"Actually, no," he answered. "I specifically remember her saying that you were like a gentle, calming breeze over Broadhurst, and that the whole of the estate would bend to your care. Whereas she, who was anxious and fretful, could never tame it. Nor did she care to. In truth, she really hated the country." Jane stared off at the remarkably low ceiling. A subtle smile crossed her lips.

"We all have our talents and abilities, don't we?" She dabbed at her nose with her napkin and sniffed. "Now, "she said loudly, "how about another drink?

CHAPTER FOURTEEN

"Like manna from heaven, I do believe we have saved ourselves from ruin with this greatest of news." C.W.B. 1779

Duke Parker burst into the tavern like a bull in a china shop, shattering the early morning calm with a curious noise one might only describe as a rebel yell. Such a sound was, of course, entirely out of place in Connecticut.

Jillian Garrett and Josie Graham stared up at him from their places at the small window table where they had been planning the Harvest Party menu. Had it been anyone other than Duke making such a racket in this place, the police might have been called, but seeing as it was only Duke the pair quickly returned to the task at hand.

"Well, well, well ladies," Duke snarled enticingly as he sauntered in their direction, "I'll bet you're dying to know what I just found."

"Not if it's a snake," replied Josie flatly. "I don't like your snakes. And I don't care what kind they are or where you found them. I don't care what color their stripes are, or what shape their head is, or what they eat for breakfast. If they're snakes, I don't like them."

"Ditto," said Jillian tersely, scribbling feverishly on a pad of note paper and pushing her glasses back up on her nose. Duke flipped his bandana-rimmed eyes to the ceiling and let out an audible sigh.

"My work is so undervalued," he muttered in disappointment, circling around behind the bar and helping himself to a handful of green olives. Once again, the tavern settled into quiet. Jillian and Josie scribbled and flipped at piles of papers before them. Duke stood there, casually popping olives into his mouth as others might eat peanuts, hoping someone would notice him. Jillian? Josie? He eyed them from the corner of his peripheral vision as he chewed. Still, they would not submit.

"Oh, come on ladies," he said at last with exasperation. "This is good stuff."

Jillian looked up smiling from her paperwork, savoring the victory over Duke's patience. She stared at him with soulful eyes that stopped him short.

"Wow," Duke uttered. "What's wrong with you? You look terrible."

"Thanks," Jillian said. "You're sweet to say so."

"Seriously," he pressed on, edging forward.

"Seriously?" she asked back. "Oh you know. Death of a dream. Patriot turned assassin. Ten years of my life that I'll never get back wasted. Just the usual stuff."

"Hey," he offered gently.

"I don't want to talk about it," Jillian responded quickly, brushing it off. "Go on. Thrill me with news of something wild and exciting. We're brimming with excitement around here."

Duke edged forward, hands on hips and feet squarely planted on the worn floors. It would be reasonable to guess that he now stood in a spot where Catherine Wentworth Brownley had stood over two centuries before. The great patriot of Wetherton. Much-loved and adored by everyone who knew her. Throughout more than two centuries, locals would brim with pride at the mention of their heroine. Her passion as a patriot had never been doubted. Or at least not until recently. Who could imagine that historians for all these decades had gotten it wrong.

There was a night, in 1775, when Tories from Ridgefield sought lodging at the Tavern. John Brownley, at the insistence of his wife, would have the three men dragged "arguing and most belligerent" from the Tavern while commenting that "the display of hypocrisy required to tolerate such visitors would no longer be available from the Brownleys." This fact was well-documented by two locals who wrote of the account in their personal letters.

Catherine stood squarely behind her husband in this declaration.

Just one year earlier, it was Catherine who refused to serve tea at the Tavern, in the wake of nearby Boston's tea party. The resulting closure of Boston Harbor only added to the fuel of her anti-British sentiment.

Catherine's simple reply, often quoted thereafter in history books and writings, was, "I do so tire of tea, as do we all here in the colonies, and long for some new and far more interesting refreshment that is not in any way English."

The people of Wetherton were almost entirely unified in their thirst for freedom from British rule. A committee of correspondence was selected, so that Wetherton might effectively participate in battle plans now brewing in Hartford. Similarly, a committee of inspection was created to root out British loyalists. Both Catherine and her husband, John, were keen to help in this matter and were often described as "the ears of Wetherton."

Of course, as a woman, Catherine's role as wife and mother were paramount to any other interest, including that of patriot. There were no women serving on any committees or traveling to Hartford for meetings or ferrying much-needed supplies to their neighbors in Boston. Women stayed at home in support of those who would take a more visible role. Catherine understood her duty and used it to her best advantage whenever possible.

It was in the spring of 1781 that General George Washington returned to Wetherton for the second time. His first visit, just one year earlier, had held such pleasant memories for the General of "food, wit, generosity and the excellent care from the citizens" that prompted him to choose this town yet again for his meeting with Rochambeau. He graciously accepted the hospitality of his previous hosts, John and Catherine Brownley.

On this occasion, it was said that Catherine Wentworth Brownley offered her greatest service to the cause of freedom. During their four-day visit to the small town, Catherine attended to each and every need of her guests. It must have been exhausting to plan and prepare the meals for at least 50 extra men, but Catherine never broke her pleasant demeanor or showed the tiniest hint of tiring in her efforts. On the contrary, she seemed fuelled with energy by the prospect of aiding the patriot cause.

Over the course of three days, meetings were held at several locations around town. On May 22nd, one of the most important meetings took place at the Brownley Tavern between General Washington and Lt. General Rochambeau. Catherine kept a watchful eye over the closed door throughout the two-hour discussion.

As one of "the ears of Wetherton" she learned the identities of a few individuals in town whose loyalties seemed dispassionately unprofessed. Catherine was startled on that day to spot one such person, Ezekiel Smith, wandering close by behind the rear tavern entrance. Allowing no room for error she instantly called out loudly, "what news of this day Mr. Smith? Why do you walk behind the tavern in such a way? You know you are always welcome at the front door."

Upon hearing his wife's voice, John Brownley and five military guards quickly emerged from the closed door session. They flew to the rear door where Catherine gave way and found Ezekiel staring dumbly before setting off through the fields that surrounded town. A chase soon gave way to his capture and the discovery of a long land musket he had stashed in the tall grass near the White family garden.

He never confessed, but corroborating stories were offered from two colleagues. It is believed, but not proven, that Ezekiel Smith intended to assassinate both General Washington and Lt. General Rochambeau on that day. Had it not been for the quick and decisive action of Catherine Wentworth Brownley, with a bit of luck, he may well have succeeded.

Duke Parker now circled around to face Jillian and Josie, standing directly in front of Catherine's portrait. He chewed his last olive and raised his eyebrows up and down in anticipation.

"I think you're going to like this," he said. "I think it will cheer you up."

"OK, any time today. In fact, any time this morning would be great," Jillian responded to his final eyebrow maneuver. Duke edged forward, grabbing a chair for himself and cozying up to the table. Josie offered a bored glance at Jillian who shrugged her shoulders in defeat.

"What do we know about Margaret Woodsmith?" Duke began quietly, with an almost maniacal look of intrigue. Jillian slumped back in her chair, drumming the pen to her lips and trying to place any recollection of the name. Josie, who was a culinary school student working part-time in the tavern kitchen while she finished her degree offered a forlorn look of "who cares?" to no one in particular.

"Ah," Jillian sighed finally in frustration, "I can't place her. Who is she?"

"You mean, who was she," Duke smiled. Jillian's lips curled down at the corners.

"OK smartass, who was she?"

"She was the first wife of Horatio Beckwith," Duke answered, rays of sunshine beaming from his great smile. Upon hearing the name Beckwith, Jillian threw her pen on the table and leaned forward with her undivided attention.

"Go on," Jillian said, silently aware of the undying hope that every historian conceals, which is that a needle in the haystack can actually be found.

"Married in England, County Kent, April 1769. Arrived here as newlyweds in September of that year." Jillian's wide brown eyes filled with enrapt interest, while Josie doodled rainbows and happy-face flowers on the corner of her notepad.

"Where did you get the name Woodsmith?" Jillian asked. "I thought all we had was Margaret?"

"We did, but then I came across this amazing website, which, can I just tell you it blows my mind what's out there on the web today," Duke said nodding for extra effect. "There it was, right in front of me. This notation, in beautiful script, I mean that was really writing the way writing was meant to look, it's like art man, it's beautiful," he paused. "Anyway," he began again, "it was right there with every other recorded marriage and christening and I said to myself, Duke, this is it."

"Wait a minute," Jillian said cautiously. "First of all, how do we know this is the same Horatio Beckwith? And second of all, other than uncovering something new, which is always great," she added with purpose, "what does it tell us? How does it help us?" At this, Duke raised a pointed finger straight in the air. He then proceeded to pull an 8 ½ X 11 sheet of paper from his rear pocket, which was folded into a 1 X 1 inch square. Slowly, like a magician performing at a child's birthday party, Duke unfolded the paper, pausing after every few unveilings for dramatic effect. Jillian massaged her left temple with her fingertips and sipped at her coffee which had long gone cold. At last, the paper, in a wrinkled state of imperfection, was presented before her. Jillian pulled her glasses off her nose and studied the document in her hands.

It appeared to be a passenger log from the ship Mary Constance. Mary Constance made several transatlantic voyages between England and the colonies in the mid to late 1700's until she wrecked in a storm off the coast of Spain sometime around 1780. Jillian stared in disbelief.

"Where, in the name of God, did you find this?" she asked at last, truly amazed.

"It's the Internet baby, it is just out there just full of life and information. It's wild and free and crazy," Duke answered in equal awe. "Some guy had this old chest in his attic and when he opened it up it was like, wow, man, 300 years of history just sprang out at him. What a trip, huh?"

"Is it credible?" Jillian asked with concern.

"That," he implored," is an excellent question. Dahlia has a friend working on it right now. But, hey, we can only hope, right?"

"Yes," Jillian said, now rubbing her temple and her forehead, "but Woodsmith isn't a name I've ever heard in Wetherton, or even Connecticut."

"Ah ha!" Duke said, interrupting her before she could finish her thought. Again he reached into his rear pants pocket, this time on the opposite side, and produced an equally small square of folded paper. Jillian forced a smile of encouragement while Josie excused herself to the kitchen. Duke unfolded, and he unfolded, while beads of exasperation welled on Jillian's brain. She was almost unable to restrain her urge to rip the paper packet from his hands.

"Can you dig this?" he said at last, placing the paper before her. This time, Jillian reached for her glasses and placed them on her nose. The writing was smudged in spots, but still entirely legible. She stared at the paper for a long and healthy moment, before finally allowing herself to exhale an enormous sigh.

It was record of marriage. That fact was plain enough.

CHAPTER FIFTEEN

"Such a tedious business is this of deceit. One must always wonder if some small bit will lead to the exposure of all." C.B. 1772

James looked up anxiously at his computer screen, startled by the little bell that announced the arrival of a new e-mail message. He could hardly believe he would stoop so low, and yet, there he was monitoring Aunt Jane's e-mail account like a parent watches over a child. It was only 5:30 in the morning, and he felt confident that Aunt Jane would still be fast asleep at this hour. He wasn't spying on her, not really. He was only protecting her from the dangers she could not possibly understand. Thus far, he had found only the pesky American woman in her mailbox and loads of spam which he filtered out instantly.

A quick check revealed Jillian Garrett again. He clicked to read the message quickly, but found nothing harmful in their communications. He doubted this woman would present any risk to Aunt Jane or the Broadhurst estate. Maybe Aunt Jane was right. Maybe he was paranoid. A pang of guilt tugged at his throat and he swallowed hard to reassure himself in this questionable task.

Dear Lady Rochester,
We have recently discovered that the wife of Horatio Beckwith was named Margaret Woodsmith. We believe the Woodsmith family may be related to the Wentworth family. Do you have any information regarding this connection? As always, we are deeply grateful for your assistance.
Sincerely,
Jillian Garrett
Wetherton Historical Foundation

James scratched at his mop of curly brown hair and sighed. Clearly no one of interest was communicating with Aunt Jane via e-mail. Not yet anyway. That was a blessing to be thankful for. His next step, dare he take it, would be to ring his good friend Peter for advice on how best to proceed with his surveillance. Spyware. He had heard of it, but not in his wildest dreams had he ever imagined such a thing would be necessary.

Absently, the name Woodsmith stuck with him, but he couldn't place it. Where and when he had come across the name? Had it been in the ledger of 1760 – 1770 or had it been in the church records of some time prior? Perhaps the personal correspondence he had found, much to his surprise, in an old collection of engravings of that period. It escaped him.

He was tired, very tired and very worried. This computer, he now realized, had been a monumental mistake. Perhaps he could have her Internet connection disabled. No, he must remain calm and alert. Sooner or later he would find an opportunity to get rid of the bloody thing and return Aunt Jane to her quiet country existence. He nodded to himself in resolve.

It was 5:46 am and Jane Wentworth Rochester unlatched the door to the barn. She felt invigorated and refreshed and couldn't wait to be outdoors. Dr. Latrell had made her swear to almighty God that she would walk for no more than 15 minutes and even Jane, who was not one for bargaining with anyone, had agreed to his terms. She had to admit, for the first time in her life she was beginning to feel old and it was not pleasant to her. Just the other day, for instance, she could not reach the top shelf of her closet. What a silly thing. Were her arms shorter, her shoulders less flexible? Was she shrinking? She shook her head in disgust. What next? Would all of her teeth fall out?

The air outside was cool and damp and she breathed in fully. Dudley wagged his tail enthusiastically and ran a few feet ahead.

"I'm coming old friend," she answered with equal enthusiasm. "Where shall we go on our little journey today?" Dudley led the way down the path to the pasture and Jane laughed at him with pure joy. She was in an inexplicably good mood and filled with energy. She walked along, slower than in the past but still at an impressive pace for a woman her age, and glanced at the familiar beauty all around her. True to her word, she checked the watch on her wrist and recalled her dog to her side.

"Sorry old friend, but you know what the damnable Doctor said. If they find my dead body further than 10 minutes walk from the house they'll know I didn't keep my word. And I always keep my word." Dudley wagged an encouraging tail and let out a loud bark, but to no avail. "Not today old boy. Come on then."

Back in the house, her hair wild and wispy from the breeze outside, she settled in the library and turned on her computer.

"Have a nice walk this morning?" asked Liza. "I'll bet you're happy to be back out and about."

"Yes, yes, yes," Jane said smiling and typing away at her keyboard.

"Shall I bring your breakfast in here Mum?"

"No Liza, thank you, but I'll be along shortly. Just have a bit of catching up to do." Liza looked puzzled.

"Catching up?" she asked.

"Won't be long," Jane answered without looking up, typing away under Liza's curious gaze. She had not heard from "THECOLONEL" in a few days and was wondering if he would be online this morning. She was also worried about "PINKY" who had not been heard from since last Tuesday when she was off to meet the parents of her newest boyfriend. She was, apparently,

158

from California and while Jane did not post messages to her very often she delighted in reading what "PINKY" had posted for the world to see.

She frowned. "THECOLONEL" had written that he would be traveling for the next week and would not be online until he was back. "A shame," Jane muttered. She had been looking forward to his views on the Middle East peace process. He was clearly a remarkably intelligent fellow.

She clicked onto her e-mail account and found a message from Jillian. As she read aloud, she was startled by the instant message which flashed to one side of her screen. "Heavens," she muttered quietly, withdrawing her tentative hands from the mouse. What was this? The message read:

Lady Rochester. This is Jillian Garrett. I happened to notice that you were online and I was wondering if you had any news regarding my query of the name Woodsmith. Do you mind if I instant message?

A happy smile crossed Jane's lips. How wonderful! Instant messaging! She had heard of this. Fascinating. Carefully, she maneuvered the mouse so that she could reply.

I have just now read your message and will have to think back upon it. I do know that the Woodsmith family married into our family from a connection in the eighteenth century. I believe it was a woman named Louise, but I will confirm this fact.

She paused a moment, then added:

How is the weather in Connecticut?

The reply was swift:

The weather is lovely. It is a chilly fall night. Thank you again for all of your assistance. We are battling against the possible loss of one of our oldest homes, built circa 1740, and are trying to determine the historical significance, if any, that the home might have in order to protect it.

Jane frowned. 1740? Was that an old home? Good God. She owned breakfast dishes older than that. And why should anyone have to prove historical significance to save a house?

I am puzzled as to how the Wentworth family could help you in this. Were you not inquiring with regard to Catherine Wentworth Brownley?

She hit send.

We are. And continue to be interested in any information you may have about her. Much to my surprise, we also believe that your family may have some connection to the Beckwith house through the Woodsmith family and I am now also interested in this as well. I'm sorry to bother you, but any help you could give would be greatly appreciated.

Jane frowned again. How odd, she thought, that her family should have any connection to this little American town.

I shall have my nephew assist in this matter and will reply with any information that is available. Now, tell me more about that friend of yours from Texas.

She hit send and proceeded to have a lovely chat with her newest young friend over breakfast.

CHAPTER SIXTEEN

"It has often been said that when we wish for one thing too keenly it will only lead to disappointment. I find this to be altogether true, and am henceforth determined to find joy in the everyday. Still, I pray that God will send us some amusement here. We are sorely lacking at present and it would do us all much good." C.W.B. 1780

The late October sky was a brilliant blue and the air held a crisp, biting chill filled with the smell of falling, decaying leaves and chimney smoke and baked apples. It was now officially what the experts declared to be "peak leaf season" in the Connecticut River Valley and the trees were a feast for the eyes, boasting grand displays of vivid reds, oranges and golds. God and Mother Nature had smiled upon the tiny little town, and in so doing, had created the perfect day for the Harvest Party.

"Finally," Jillian said smiling to herself as she walked past the old cemetery, "finally, something is going right around here." Later, she would be obliged to don the Catherine Brownley costume of green and blue silk that she wore only on this day, on the occasion of the Christmas party and for special tours for supporters who pledged $1,000 or more. Needless to say this third opportunity was remarkably rare. For now, she hurried along in denim and polar fleece, never bothering to worry whether or not it was fashionable or flattering. Wethertonians never gave fashion a second thought. If it fits, if it doesn't have too many stains or holes, if it keeps you warm or cool, you wear it. That was pretty much the extent of fashion. Of course, in the true colonial Wetherton, fashion had been essential. It defined the classes, it defined the self and it most certainly defined the occasion.

It was funny, Jillian thought, but somehow over 200 years, fashion had become curiously unimportant. Even a

15-year-old green corduroy jumper could elicit rave reviews with the right audience. 18th-century ladies would be rolling over in their graves to see the unkempt, haphazard mess of frumpy clothing that now shrouded the Wetherton woman. From a time when women would not step foot out of their home without the proper fan, to a time when women would wear the same college sweatshirt for 20 years, the standards had slipped to a remarkable low.

After her customary right turn on King Street, Jillian cut through the back path of the Scott house, a shortcut she rarely used since the family that now owned the home had a nasty little dog that was part Chow and part terrorist. Although the Brown family was lovely, their dog was not, and it was only in the wee hours of early morning that Jillian would dare to make the trip. Thankfully, PeeWee, if any name could be less telling, was still indoors and unable to snarl his familiar greeting at her.

After a turn onto Walker Lane, a tiny little stretch of just two tiny little houses, built sometime around 1865 for returning Civil War veterans who were too disabled to build homes for themselves, she circled around behind the Treat house.

"Morning," she heard called out to her in an oddly unfamiliar voice. She turned to look up and see the incredibly cute roofer, once again piecing together his cedar shakes to assemble a perfectly recreated colonial roof. Jillian gazed up at him and snapped her mouth shut.

"Uh, good morning," she offered back, psychotically aware of the fact that this was the first cute guy under the age of 70 who had said hello in many months.

"You must be excited," he said in return.

"Sorry?" Jillian answered back, edging a bit closer. She watched him climb down from his perch on the roof, breeches, stockings, buckled shoes and all. As he hit the ground, he wiped his face with the scrap of red cloth he pulled from his pocket. Holy crap, Jillian thought silently, he was amazingly handsome.

"Aren't you the lady in charge of the party?" he asked politely.

"Uh, yes," Jillian stammered. "That's me," she added shyly. "I'm Jillian. Jillian Garrett." She raised her hand to shake his, but he bowed gallantly before she could make the gesture.

"Thomas Sloan," he offered. "A pleasure to make your acquaintance."

Jillian smiled and curtsied in return, although she felt a little funny in her jeans and hiking boots.

"The pleasure is mine, Mr. Sloan."

"Great day for a party," Thomas said. "I only hope I can finish this roof in time to enjoy some of it." Jillian glanced up at the roof which she judged to be at least 3 days away from completion.

"I'm sure you can slip away for a little punch," she answered. "We're not tyrants here in Wetherton." He smiled back, a bright white perfect smile.

"I'm looking forward to it. Will you be at the tavern?"

"Me?" she asked somewhat meekly. "Uh, yes, well, eventually." Maintain composure, do not make an idiot of yourself. "I pretty much have to be everywhere today, but eventually I'll make it over to the tavern."

"I hope to see you there Miss Garrett," Thomas said, again flashing that perfect smile. The blonde curls of his hair, caught in a ponytail at the back of his neck, were almost luminous in the early morning sun. He bowed again as she began to walk along her way.

"Yes, well, see you later then," she stumbled, nearly tripping over her own feet in her clunky boots. Why couldn't she be wearing something fabulous? Why did she have to look like a lumberjack? She self-consciously pulled at her hair and hurried on, smiling to herself at the prospect of seeing Thomas at the tavern later tonight. She glanced back at him and his painstakingly slow progress on the roof. Jillian shook her head. "Who gives a damn about a roof," she muttered aloud, and hurried over to the town green to check on pumpkin crowns and candied apple flashlights and all the other very important details of the morning.

She found Carol amid a sea of orange, red, yellow and brown balloons, all strung together to form a rainbow entrance to the historic district. Henry was painstakingly testing miniature lights to find bulbs that needed replacing and Tricia was lighting kindling in a stone fire pit to warm caramel for hand-dipped apples.

Adelle Barth unloaded dozens of pies from the back of her station wagon. Timmy Bartlett painted a baked goods sale sign with spray paint and Judy Gardner put the finishing touches on her display of scarecrows, witches and other handmade Halloween décor. Her dogs Calico, Buster and Maria Luisa all watched from the windows of her SUV.

Sue Scotts offered homemade muffins for fortification against the grueling day of fundraising and frivolity that was ahead of them.

Down the hill beyond Butler's pasture was this year's newest addition to the festivities. The Corn Maze, which stretched through four acres of Jerry Tate's farm, and promised over one mile of twists and turns through scarecrows, hay bales and withered corn stalks. Jerry himself had designed and implemented the maze only just the night before. While he hadn't exactly found his way through successfully, he steadfastly confirmed that "he just knew there had to be a way out of there." At this late hour, that would have to do.

Duke Parker glided up the street on his moped, the whitish blonde wisps of long, thin curls flowing behind him in the breeze. He was resplendent in his trademark shorts, work boots and Harvest Party orange tie-dyed t-shirt. He smiled his greeting from behind mirrored aviator sunglasses circa 1972. Even on a moped, Duke was compelled to be a hyper-miler, squeezing out every last drop of forward momentum and appearing to be entirely ignorant of a little thing called brakes.

"Man," he beamed, "what a ride! I cruised all the way down King Street from West."

"Hit any squirrels?" Jillian asked politely.

"Not today," Duke affirmed, removing his shades and hanging them from his collar. "Is this weather far out or what?" Jillian smiled.

"So freaking far out I can't even describe it," she answered.

"It's gonna be a great day," Duke said, dismounting and parking. "Where you headed?"

"Tavern," Jillian replied, gulping her coffee with skim milk and six sugars. The cup warmed her hands right through her knit gloves. "George said something about bread pudding gone bad. Thought I'd better check it out."

"Bread pudding!" Duke gasped with exaggerated alarm. "You don't have a moment to lose," he added, giving her a little shove in the right direction. Instead of her usual pithy comeback, Jillian just giggled and protected her coffee with both hands. She was in a fantastic mood. Maybe it was the sun, the cool fall air, or maybe it was the relief of having another successful Harvest Party to afford another year of keeping historic Wetherton, Connecticut in the black. Although what did it matter if Catherine Brownley turned out to be nobody? Jillian pushed the thought from her mind.

She turned her attention to the prospect of having Brownley punch at the tavern later this evening with Thomas Sloan. "Who knows?" Jillian thought aloud, "and who cares? It's going to be a great day and, for once, I'm going to enjoy myself."

She waved greetings to the Graham family, and the Tate family and the Sulkowskis. Before she reached the tavern, Jillian must have greeted every Wethertonian who passed her way. She never thought of it before, but now had to admit that it was nice to know nearly everyone in town. Her spirits soared even higher as she dwelled on her apparent popularity. Jillian whisked past a young couple parking their car and packing their fleece-bundled baby into her stroller. New Englanders couldn't resist the urge to be outside on such a beautiful fall day. Jillian imagined hearing the bells of a cash register drawer tinkle in her head and she knew that receipts should be strong. She raised her eyes to the skies and silently thanked God for their good fortune.

It wasn't long before the doors were open full swing and the crowds of revelers came pouring into town and Jillian's team of volunteers fired off their duties like a well-drilled military machine. Apples were dipped in caramel and rolled in chocolate chips. Cherubic little cheeks were painted with black cats, pumpkins and ghosts. The smell of barbequed chicken, hot dogs and hamburgers filled the air.

By noon most children, and many parents, donned the obligatory $4 pumpkin crown. Cha-ching, cha-ching, Jillian muttered. Although sunny, it was not a warm day and many folks stopped by the bonfires scattered around the green to warm up and greet their neighbors. Dahlia's booth full of painted glass and wooden items was a huge success. Nearby, Mary Forest's photo booth, where folks dressed in period costumes and posed before a backdrop of colonial onion fields filled with scarecrows, was also drawing big crowds.

Jillian hadn't been able to make it down the hill to the corn maze or the pumpkin catapult, but heard on her walkie-talkie that the crowds were huge. Imagine paying money to watch a pumpkin hurled through the air via catapult, she thought. After a quick trip to the tavern she would go down and check it out personally.

In the blink of an eye it was half-past four. Candied apple flashlights were beginning to bounce through the crowds like little fireballs of red. The smell of hot, mulled apple cider and spice cakes mingled with shepherd's pie and beer. The great bonfire in the center of the Green was lit, to the delight of a record-breaking crowd, and Judy Sanford reported receipts of nearly double last year's.

Over 30 families complained that they could find no true path out of the corn maze and resorted to following the sun and pushing aside scarecrows to blaze a path of their own. Still, the authentic Colonial experience of foraging for survival left them invigorated by the challenge, and only one family from New York really raised a stink about the course.

Jillian smiled satisfaction as she admired herself in the mirror. She didn't know what was better, a record-breaking Harvest Party or wearing the blue and green Catherine Brownley silk gown for the evening. Nathaniel Davids would be playing John Brownley tonight, a choice that made Jillian feel sadly empathetic for her late heroine. Everyone agreed that Nathaniel bore a remarkable resemblance to the great patriarch, right down to his enormous belly, hairy ears and yellow teeth. Still, he was an awfully nice guy and played to the crowds like a pro. Jillian admonished herself for being shallow and judgmental as she swished and swirled in the fabulous Brownley silk gown.

She checked herself for make-up, something she rarely ever worried about, but tonight she wanted to look her best. Was she worried that Archibald Mack might show up unexpectedly? Perhaps. Was she determined to look her very best in the interest of portraying Catherine Wentworth Brownley to perfection? Maybe. Did she wonder if maybe, just maybe, the handsomest and most adorable roofer in the history of Wetherton might be waiting in the tavern for her? Most definitely. And so, she lingered for that extra moment, to be sure that every seam was in place.

Then, she was off. She was out the door and down the street and across the lane toward the tavern. Seemingly hundreds of pumpkin-crowned well-wishers requested a photo.

"Would you please let me take a picture with my daughter?"

"Oh, please, could you stop for a picture with Uncle Ed?" She could hardly disappoint them. Every happy customer was a paying customer. In the spirit of Catherine Wentworth Brownley, Jillian accommodated each request with a gracious smile.

CHAPTER SEVENTEEN

"Spies and demons are among us I fear." C.W.B. 1776

James walked closely alongside his Aunt Jane while the two stomped through the fields on the south end of the property. Dudley was well ahead of them, stopping occasionally to glance back and make sure he was still being followed. Humans! He barked with joy, tendrils of steam floating from his gaping mouth.

James could hardly remember the last time he went for a good long walk. Although he was born and raised in London, the countryside surrounding Broadhurst Hall suited him very well. For her part, Jane was pleased to have his company. He didn't talk too much. That was a blessing. She always hated walking with a chatterbox. She also had to admit, it eased the burden of worrying that she might die in some undisclosed corner of the property where her body would be ravaged by nature before she was found. She preferred to be buried in one piece, whole and unravaged. Thoughts such as this had never, ever entered her mind before. Yet, since her illness, she was just a touch cautious about being alone too far from home.

They cleared the little knoll by the fence and surveyed the land that spread before them. This was the highest vantage point on the entire property and it was an incredible sight to see. Neither of them spoke. They simply breathed in the beauty.

Roger Wentworth certainly knew what he was doing when he chose this land to build his great monument. It was breathtaking. For centuries, Wentworths had come to this spot to drink in this view and enjoy their privilege of ancestry. Today, James and his Aunt Jane were no different than any of the hundreds who had been here before them.

"I love it here," Jane almost whispered. "I always have." James nodded.

"It is remarkable," he offered, settling his hands on his hips and turning around to take in every angle.

"Do you understand the tremendous responsibility you will one day inherit?" she asked. James looked down before answering.

"Do you think I'm the right man for the job, Aunt Jane?" he asked. "Honestly?" Jane shrugged.

"You'll have to be, won't you?" she answered. "It is your responsibility. It is your duty." James exhaled loudly. It was a massive amount of responsibility. How would he manage it? He couldn't even manage Aunt Jane. "You'll be just fine," she assured dismissively. "Come on then, I haven't all day to stand here in the mud with you. We have work to do."

Dudley, not surprisingly, was the first to arrive. They came upon him lying in the grass, curled up into a giant ball of fur. Although it was nearly lunchtime, they agreed it would be best to begin their research in the library. Jane walked ahead and took the seat by her computer. James tensed, ever so slightly. He watched her in amazement as she typed and clicked.

"My God," he blurted out, "you've become very proficient haven't you?" Jane chuckled.

"I have indeed!" she announced. "It is very exciting."

"Exciting?" James asked, trying to sound casual. "How so?"

"Heavens," Jane murmured to the portrait above her. "Such a silly boy." James frowned.

"I'm sorry?"

"Exciting, James. Think of how exciting it is for an old woman like me to see the world again in this new way. It's marvelous." James forced a laugh.

"Aunt Jane," he said with caution. "You are being very careful about using this. You're not getting onto crazy websites or anything?" He bit his tongue.

"Crazy websites?" she asked, looking above her glasses at him. "Certainly not!" She turned her attention back to her computer to access her e-mail account. James edged in closer for a better look.

"Ah!" Jane announced, typing away with surprising speed. James edged in again.

"What are you doing now?" he asked. Jane seemed to pay no attention. "Are you instant messaging?" James asked with growing alarm. Jane looked up smiling.

"I am," she said with pride. "Imagine that!" By now, James had edged up against the back of her chair, a look of shock and awe transforming his face.

"Who, may I ask, are you instant messaging?" he asked. Jane frowned.

"Jillian Garrett, of course. Why do you think we're here?" She eyed him cautiously. James was nearly speechless. He scratched his head, tousling the mop of brown curls, a mild laugh escaping from his lips.

"How on earth did you learn this?" he asked with genuine surprise. Jane shrugged.

"It wasn't difficult," she said. "I may be old, but I'm not out." She looked up at the portrait. "Darling, he thinks I'm bumbling."

"I do not," James protested, not knowing if he should address the portrait or his Aunt. "I'm surprised, that's all. Computers are very new to you and I'm surprised that you've adapted to them so quickly." Jane finished typing and awaited her response. James leaned forward to wait with her. In mere moments the answer, from Jillian Garrett in Wetherton, CT arrived.

"I enjoy our conversations very much," Jane said. James stared in disbelief.

Good morning Mrs. Rochester. Today I will be busy all day with our annual Harvest Party, but please send me any additional questions via e-mail and I will be happy to answer them later this evening. I hope you are feeling better after the fish yesterday.

"The fish?" was all James could manage.

"Yes, well, you know, Liza makes a terrible fish stew," Jane answered. "Set me a bit off yesterday."

"And an American woman, whom you've never met, knows this about you?" She looked at him, her expression blank and innocent.

"Yes," she said finally, "I suppose she does." Jane smiled pleasantly. "Come now James, let me fill you in on what we're looking for."

Jane chattered and talked for several minutes, gesturing wildly to the leather bound volumes that resided near the ceiling and complained of their inaccessibility. Would he be able to reach them if she needed to see that red one over there? Would he be able to help her decipher this peculiar handwriting in the brown volume over here?

James listened, trying to focus on her requests. Aunt Jane was a whirl of activity and excitement. She jabbered on about a woman named Woodsmith and something about a marriage. He reached for volumes and helped her interpret illegible handwriting. Yet, all the while he could not shake the notion that an American woman named Jillian Garrett had befriended his Aunt Jane and was asking about last night's fish stew.

CHAPTER EIGHTEEN

"Diversions are sorely needed in these trying times. When pleasant moments find us, we seize them with greed." CWB 1777.

Candlelight filled the tavern and the windows glowed with festivity. The sound of laughter hummed from within. Jillian could see every breath exhale before her in a steamy puff as she crossed the green and hurried toward the party. The night air had dipped from pleasantly crisp to nearly freezing.

It had already been a very long day for all the volunteers and the handful of paid employees, but the tavern party was an event not to be missed and everyone rose to the occasion. This year, in particular, found everyone in need of a good excuse to relax and be merry. The imminent destruction of the Beckwith house pressed in on their collective history-loving souls. Not to mention the prospect of revisionists re-writing Catherine Brownley out of history entirely. Jillian shook her head and pushed the thoughts from her mind. Tonight she deserved to have some fun. Just inside that tavern door was a glass of Brownley punch with her name on it.

The front door stood wide open with Nathaniel Davids playing the role of host, John Brownley, his resplendent belly protruding through the doorway before any other portion of him could be seen. In years past, he had a tendency to drink a little too much punch and wander off of the job. In fact, three years earlier, many disappointed revelers were unable to have their photos taken with the famous figure because he was sleeping off a few too many in the barn out back. Still, he was the best man for the job.

"Good wife," he said to Jillian with a smile, "we have many guests to attend to. Where have you been?"

"I went to London to visit the Queen," she offered glibly, moving quickly past him and into the noisy crowd. It was a sight to behold. The room smelled of wood smoke from the fireplaces and rum, nutmeg and cinnamon. Candles burned brightly in every corner, filling the rooms with soft beautiful light that drew dancing shadows on the moss green paneled walls. The aromas of roast chicken, shepherd's pie and harvest stew, along with fresh-baked bread and ginger cookies mingled with strong dark ale.

She was late in her arrival, mostly because two families were lost in the corn maze, but also because the pumpkin catapult was such an overwhelming success she decided to keep it open for an extra hour for the windfall profits. By now, many of the visitors were gone, exhausted from their day of fresh air and good old-fashioned colonial food and fun, leaving just the locals to fill the tavern that night. By the look of them, many had been here for quite a while.

Jillian wound her way through the crowd, stopping to thank everyone along the way for baking, selling, bartering or volunteering something to make this year's Harvest Party the best ever. Her eye scanned the room for Archibald Mack who was, predictably, a no-show. Jillian was surprised to feel a sense of disappointment. She continued to work her way toward the bar where Meegan Graham manned the punch bowl.

"You look like a woman who needs a drink," she yelled over the crowd, handing her a glass of the spectacularly golden brown elixir with a wedge of orange rind floating on the top. She winked at Jillian and ladled another glass for another customer. Jillian breathed in the spicy sweet scent and sipped a good long swig. Ah, the nectar of Wetherton!

The town was originally settled by Puritans who moved down from the Masschusetts colony in the mid-1600s. In spite of this puritanical heritage, Wetherton was long known as a town fond of its libations and only a few men throughout history thought to challenge the town's taste for "drink". The Reverend Charles Abingdon, on travels through Wetherton from Manhattan, sometime around 1680, spoke openly and critically of the town's "drinking of rum and other spirits debilitating for the soul and the mind." Thereafter, finding himself unable to secure lodging anywhere in Wetherton, he would be forced to move on toward Boston, predicting the downfall of the town as he left. Over three centuries later, Wetherton was still alive and well.

"Jillian! Jillian Garrett!" came the voice of Burt Payne from behind her. "It's a great day for Wetherton, wouldn't you say? Even in the middle of all this mess, we can still pull together, can't we? Boy, I wish old Murton was here right now. We'd give him a dose of good old-fashioned Wetherton whoop-ass, wouldn't we? Huh? Huh?" Jillian gulped another slug of punch and smiled.

"Yes sir," she replied with a forced cheeriness.

"If he could see this right now with all of us right here. If he could see how we all just pull together and get the job done. Well, hell, I bet he'd run crying all the way back to Greenwich. Don't you think?"

"Well," Jillian offered vaguely, "I don't know about that, but I am very proud of all our hard work today." Another big gulp of punch.

"Come on now," Burt prodded. "You can't keep a bunch of good Wethertonians down. Our great, great, great, great granddads were patriots. We built this nation. We sure as hell built this town." Burt smiled with ancestral pride.

Yes, it was true that Wetherton had weathered many storms. There had been hurricanes that should have blown the town off the map, and yet it survived. There had been bad crops, failed harvests and drought that should have starved everyone out, and yet they found a way. There had been disease, dysentery and filth that should have left them all for dead, and still they lived. There had been war. Revolutionary war. Wethertonians had risked everything, their homes, families and their lives, for a chance to live free of a king who would tax their labors and hard-earned existence down to their last pennies, and they had won. God had smiled on this tiny town throughout the centuries and had filled its residents with the strength of commitment and perseverance needed to win the day.

Now, there was a new fight. Not one that could be won with strength of brawn or character. This was not a fight that could be won with sheer determination and a will to succeed. This fight would require a founding father's intellect and a king's purse. Jillian knew they did not have the latter.

"Burt," she said, gulping the last of her drink, "I'm going to get more punch. I have to catch up to the rest of this crowd."

"Oh sure, yup, sure. That's right. It's a great day. What a party, huh? I'll tell ya." Jillian smiled and ducked between two costumed men next to her. They mumbled congratulations as she squeezed past and out of the reach of Burt Payne. She looked toward the edge of the bar where Meegan continued to ladle away.

"Refill?" Meegan asked happily. "Goes down pretty smooth, doesn't it? But watch it. It's got a way of sneaking up on you."

"I'll bear that in mind," Jillian said knowingly and greedily grabbed the glass that was handed back to her. "Have you seen Duke?" She shook her head.

"He was eating upstairs about an hour ago, but I think he left."

"Already?" Jillian asked.

"I think he's coming back with Dahlia. She needed some help cleaning up her booth." Jillian was disappointed. She scanned the room looking for some much needed pleasant conversation, and was willing to

176

talk to anyone about anything other than Arnold Murton or the Beckwith house. From the corner of her eye she caught him, standing near the fireplace against the opposite wall of the room. In the glow of the flames his brilliant eyes flickered with soft blue and gold light. He wore a crisp white shirt, brown vest with brass buttons and britches that matched. His sandy blonde hair was held at the back of his neck in a ponytail. She caught his eye and he grandly bowed in her direction. It was Thomas, her favorite roofer.

He threaded his way through the crowd, never losing sight of her. Jillian gulped hard at a lump in her throat and sipped at her punch.

"Good evening, Miss," he said politely, playing the role of colonial gentleman exceedingly well. "It's a great celebration tonight."

"It is indeed," she returned. "Are you enjoying your first Harvest Party?"

"Very much," he answered. "Although, I must leave tomorrow for my time here is almost gone."

"Really?" Jillian stammered, trying to hide her surprise. "I didn't realize you were leaving so soon."

"Sadly, yes. But I believe I might be back in a few months." He smiled shyly. "That's a beautiful gown you're wearing. You look lovely." Jillian could feel her face flush.

"Thank you," she almost yelled over the crowd.

"Everyone here says that you're the woman responsible for this great day. Is that true?"

"No," she answered modestly shaking her head. "Everyone works very hard and everyone deserves the credit."

"More punch?" he asked, helping himself to another glass.

"Yes please," Jillian answered without a thought.

Amid the chaos, the room next door was clearing way for the entertainment to begin. Frank and Keri Reed, who moved to Wetherton from New York the year before, played everything from the guitar to the violin to the tin whistle. In moments the room filled with the sound of 18th-century colonial favorites. The floorboards began to shake as Grace Connor organized a group to dance a localized version of the Virginia Reel.

"Do you dance, Miss?" Thomas asked politely.

"Not at all well, I'm afraid."

"I don't mind," he responded with a wink. "Would you do me the honor?" He held out his arm for her.

"I really don't dance," Jillian protested with mild panic, sipping another gulp of punch. "I'm a classic case of two left feet. My mother says I get that from my father."

"I don't mind," Thomas protested. "I'll teach you." His smile was so pleasant and encouraging. He seemed so polite and gentlemanly. It had been so long since any man had shown her any attention, other than Archibald Mack. She couldn't help herself. In one of those "what the hell" moments that anyone could live to regret, she threaded her hand through his outstretched arm and followed him to the makeshift dance floor.

The room was pounding with music and sound of stomping feet. Most Wethertonians, it was clear, danced no better than Jillian. Yet, everyone seemed willing to take their turn spinning and twirling and stomping this way and that. Thomas grabbed Jillian's hands and whisked her in circles. Her massive silk skirt twirled around her legs. Everyone was drinking and dancing, clapping and laughing. Jillian spun to her left, clapped her hands and spun back to her right. So many dancers were in colonial costume it was almost as if the centuries had been turned back entirely. Catherine Wentworth Brownley stared down at them from her portrait with pride and pleasure.

Thomas grabbed her hands again, this time pulling her toward him with one hand on her corseted waist. He held his left hand high for her to touch and led her around the dance floor in a waltz.

"You're a very good dancer!" Jillian shouted.

"Fifth grade," Thomas replied with a smile. "My mother made me learn. She always told me that some day I would thank her for it, and I think I finally will." He smiled again. Jillian was utterly enrapt. How could she have allowed this incredible man to wander all summer through the streets of Wetherton right under her nose? What would Taylor say?

It was a Harvest Party never to be forgotten. Hours later, long after Frank and Keri had retired their instruments, a hearty band of determined revelers kept the spirit of Wetherton dancing and celebrating far past midnight. Colonial music gave way to a selection of country western, classic rock and a little reggae. The more she danced the more she laughed and the more punch she drank. Jillian was officially having the best time of her Wetherton life.

Well past 2:00 am the Brownley punch began to dry up and last call was shouted. The fires in each hearth burned low. Jillian and Thomas were the last couple to leave the dance floor, shuffling and twirling to the sounds of reggae. They were an odd sight. Both drunk. Both dressed in colonial costume. Both singing to the steel drum tune with gusto.

"I'm locking up," Meegan called out to them, "unless you want to stay here all night."

"I guess it's time to go," Jillian said disappointed. "I can't believe it's over already. I feel like I could dance all night."

"You did dance all night," Thomas replied. "And you're the girl who said she couldn't dance."

"I know," Jillian replied with drunken enthusiasm. "But I'm not the least bit tired." She grabbed for her wool cloak in the back room. Thomas pulled on a down jacket and picked up his duffle bag.

"Can I walk you home?" he offered politely, slurring his speech into something that sounded more like "kin I work yoam". She spun around to see him standing in britches and a ski parka, his tri-corner hat fitted nicely on his head, and dismissed the notion that he looked suddenly odd.

"That would be nice," she said happily and they braced themselves for the shock of cold air that was waiting outside.

"Whoa!" Thomas yelled like a southern California surfer. "Ah, that air feels awesome." He offered Jillian his arm and they wandered down the street. "Which way?" he asked. She pointed in the direction of home and they walked, or stumbled, across the green.

It was only a ten minute walk, but it seemed to take forever. Jillian shivered with cold and Thomas kept coughing. Clutching each other, they could barely manage more than two steps in a straight line before they would veer and sway off the chosen path. They giggled and sang, loudly, causing the occasional dog to bark and the front porch light at number 75 to come to life.

"Whoa," Thomas kept saying. "I seriously drank too much of that punch." Jillian nodded agreement, realizing now that she was no longer enjoying the elated feeling she felt back at the tavern. They stumbled up to her front gate.

"Here it is," Jillian slurred. "This is me." She turned to unlatch the gate, but couldn't seem to recall how to work the mechanism. "Uh oh," she mumbled. "Somebody changed the lock."

"Let me do it," Thomas offered feebly, banging at the gate with his foot. "Nope," he said with resignation. "Broken. We'll have to go over." Without another word he hoisted Jillian like a feather over the gate, sending her to the ground with a whimper.

"Ow," she protested, watching Thomas attempt first one leg, then the other and finding him quickly on the ground next to her.

"Whoa," he said again, looking up smiling. He was very cute Jillian thought. Although not quite as cute as he was at the tavern. His hat was now missing and the rawhide tie that held his ponytail had fallen off. His hair was just kind of messy and stringy and, hmmm, maybe dirty, she mused. He leaned up on one elbow and reached for her face with his other hand, pulling her close to him. She breathed in the steamy air of his kiss and felt her head swooning. Was it a great kiss? No. A nice kiss, but not a great kiss. She suddenly realized she felt very ill and the swooning was not from the kissing. It was from the punch. She moaned.

"Let's go inside," she said meekly, hoping she could manage another five steps to the front door. Thomas followed behind her on wobbling legs.

"Jill, yo Jill," he said, I think I'm gonna be ....." And yes, he was. Sick. Very, very sick. The corners of Jillian's mouth turned down with her own nausea.

"Oh dear," was all she could manage. "I'll get you a towel or something," she mumbled, heading into the house. She fumbled around in the powder room for a towel and a cup of water, turning to find him stumbling into the house behind her.

"It's OK babe, no worries," he said. Jillian frowned. Had he just called her babe? "I'm a trooper with this. Happens all the time. Just give me a few minutes, I'll be good to go."

Jillian's alcohol-soaked brain tried to reason through what he just said. Happens all the time? Jillian couldn't remember the last time she had been in such bad shape. Yale, no doubt. In a few minutes he'd be good to go? Go where? Great God in heaven, she thought, panic beginning to take over. She followed him into the living room, where he was passed out on her floor.

"Uh, Thomas," she whispered, stumbling through the darkness to find him a blanket and a pillow. "OK. You just rest right there. Here you go," she said, doing her best to cover him up, but landing the pillow on his feet and covering only his head with the blanket. "Good night," she whispered, clutching at the stair railing and praying that he didn't wake up.

With extraordinary effort she reached her bedroom, closed and locked the door behind her. She fumbled at the tiny buttons that required such great patience and care and tugged at the tangle of strings on her corset. After what seemed an hour of undressing herself from the 18th-century, she flopped down into her bed, covered her head with her comforter and waited for the room to stop spinning.

CHAPTER NINETEEN

"I'll not be treated as a child nor will I be silent in the face of tyrants. I accept only the respect that I deserve for the woman I am and the choices I have made." C.W.B., 1771.

Lady Jane Alexandra Wentworth Rochester greeted her nephew that morning with an uncharacteristically cheerful hello. It was, in fact, so surprising that James stopped short, pausing to drink in her pleasant tone before continuing on.

"Good morning Aunt Jane," he offered, proceeding even more cheerfully than usual himself in return. "I have found an interesting bit of information on the Brownley woman that I think you'll like."

"Excellent," Jane replied enthusiastically. "We shall certainly send off a note to our American friend. What, pray tell, is this bit of information?"

"It's fascinating," James answered, grabbing a perfectly toasted slice of bread and slathering it with butter and strawberry jam. "Apparently there was indeed a Catherine Laurel Wentworth born in this very house in 1755, to Howard and Anne on April 26th and christened a few weeks later in May."

"Marvelous," Jane said evenly.

"Indeed," James went on, "although curiously, there is no other mention made of her, not anywhere that I have found."

"Perhaps she did not survive infancy, James," Jane offered sympathetically, knowing fully the perils of early childhood diseases in the 1700s.

"Yes, well I thought that myself," he went on with enthusiasm, "but Howard Wentworth was renowned for his fastidious record-keeping. Apparently the man was something of a tyrant. Every birth, death, christening, marriage and the like are all dutifully recorded in his personal bible. I have it here with me," he said, patting the black leather attaché he had carried in with him that now rested by his side. "I borrowed it from your library."

"Borrowing books, are you?" Jane asked, surprised and imperious. James frowned.

"Why yes Aunt Jane," he offered uncertainly. "I did not think you would mind."

"As a matter of fact, I do," she said tersely. "It is only a small matter, but I like to keep my things, which are indeed my own personal property, here at Broadhurst where they belong. I am unhappy to think of my personal property being displayed hither and yon in the far reaches of your piddling little townhouse in Chelsea." Jane eyed him sharply, her blue eyes darting with a shrewd glare. James appeared positively unglued, staring back open-mouthed and uncertain how to respond. Instantly, Jane softened.

"Nevertheless," she went on, once again smiling and recapturing her remarkably pleasant tone, "I'm sure it won't happen again, and how fortunate indeed that you stumbled upon such a treasure trove of information." She smiled and winked in a most uncharacteristic gesture. James smiled back with trepidation.

"Yes," he said finally, "well, I do apologize. I certainly won't think of borrowing anything else without your express consent." Aunt Jane nodded happily, wrinkling her nose in approval, which James noticed was yet another oddly un-Janie thing to do.

"Now then, what shall we conclude from this curious lack of account with regard to the fate of our dear ancestor Catherine?" Jane smiled sweetly. James attempted to brush off his rising confusion, and refocused on his discovery.

"What indeed?" he answered with cautious enthusiasm. "I asked myself that very question, and had nearly given up on finding any satisfactory answers, when I came across a notation in an accounting ledger that gave me concern."

"Do go on," Jane said encouragingly.

"I can show it to you," James said excitedly, "I have a photocopy right here." He reached down into the attaché and revealed a stack of papers neatly clipped together. He shuffled through the first five or six pages before finding the page he required, and handed it over to his Aunt for her perusal. Jane slipped on her reading glasses, which hung from a gold chain studded with pink crystals around her neck, and reviewed the document in hand.

"Ah," she said finally, "perhaps this is a clue. Do you think we should send this information to our new friend, Miss Garrett?"

"I do, yes," James replied enthusiastically.

"Well then, when you've finished let us proceed to the library and convey our findings."

"With pleasure," James said happily, biting into his last bit of toast. He had truly enjoyed this historical quest they had shared and was fascinated by every morsel of information they had uncovered.

"Do go on ahead," Jane smiled, "I'll be along momentarily."

"Very well," James said, wiping his mouth with the perfectly starched white napkin and adjourning to the library where he could turn on the computer and begin the day's work. At last, he could access the computer! Jane followed cautiously behind, eyeing him with her piercing blue eyes, a twisted half-smile curling her lips to the left.

She found him standing next to the computer, leaning forward, hands tapping lightly away upon the keyboard again and again. Jane sidled closer, quietly enjoying his perplexing predicament, the little bow-tied imbecile.

"Are we ready then?" she asked casually, startling James from his concentration at the keyboard.

"Aunt Jane," he said cautiously, "there seems to be a problem with your computer."

"Really," Jane answered with exaggerated surprise. "Whatever do you mean?"

"I can't seem to access your e-mail account," James stammered, panic rising in his voice as the words tumbled from his lips. Jane half-smiled triumphantly.

"I believe that is called a loser error James," she answered smugly, remembering what "RAZORCLAM" had instructed in their chats on the matter. James looked up in alarm.

"Pardon?" he answered feebly.

"Yes, loser error. It's a surprisingly appropriate term used when an individual blames his computer for an error that he actually caused." Jane raised her eyebrows at him as if all the secrets of the world were known to her. James exhaled an enormous sigh of panic.

"Aunt Jane," James said quietly, after a long, courage-building pause, "how do you know of such a thing?"

"I learned it on my computer James," she answered nonplussed. "A computer is a wealth of information for a poor old shut-in lady like myself."

"Aunt Jane," James began with slow but rising determination, almost not believing what tumbled out of his mouth, "are you a chatfly?" Jane gasped and her mouth dropped open in horror, her own adrenaline now rising by the sudden surprise attack.

"How dare you," she answered in defiance, feeling around feebly for the back of a chair to support her.

"I must know," James pressed on.

"How dare you ask such a thing of me, you, you, you," she blustered for a moment, uncommonly incapable of thinking quickly, "you spy!"

"I am not a spy," James protested loudly.

"And I am not a chatfly," Jane protested with equal vigor. Liza, upon reaching the door, let out a feeble, "Lord help us" and beat a hasty retreat back down the hall.

"How dare you access my e-mail account and check up on me as if I'm some reckless schoolgirl."

"I was worried about you," James shot back in despair. "You know nothing of these things." His face was twisted into pain and panic. His stomach churned with anxiety and his heart felt as if it would burst at any moment. "The world is a dangerous place Aunt Jane," he went on, "and technology has made it ever more so."

"You had no right to invade my privacy," she shot back with fierce indignation. "And to hell with you if you think I'm some doddering old maid who doesn't know anything of the world or her own mind."

"It's not your mind I worry about," James begged, "it's the twisted mind of every sick madman out there, here in England or beyond, who would take advantage of a kind soul like yours for cruel amusement."

"You know nothing of it James," Jane shouted wildly. "I stood on the south lawn of this very house and watched Hitler's Luftwaffe send bombs down upon us. My littlest pinky finger has lived a life greater than your entire being will ever live. Do not tell me I know nothing of the world."

"Aunt Jane," James went on determinedly, "this is not 1943. The world is changed forever. And while I respect and appreciate the length and breadth of your experience in this lifetime, you must let me help you navigate these new roads."

"I've never asked for help from anyone in my entire life, and I will not have a sniveling, bow-tied bore of a nephew taking charge of my circumstances without cause or invitation." Jane panted with exhaustion. She could barely remember the last time she had been so provoked into a row. It was exhilarating, really. But no, actually, it was not. She glanced at James' dejected face and knew that she had caused the pain that now lined his brow. His head was bent in resignation, in a most hurt and dejected manner. He seemed to her like a child who had offered his greatest achievement for praise and had received only ridicule and criticism.

"I am truly so very sorry," he whispered finally, pulling back his curly brown hair from his forehead. "Please forgive me. I only felt it was my duty to take care of you as best I could. And I've always believed that one's duty is paramount above all else." The words cut to Jane's heart as none other could do. She herself knew it was true. Duty was the watchword of every Wentworth who had ever been or ever would be. He stumbled to the door in the face of his Aunt's austere but wavering glare, wandering aimlessly down the hall toward the kitchen and out into the grey morning of late autumn.

Jane stood motionless, unable to decide what she should do. Part of her felt elated and triumphant, and yet part of her felt extraordinary pain. She was not at all inclined to feel remorse and guilt with ease. The weight of what she had said and done began to press in upon her.

It was true, she knew, that right was on her side. She was 86 years old and a Wentworth, by God, and she neither needed nor invited any protection from James or anyone else for that matter. It had been nearly seven decades since she required a chaperone to conduct herself and she would not bloody well allow anyone to believe she required their care or supervision now.

She was Jane Alexandra Wentworth Rochester, lady of the house, heiress of Broadhurst Hall, keeper of the legacy and protector of the family heritage. The Internet, she reasoned, was nothing more than the latest gadgetry. If England could survive World War II, it could certainly survive the Internet.

A loud exhale released from her nostrils. Her piercing blue eyes were fixed in an intense glare.

She raised her chin in resolve, displaying the strong jaw of Wentworth determination that ran in her blood, and seated herself before her computer. Quickly typing in the new password, she composed a short note to Jillian Garrett, her new friend from Connecticut.

Dear Jillian,
My nephew, James, has uncovered some information which you may find helpful. I shall have it sent to you by post immediately. I am afraid I am unable to offer any further assistance as James, who has a keen mind for research, is no longer able to devote his time to this task.

She paused for a moment before adding the next line.

I would enjoy a chat later today if you are available.
Sincerely,
Jane Rochester

She clicked send and dabbed at a tear in the corner of her eye. Imagine! Lady Jane Alexandra Wentworth Rochester weeping. She hated to cry. Great bloody hell, if anyone saw her at this moment she would be simply beside herself.

In truth, she had enjoyed her time with James rummaging through the library for bits and pieces of nothing in particular. Although his bow ties were excessively bright and exceedingly random in choice, she had to admit they had grown on her somewhat lately. It was an exciting new time. She supposed she should probably call after James, but that would do no good. She imagined that he was already at the train station. She sat quietly for a good long while, considering all of the options that were before her until the little bell chimed within that strange and wondrous computer, alerting her to a new e-mail just received.

CHAPTER TWENTY

"Regret is not an emotion I am inclined to entertain. I prefer the business of what I do well rather than what I did not do or did not do well. I am content to know I have always followed my passions for better or for worse." C.W.B. 1780.

Jillian woke with a start. A brilliant blue sky beamed through her window and she momentarily shielded her eyes against the glare. Rubbing her head and smoothing her hair she scratched at her neck and pressed her finger to her temples. A throbbing pain filled her head along with the strong feeling of nausea. Her mind was a jumble of confusion. For a moment, she couldn't seem to remember anything at all, not even what day it was. But then, like a slow fog rolling through her brain, it hit her and spilled forth into the conscience of the morning after. Brownley punch. The devil's brew. The nectar of Wetherton.

"Brownley punch," she moaned softly, shaking her head ever-so-gently and flipping back over onto her side, pulling the sheets and blankets up over her head. She lay there like a lump for a good little while until something caused her to spring life-like again and sit straight up in her bed.

"Thomas!" she muttered with alarm, pulling her hands up over her mouth. "Holy crap!" she blurted out in a panic. Had he left? Had he stayed? Had he thrown up on her favorite needlepoint pillow? She could not possibly guess. Jillian rustled around under her sheets, struggling to free herself from the tangle of linens that grabbed at her legs.

Cat-like, she crept to the door of her bedroom and gently nudged the handle. The door let forth, offering the predictable screech of 150-year-old hinges and a frame that was entirely out of plumb. Jillian rolled her eyes. So much for cat-like.

She wore a nightgown that looked like a floor-length long-sleeved t-shirt and wool socks that scrunched-up around her ankles. Her backside slid along the wall as she clumsily maneuvered the narrow hallway that lay between her and the staircase. At every doorway, of which there were three, she stopped abruptly to check the room for any possible inhabitants.

Door number one, the blue room, yielded no unwelcome guests. Thank heavens, Jillian thought, as this was very much her favorite guest room and she would have been extremely alarmed to find Thomas snoozing among the exceptional Egyptian linens she saved for months to buy.

She continued on, sliding her bottom along the wall for support. A painful throbbing filled her temples. Door number two, the bathroom, also yielded no unwelcome guest or, thankfully, evidence thereof. This left door number three, the green room, as the number one suspect in the search for her missing Harvest Party date.

Her head swooned with a queasiness for which she could only curse herself and the damnable Brownley punch. Never, never again would she drink it, so help her, may God strike her dead.

She leaned back and steadied herself against the wall before proceeding. What would she do when she found him? Would she wake him? She frowned. Certainly not, she decided logically. She would run to the Foundation offices and pretend she was positively immersed in extremely important business for perhaps 18 hours or more, until Thomas would leave for want of company or food or the need to catch his flight, whichever came first.

She licked her lips with determination and crept toward the door to the green room. Did she hear anything? Any breathing? Vomiting? Any signs of life? She waited a moment before determining that all was quiet. She gripped the door frame and peered inside.

With a great exhale, she realized the room was undisturbed. Perhaps, she reasoned, Thomas had found his way home last night after all. Then again, perhaps he was still on the floor downstairs where she had left him. Was that where she had left him? She thought so, but couldn't be sure. Down the stairs, on tip-toe feet with floppy socks she peeked into the living room. No sign of him. Strange. Where the hell did he go? With a lighter heart, but no lighter a head, she found her way across the room and flopped down on the sofa. More throbbing and pain. It was only then, when her nightgown had flown fully up over her hips, that Thomas presented himself.

"Morning," he nearly shouted upon seeing her enter the room. Jillian scrambled to attention like a student caught sleeping in math class.

"Whoooo," was the only intelligible sound to be heard from her lips. Thomas smiled.

"I hope you don't mind if I helped myself," he offered, leaning forth a plate of runny eggs combined with something red and unidentifiable. The corners of Jillian's mouth turned uncontrollably downward.

"Of course not," Jillian offered meekly, covering herself with an afghan crocheted by her grandmother in 1978.

"You haven't got any beers around, have you?" Thomas leaned toward her and spoke softly. "Hair of the dog, you know?"

"Sorry," Jillian whispered, "no beers." Thomas shrugged and seated himself spread eagle on the ottoman before her. Jillian frowned. Was this really the same man who had seemed so irresistible just hours earlier? Was this the same man who had so captivated her? Gone were the breeches and vest, replaced by grey gym shorts and a t-shirt that read "Chicks are my life" across the chest. Gone was the tricorn hat he had tipped so gallantly as she walked by. He hunched over his plate in a pose she could only describe as caveman-like and consumed the runny eggs almost without breathing. He looked up at her and nodded a smile, bits of egg stuck to his chin and cheeks.

"I had a great time last night," he said. "Sorry I passed out," he added with a wink. Jillian laughed nervously. "You're quite a dancer."

"Am I? Yes, well, so are you," Jillian said, searching her mind for some shred of a memory of dancing.

"Too bad I have to leave today," Thomas said, speaking with his mouth full of food.

"I know," Jillian answered with exaggerated despair. "I'm sorry we won't have a chance to get to know each other better."

"I've got about 40 minutes now," he said, glancing at his watch, and turning back to her with a look of anticipation. "My flight's not until noon." Jillian let out a panicky laugh.

"Yeah, well, sorry," she said, "I'm a little hung over. And, uh, I'm not really that kind of girl." Thomas shrugged his shoulders.

"I don't know," he said, rising with his plate and fork, "you're one hell of a dancer, I'll tell you that." Great God in heaven, Jillian cursed herself silently, what's with the dancing? A foggy memory of twirling around and stomping her feet filled her with nausea. She pulled the afghan up over her head as Thomas shouted from the kitchen.

"Maybe I'll come back in a few months," he went on. "Since I got kicked out of school my parents kind of cut off the old cashola, know what I mean? So my aunt tries to help out when she can. Roofing's not a bad gig. Especially in this little town," he added with a wink. Jillian's mouth hung uncontrollably open.

How many times had she been reminded to never judge the book by the cover. It's what's on the inside that counts. She knew this. She was not stupid, and yet, she had fallen for a frat boy in a colonial costume. Was there no hope left for her?

He circled around behind the sofa and pulled the afghan from her face.

"Are you sure I can't talk you into a do-over to make up for last night?" Jillian swallowed hard at the lump of nausea in her throat.

"Sorry," she said meekly. "Just not up for it." Thomas shrugged.

"I really do think you're a great chick," he said, offering her what she imagined was his ultimate compliment. He leaned over and kissed her cheek. "Take care Jillie. I gotta run." Jillie? Had he called her Jillie?

"Have a good flight," she said quietly. "Forgive me if I don't walk you out."

"No worries," he called back over his shoulder. "Take care of that hangover and, uh," he paused for an awkward moment, "keep on dancing." She forced a feeble head nod and a smile.

The door shut behind him and he was gone. Jillian slumped back into the sofa drained of strength. Her head ached, her body ached, her very soul ached. She was utterly and completely disgusted with herself. She threw herself back down on the sofa cushions and huddled under the afghan like a child pretending to hide.

"I am on the edge of ruin," she muttered softly, mentally taking note of everything she would never do again, including drinking Brownley Punch and, above all else, dancing.

At some point, after quietly considering her wretched state of affairs over and over in her head, Jillian must have drifted off to sleep. The sunlight was warm and welcoming and the afghan of her childhood was like a blanket of comfort all around her. At 1:25 in the afternoon, the telephone startled her awake again. She couldn't bear to get up from her sofa, not only because she was tired, but because the pounding in her head had continued on like a bongo drum. She licked her lips and realized she was desperately in need of water.

The answering machine beeped as she rose to an upright position, her brown hair uncharacteristically snarled into a makeshift beehive, and stumbled her way toward the kitchen.

"Jillian, Burt Payne here. Just got a call from Murton who says he's in town and wants to talk. Don't know what that's all about, but, by God, I think it could be good news. I've asked him to come down to the office at 4:00, 'course Dahlia's coming. Wouldn't want to meet that old snake in the grass without our attorney. Any who, I was hoping you'd join us. Shouldn't take too long. Call me back, will ya?" Beep.

Jillian raised her eyebrows and gulped a pint of bottled water without stopping. Then, without any attempt to conceal her mouth with her hand, she belched. "Lovely," she said softly, shaking her head in disgust. "I've become a sewer rat. Just lovely." She grabbed at the aspirin bottle and poured out two caplets, tossing them onto her tongue and swallowing hard.

Jillian agreed with Burt Payne. Arnold Murton was a snake. But unlike Burt, she could see no immediate reason to believe that Murton's desire to talk meant good news. When the serpent wanted to have a little chat with Eve, was that good news? She wandered out of her kitchen and back to her sofa. It wasn't even two o'clock yet, she reasoned, and with a shower and maybe some eggs and bacon, her hangover meal of choice, she might be able to make it to the meeting. She decided to ignore Burt's message for the moment and flipped on the television.

Public television was staging their annual fundraiser, with eager hosts smiling toothy grins at the camera and reminding viewers that no gift was too small. Jillian assessed their fundraising technique, and felt their twelve volume DVD set "Adventures in the Orient" was good value for a two hundred dollar donation. She momentarily toyed with the idea of a Wetherton DVD, then flipped the channel.

Republicans and Democrats bickered away like children on a playground. "Did not, did too, did not, did too," they taunted each other. She didn't recognize any of the faces or names, except the guy from Florida with the ridiculously dark, orangey tan. She couldn't remember his party affiliation, but it didn't really make a difference. They were all the same. She flipped the channel again.

A reality show re-run caught her attention for a few minutes. Housewives, dressed like teenagers, but fooling no one, were seated around a large table with enormous glasses of wine arguing about something Jillian couldn't quite make out. Apparently, one of them had said something about another to someone else and now everyone was angry. Jillian squinted and tried to settle into the story, but soon gave up trying and made a mental note never to go blonde. She turned the television off and flipped on her back to stare at the ceiling.

Her eyes traced a crack in the plaster that ran all along the corner by the fireplace. Josiah MacDougal built the house in 1799 for his new bride, Mary, who was from Albany. It was not a grand house, but it was extremely well-built as Josiah himself was a master carpenter and builder. Mary MacDougal would die in childbirth, in the room Jillian now called the green room, bearing her second son. Josiah went on to marry Carolyn who bore three more sons before her own untimely death, at the age of 27. The home had passed from son to son for nearly 100 years before its purchase by the Mitchell family in 1915.

Jillian considered herself beyond lucky when, upon her own arrival in Wetherton, she found the antique "fixer-upper" on the market.

"Needs an awful lot of work," the home inspector said, "but the foundation and framing is rock solid. No rot, no termites, but good Lord young lady, you're talking roof, electrical, plumbing, the works." Jillian was not daunted.

She bought it for a bargain price and moved in within weeks. Everyone in the neighborhood was so polite and helpful, bringing her brownies and offering the names of their in-laws and relations who were plumbers and painters. The man at number 75, of course, offered only the occasional grunt or head nod, but Jillian didn't mind. It wasn't until her second week of homeownership that she realized the party was over.

Rain pelted the town along with the tiny little house that Jillian now owned, and the need for a new roof became exceedingly apparent. Every pan, bucket and bin was used to catch drips from the attic down to the first floor, and nearly every last penny was depleted from her savings to pay for the work. She instantly recognized the need to bone up on her home improvement skills, and spent nights running up to the big hardware store in Hartford to take classes in tiling, plumbing and plastering. She must have patched that crack in the living room ceiling at least four times in the last ten years, and yet every winter it re-emerged like a crooked smile laughing at her from the corner. She had finally given up and decided that if the house could accept her and all her flaws then she could do the same.

Jillian glanced at her clock. It was 3:05. She exhaled loudly. Although she was feeling better, she simply didn't know if she could muster the strength to deal with an Arnold Murton meeting. She toyed with the idea of just pretending she never received the message. "I just need a break!" she shouted out to no one in particular. She waited, limp and lifeless, to see if anyone would answer. Nothing. So, with angry resolve, she hoisted her body up to the shower and readied herself for battle.

Jillian could see the brightly lit windows of the Wetherton Historical Foundation from the distance as she approached. The afternoon air was fresh and invigorating. Evidence of the Harvest Party from the day before had been almost entirely cleaned and cleared away, save the jack-o-lantern-headed scarecrows that would remain until after Thanksgiving. Her head was beginning to clear, thanks to eggs, bacon, water, aspirin and a good long nap on the sofa. Still, she wished she could be home in bed instead of heading into another meeting. Especially a meeting where Arnold Murton would be present. She decided she'd take a back seat and let Dahlia and Burt do most of the talking.

There were only a handful of people in the room. Dahlia nodded hello from her seat at the table next to Burt, but it was Duke who swooped over to greet her. "Diabolita," he snarled. "My little dancer."

"Dear God," she sighed resignedly shaking her head.

"Seriously," Duke persisted. "I had no idea. Did you take lessons, or what? I mean that was far out." Jillian turned to face him.

"I will kill you with this pen if I have to. I don't want to, but I will. So zip it." Duke smiled.

"Touchy. Touchy. I guess that means salsa lessons are out of the question." She raised her pen like a sword.

"What's going on?" she asked, heading for a chair at the far end of the large table. Duke trailed behind.

"Apparently," Duke whispered, "he's offered to let the Foundation move the Beckwith house across the little stream to the other half of the property if we will let him subdivide the other half out of the historic district." Jillian frowned while she processed the latest information.

"So he gets his five acre parcel," she said at last.

"For 'affordable' housing," Duke broke in, with two fingers on each hand arching up and down to emphasize the word affordable.

"And we get to keep the Beckwith house," Jillian finished. Duke nodded.

"Of course, moving a house like that isn't cheap," Duke went on. "Eighty, maybe a hundred grand."

"No!" Jillian said in a shocked whisper. "That much?"

"Sure," Duke nodded. "And maybe it can't even be moved intact. To get it over the little bridge we might have to take it apart and move it in pieces."

"But then it would be ours? The Historical Foundation would own it?"

"That's what he says, but Dahlia wants to look over the deed." Jillian slumped back in her chair. One hundred thousand dollars. Maybe more. That was an awful lot of money to come up with. Archibald Mack instantly popped into Jillian's head.

"Folks, why don't we take our seats and get started," Burt called out. "This is a somewhat informal meeting and I know a few of you are probably nursing a fine hangover from yesterday." The room collectively turned to look at Jillian. Her eyes widened with alarm.

"I'm fine," Jillian offered meekly but defensively. "Really." She knew she heard a few snickers, but couldn't be certain where they had come from. She scowled at Duke from the corner of her eye, who immediately looked innocently away.

"For those of you who have not met," Burt continued, "I'd like to introduce Mr. Arnold Murton, present owner of the Beckwith house."

"Murton house," Arnold Murton interrupted with a smile. "I like to call it the Murton house." Burt paused for a moment.

"Very well then," he continued. "I guess you can call it what you like, but for over 200 years we've been calling it the Beckwith house, so forgive me if it takes some getting used to."

"No need to get used to it," Murton went on. "The truth is, if we can't come to some sort of agreement pretty quick, it won't be here much longer anyway." Jillian felt her face begin to flush with anger, but Arnold Murton pressed on nonplussed. Clearly, he was not the sort of man to care whether or not he made any friends in life.

"I know you all love that house, God help you, rat-infested, rotten broken-down death trap that it is." He scratched at the wispy blonde hair on his balding head. "I've handled a few tree-huggers in my time, but I never met a bunch of house-huggers like you people turned out to be," he laughed to apparently no one but himself. "I don't pretend to understand. And the truth is I don't care." Duke squinted at Murton with a placidly calm expression.

"I'm here because I build quality, affordable housing for people who couldn't otherwise even dream of living in Wetherton. I don't care about some run-down old house, when I can provide a safe, wonderful environment for families to raise their children and live the American dream." Duke coughed loudly. Jillian couldn't be sure, but she thought she heard him mutter "bullshit" under his breath. Murton glared and paused to regain his calm.

"Nevertheless," he continued, "nobody likes to be a bad guy. Not even me. And I was talking to my engineer the other day and he said 'why not let them move the house to the other side of the property' and I thought that was a fantastic idea."

"How would we move that house, Mr. Murton?" Burt asked innocently. "We're not builders or architects here. We'd need some time to investigate." Murton raised his hand in a gesture likened to a school crossing guard.

"I'm happy to help you with that," Murton said smiling. "My team has moved dozens of old houses. We can move that house tomorrow. Or I can knock that house down in just a few more weeks. It is my house after all folks. I can do what I want with it. I'm only here, offering you this deal, because I'm trying to be a nice guy."

For a long awkward moment, no one spoke. The room was completely silent. No one was sure how to proceed. Should they take the deal? Find a way to raise the money to move the house? At least it would be saved.

Colonial Williamsburg had moved several structures during their restoration. The result had been very successful.

"Are you saying that you're willing to give the Wetherton Historical Foundation the house and the property on this side of the creek if we pay to move the house?" Jillian asked finally.

"That's right," replied Murton. "Just as long as the town is willing to redefine the limits of the Historic District so that the other half of that property can be moved into the business zone. You get what you want and I get to build housing for dozens of families. Everybody's happy."

"How much do you think it would cost to move the house?" Burt chimed in.

"Aah," Murton mused, "I could give you an estimate tomorrow, after my engineer has another look at it."

"Ballpark," Burt pressed. Murton leaned forward and folded his hands.

"I'm guessing ninety, maybe ninety-five thousand." The room let out an audible gasp.

"That's almost half what you paid for the house and the property all together," Dahlia interjected, speaking in her calm, measured tone. Murton shrugged his shoulders.

"Hey look, I'm not going to lie to you. It's expensive to move a house," he nodded for emphasis. "But you folks are the ones who want to save it. It's entirely up to you."

"We'd need some time to consider our finances," Burt answered. "We simply don't have that kind of money lying around." Murton leaned back in his chair, pushing away from the table.

"Like I said, I'm trying to be a nice guy here. The truth is, in thirty three days that demolition delay you slapped on me is going to expire. And when it does, that house is coming down, whether I get to build my apartments or not."

"But why would you knock it down if you couldn't get your building permit?" Jillian blurted, instantly kicking herself. Murton leaned forward again.

"Do you really think you can stop me from getting a building permit? Is that what you people think?" He chuckled and looked around the room. "I feel sorry for you. I do. You're in way over your head here." He lowered his voice just a bit and glared at the room. "I don't like thorns in my side and I don't like to lose. Move it or lose it, I don't care, but that house is gone." He rose to his full six foot two inch height and straightened the belt on his expensive khaki pants.

"I'll look forward to hearing from you tomorrow on this. Or I'll take this deal off the table. I've got a lot of projects in the works and this is only one of them. I'm not spending any more time in Wetherton than I have to." He nodded his head and sauntered out the door with his two equally large colleagues in tow. Dahlia shook her head.

"He's a very shrewd man," she said quietly. "We'll pay for the cost of moving the house and save him the expense of tearing it down. He'll get the land he wants for his apartments and end up making money on the deal to boot. Very shrewd. Very shrewd." Burt Payne shook his head.

"I just don't know folks. What do we think?" he asked looking anxiously around the room. Duke was the first to answer.

"Well I don't know about the rest of you," he said, "but I think we shouldn't go running away from the fight with our tails between our legs." The room exchanged nervous glances. Burt shook his head.

"I don't like it any more than you do, but we've got to face facts." He paused and rubbed the bridge of his nose. "Jillian, what do we know about any historic significance in that house? Anything new or promising?" Jillian shrugged.

"We have the name Woodsmith that I'm following up on, but that's the only new lead." She looked down, unable to bear their forlorn faces. "Honestly, I think we have to start to come to terms with the idea that we're going to lose the house." More gasps could be heard around the room. The reality of their reality had begun to bear its weight upon them. Hal Walker, owner of the hardware store, cleared his throat for attention.

"I have to say, I agree with Jillian," Hal began. "We should just let this one go and move on. Maybe we'll get the next one." Now the room nearly erupted in response. Duke threw his hands up in the air in an angry gesture. Burt Payne simply shook his head in resignation. Maggie, the recording secretary, scribbled away at her notepad looking up to offer the occasional worried glance as she scribed.

"All I'm saying," Hal went on in a much louder voice, "is that we don't have the money for this. And frankly, well, I gotta tell you, it wouldn't hurt my business one bit to have forty new families living across the street." Shouts of protest and argument went on for another hour or more. It was clear that no one had the answer, but it was shocking that one of their own, Hal Walker a longtime Foundation member, could be siding with the enemy. What had the world come to when a Wethertonian would take up the fight on behalf of an outsider, an encroacher!

When, at last, the group had dispersed, agreeing to meet at 9:00 am to discuss their last minute and most up-to-date plan of attack, Jillian, Duke and Dahlia agreed to disperse to the tavern for a quick dinner. Jillian's head still throbbed, albeit not from the hangover, but the newest catastrophe de jour. They walked slowly across the green, utterly silent, except for their collective breathing. Her mood was heavy, and Jillian was fighting the most profound urge to simply run all the way back to upstate New York where her parents still lived.

"I don't get it," Duke said, settling into a chair by the fireplace. "What is up with that Hal Walker?" Dahlia shrugged.

"What do you mean?" Jillian asked.

"What do you mean 'what do I mean'? I mean where does that guy come from?"

"From the world where people have to make a living," Jillian shot back. "It's his town too. It's his life, his livelihood, his future. He's obviously thinking, 'what the hell? So we lose a house, but I gain two hundred new customers' I suppose." She sipped the water in her glass greedily. All she really wanted to do was go to sleep. She was suddenly, completely and utterly exhausted.

"This is a very strange life," Duke offered finally, staring off into an uninhabited corner of the room. No one spoke until Josie came to take their orders. She nudged Jillian with her elbow.

"Nice dancing," she said with a wink. "We oughtta call you Ginger Rogers." Jillian managed a miniature smile, realizing that she would be dealing with the dancing issue for weeks to come.

"Thanks," she said lethargically. "I just can't keep these feet still." Josie leaned down near her ear.

"He was so hot!" Jillian smiled a tired, crooked half-smile.

"Oh yeah," she offered in return. "He was smokin'." Josie trailed off to the bar to bring back their drinks. Thankfully, no smell of Brownley punch could be detected anywhere nearby, lest Jillian thought she might have to leave. Had she left, however, she would have missed out on the most fabulous bacon cheeseburger of her life, and she was profoundly grateful that she had stayed. Every mouthful was like heaven. Food had never tasted so good. Slowly, her mind and her body were recharging. But recharging for what? For a job in New York at *Historic Home* magazine?

She had been in Wetherton for ten years. Ten long, hard, money-scraping, fund-raising, crazy, kooky years. Catherine Brownley was on the revisionist chopping block and Arnold Murton was bullying his way right over 250 years of living and dying history. Fate certainly had a funny way of kicking you in the shins, didn't it?

"We have three options," Dahlia explained plainly, scooping up the last bean sprouts from her salad bowl with her knife and fork working in unison. "We can find the money to move the house or we can find the historic significance we've been looking for to save the house." She paused to ingest the last of her meal and wash it down with plain tap water. "Or we can do nothing and see the house demolished. Murton isn't bluffing. He wouldn't bat an eyelash and that house would be gone." Jillian nodded her understanding. Duke nodded his encouragement of her understanding, with his crazy maniacal smile.

"Tomorrow is about one hundred thousand dollars," Jillian answered plainly, then exhaled loudly. "I'll phone the Money Mack and see if I can reach him." Jillian shook her head. "But you do realize cocktail hour started about six hours ago for him, and I sincerely doubt I'll be able to contact him before our meeting in the morning."

Duke and Dahlia nodded their understanding. As they readied to leave, Duke asked if they could give her a lift.

"Nah," Jillian said dismissively. "I like to walk. But thanks." They parted at the door, but then Duke ran back to her as she headed down the street.

"Life is strange," he said again, panting and out of breath. Jillian frowned.

"Yes, I know," she said evenly.

"But are you content to be idle and let fate have its way with you?" Duke added quizzically, regaining his wind. "Or will you fight and make your mark upon this world known?" The words caught in Jillian's ear. To anyone else, it would be a bizarre exchange, but not to Jillian. She knew the author.

'That's a good question," Jillian replied without missing a beat.

"I know," he said expectedly, a look of childlike anticipation on his face. "There's no time to waste."

"Right," Jillian answered plainly and continued on her walk home. Could she muster the fight for one last challenge? Would history remember the story of Jillian Garrett, valiant fighter for preservation of this tiny town. Probably not. Truthfully, history wasn't likely to remember any of them by name. Oh, sure, maybe somewhere there would be a plaque with their names or a record of their membership in the historical foundation, but what would history really remember of any of them? Which of their stories would be told and which would be lost to time? Jillian wondered and walked on into the night.

CHAPTER TWENTY ONE

"I miss so many old friends who are lost to us now. Has God conspired against us or will we all suffer from our own doing?" C.W.B. 1778

Lady Jane Alexandra Wentworth Rochester woke early that morning. She was restless and could not find peace. She imagined it was God's plan to ready her soul for heaven that deprived her of a full night's slumber, rationalizing that angels must do a great deal of work in the nighttime. She stared up at the ceiling from her massive bed and exhaled loudly. Dudley, just on the floor next to her, did the same.

"You're a loud old man," she whispered to him softly. "And as good a friend as any man I've ever known. Save two." She closed her eyes and allowed her mind to wander to the time when her father had admonished her for driving the car without permission. She smiled the crooked, one-sided smile. She could see her mother, her beautiful, lovely, dear mother, coming toward her with a face full of concern.

"Whatever is the matter?" she heard her sweet voice say. A thirteen year old Jane replied that is was nothing, although somewhere deep in her subconscious she knew that someone had been terribly cruel to her. Was it Richard Burke? Her first love. Jane could not remember.

"Woof," Dudley offered softly in his sleep, jarring Jane's eyes back open. She exhaled again and shifted toward the window to see fine rays of light beginning to peek around the edges of the heavy silk drapes. Goodness, she thought, how beautiful the morning would be. Something inside her forced her up and out and away, it was that irrepressible urge to be outdoors yet again.

James had not rung. It weighed upon her like a heavy fog. She felt certain that he would ring, and yet he had not. She pursed her lips as she dressed, contemplating her options and her nephew. It was not easy for her to settle her mind upon him. She was uncharacteristically confused and the need for a good walk to clear her mind begged.

She went slowly down the great staircase, grasping the rail and taking her time. No need to break a hip, she reasoned. I'll be there soon enough. The house was still, save for the panting of Dudley who wagged his tail at her from the entrance hall below. She was certain he was smiling at her, for he enjoyed his morning walk every bit as much as she did and it promised to be a lovely morning.

She almost didn't stop, scolding herself for the delay, and yet she stopped nonetheless. Dudley groaned and settled in behind her. The library had become the room where the two of them spent more time than any other room in the great house of Broadhurst Hall, and it must be said there were plenty of rooms in which to spend their time.

Lady Jane clicked on her e-mail account and found six new messages ready and waiting. Four of them were solicitations which she promptly deleted, although curiosity almost got the better of her when she noticed the last message promised bigger breasts in just two hours. Of the other two, one was from a woman in Leicestershire, who had responded to a previous inquiry, and the other was from Jillian Garret who had used several exclamation points in her plea!!! Lady Jane dragged her cursor down to the last message and clicked.

It was funny, she thought, that for so many years she had preferred this solitary, quiet existence within the comfort and confines of the Broadhurst estate. And now in this new era of her life, she was able to be quite social at the same time. It was the kind of socializing that suited her very well.

Dear Lady Rochester,

I have found a small bit of new information regarding to Margaret Woodsmith. I believe that she was the sister of Anne Woodsmith Wentworth (1720 – 1787) married to Howard Wentworth in 1739. Can you confirm this? It is very important to our preservation work here.

Thank you again. I hope the weather has improved. It is very cold here in Connecticut.

Regards,

Jillian

Jane frowned for a moment. Yes. Anne. Not Louise. Something about this stuck in her head, but she couldn't quite place it. James. It was something James had said. Something about an old journal or ledger. Her mind searched slowly. She tapped a finger to her forehead as if to jog her memory with physical manipulation. What the devil was it?

She looked up at the stack of books on the large table where James had last been doing his research. That was until, of course, their terrible row. A look of pain crossed Jane's face. She sniffed. How awful! She pushed herself up from her chair at the computer and slowly walked toward what had been James' chair for so many afternoons. It was difficult to think about it, but Jane relented. She touched the stack with her fingertips and tried to remember what he had said. She could see his face looking up at her, his enthusiasm at finding something of interest was, well, it was charming actually.

Jane touched the largest binding, flipped open the cover, but then thought better of it. It was a smaller book, delicately bound in tooled, crimson leather that caught her eye. She settled into James' chair and opened to the first page.

It was a journal. That fact was plain enough. She flipped back to the inside cover. No inscription could be found. She flipped to the back cover. Nothing. But then, on the inside of the back cover, on the very last page of well-aged linen parchment, Jane could plainly see the notation, "The Journal of Anne Catherine Woodsmith Wentworth". Jane breathed in loudly. A discovery! How exciting!

The handwriting was lovely. A beautiful script from a delicate and meticulous hand. Each entry was carefully dated, 14 November, 1741 or 26 April, 1744 and each ended with the words "may God dwell within my soul, AWW." The first entry was dated 30 November, 1739. Jane read with great interest.

Today I wed Howard Wentworth, a man I have known only these few short weeks. And yet, I am sure we will live a contented life, as he is a good man of vast fortune. My dear mother is mightily pleased, as is my father, for to marry into this Wentworth family is a blessing. I only hope I am a good wife and will give him many sons. My duty is now upon me and I am determined to show no fear. May God dwell within my soul, AWW.

"Must have been a bloody awful wedding night," Jane said softly, turning the page and shifting her head to look down her nose through heavy black reading glasses.

8 April, 1740
My husband and I have most exciting news! I am with child and, God willing, will be a mother by summer's end. My discomfort is overshadowed by the great joy I feel and I am certain I carry a boy within me. May God dwell within my soul, AWW.

"Well," Jane reasoned, "perhaps it wasn't such a bad wedding night after all." She carefully flipped through many more pages, and settled on a notation from 1768. "Well, well," Jane said aloud, "what have we here?" She rose from her seat, James' seat, and returned to her spot in front of her computer. Navigating her mouse as if she'd been using a computer her entire life, she quickly composed a note to Jillian Garrett, glancing down occasionally at the journal next to her.

Dear Jillian,
I believe I can confirm some information on Margaret Woodsmith. I have the journal of Anne Wentworth here by my side, which seems to confirm that she had a sister named Margaret. I can also confirm that this sister was married in 1768 and left for the colonies in the "new world" shortly after. I hope this is helpful.
Sincerely,
Jane Rochester

Within minutes, an instant message signaled to Jane from the upper right side of her screen. "Ah," she said with delight. Dudley, thinking perhaps it was a signal for him raised his head in anticipation. But no. His mistress hadn't even looked at him! He slumped back down to the floor for another nap.

Mrs. Rochester, thank you so much for your e-mail. Can you tell me Margaret Woodsmith's married name?

Heavens Jillian, what on earth are you doing up at this hour?

I couldn't sleep. Our deadline to save one of our house is fast approaching, and I am determined not to give up the fight!

Good for you! Give me a moment please.

Jane shuffled back through the pages of the journal, scanning each line quickly with her index finger. Ah yes, here it was.

According to the journal of Anne Wentworth, her sister Margaret Woodsmith married a man named Horatio Beckwith.

Are you certain?

Quite certain.

Thank you so much Mrs. Rochester. You have no idea how helpful this will be. May I ask if you have found any additional information about Catherine Wentworth Brownley?

Yes. As a matter of fact, I have found that she was born in 1751 and left England in 1771. Why on earth are you so interested in her?

She is a local heroine, a great patriot during the American Revolution.

Patriot? How odd.

Why is that odd? It's true, and well-documented. She was a great woman and I think you should be very proud to have such a great ancestor!

And I think you're a bit away with the fairies.

I'm sorry, I don't understand.

Away with the fairies my dear. A little crazy.

Why would you say that?

I know nothing of her patriotism, but I do know she was a little tart. Her mother's journal reveals that she disgraced the family and was disinherited. I should think I have many ancestors to be proud of, but she is not one of them!

Disgraced the family in what way?

Got herself pregnant, by some local boy apparently. Was shipped off to the colonies to marry a man that was known to her Aunt Margaret.

Mrs. Rochester, would it be possible for me to get copies of these journal entries? It will be critical if I am to authenticate these claims.

Jane paused for a long while before answering.

I will help you if I can. I will contact you later.

Thank you so much Mrs. Rochester. You have no idea how remarkable this is.

You're very welcome. And please call me Jane.

Jane leaned back in her chair, Dudley looked up anxiously. "Oh, sorry old friend," she said to him, offering a scratch on the top of his head. "Just give me one more moment and we shall be on our way. I promise." She exhaled loudly, reached for the telephone and dialed. She was nervous. How silly! She licked at her dry lips and blinked hard.

"James," she said proudly, "it is your Aunt Jane. Would it be possible for you to come and see me today?"

CHAPTER TWENTY TWO

"We are taught that to every season there is a purpose and a time for all things unto heaven. I feel this truth most keenly on this day and pray that God will protect us all." C.W.B. 1776

Jillian stared numbly at her computer screen, hardly knowing what to say or think. Was it possible? Was it true? So many answers to so many questions all neatly tucked away in a 250-year-old journal? It was almost too good to be true, and her historian's mind warned her of the old cliché. She glanced at her watch and realized it was only just past midnight.

In the morning the Wetherton Historical Foundation would once again reconvene at 9:00 am to discuss their plan of attack. Was Jillian prepared to recommend discarding Murton's proposal to move the house in the hope that they could prove historical significance based upon the say so of an aging aristocrat in England with a journal? "Yes," she blurted out to the empty room.

Truthfully, Archibald Mack was the only man who could donate or loan them the six-figure funds necessary to cover the cost. A phone call earlier in the evening had produced nothing on that end, as the Money Mack was in Barbados and could not be immediately reached. Jillian paused, for just a moment, to reflect upon the possibility of escorting the Money Mack to Barbados. The sun, the sand, the Money Mack, how bad could it be? It didn't sound bad at all to her at the moment. There was just something so charming about Mr. Mack. She physically shook the thought from her head. with a twist left and right, then moved on with her plan.

Yes, it was possible they could arrange financing for the project, but that would take weeks and the Foundation could scarcely afford to amass more debt. Of course they would have to scrap all plans for the Catherine Wentworth Brownley Visitor's Center fundraiser that was slated for the spring. It would be positively irresponsible to proceed with those plans knowing that the Beckwith house was costing an arm and a leg. Jillian's dream pushed off again.

The only option that Jillian could pursue with any reasonable hope for success was to pin her argument squarely on the head of historical significance of note and hope that the Wetherton town council would support her assertions. Now this would be tricky business, because the Wetherton town council was an oddly aligned group of appointees hand-picked by the First Selectman. To begin with, the First Selectman, Brian Palmer, was not always a friend of the Historical Foundation. He had, on many occasions, tossed aside ideas to promote the history of Wetherton as an opportunity to generate tourist revenue, in favor of building commercial enterprises that would raise his tax stream. His eight council members generally sided with his view, so success would depend upon which way the wind was blowing.

There were three women, Hazel Harrington being the only one Jillian would estimate as a troublemaker. She was retired from her job at the State Attorney General's office in Hartford, and although her work had been administrative, Hazel viewed herself an expert in all legal matters. This had proven burdensome on a number of occasions. The other five male council members, including a retired history teacher, were a conservative bunch and all past contributors to the Wetherton Historical Foundation. That was good, Jillian thought. Although, while they preferred smaller government influence and restriction, they would also, no doubt, be salivating over the opportunity to rake in all those property taxes on a new apartment building. Yet, they were proud New England Yankees who should logically bristle at the influence of an outsider like Arnold Murton. Then again, Arnold Murton was no outsider in Hartford, but rather a man of connection at the highest state levels. For every left, there was a right. For every yin, there was a yang. This would be tricky business indeed.

A hearing would be scheduled. The burden of proving historical significance of note would rest entirely upon the Historical Foundation. Murton wouldn't even have to be present if he chose not to be, although Jillian was certain he would be there with his army of experts in tow. She glanced again at her watch. It was now nearly 1:00 am. Was she ready for the fight? She exhaled loudly and wistfully, thinking again of how lovely Barbados might be at this time of year.

Drifting off to sleep was easier than she thought. Maybe it was the remnants of the hangover, the mental fatigue of their predicament with Arnold Murton, or maybe it was exhaustion from all that dancing. She smiled. It was good to be able to laugh at yourself. It was an important point of character that most people lacked. One of her favorite Catherine Brownley quotes was "I never lose an opportunity to make myself smile." And with a smile on her face, she was asleep.

In the morning, at 9:00 am sharp, the Foundation listened with great interest to everything that Jillian had to say. They collectively beamed their enthusiasm for the wealth of new information that Jillian was bringing them. Not just because it would help their argument, but because all of them, without exception, were positively fascinated by the story that she unfolded.

"Pregnant?" Maggie said in surprise. "Who would have thought?"

"I know," Jillian replied with a shrug.

"Crazy kids," Duke added, shaking his head. "Two years ago, two hundred years ago, what are you going to do?" He threw up his hands to the sky.

"I think she must have lost the baby," Jillian surmised. "Because she speaks about losing her first son with John Brownley and says "she is prepared to lose some of her children, but not all of them."

"Yes, that's right," Maggie agreed. "I think you're right about that."

"So her parents shipped her off to the colonies, just like that?" asked Burt.

"Mrs. Rochester is going to be contacting me today, I hope, to let me know about getting copies of the journal. I think once we have that, we'll be able to learn a lot more."

"It's very important that we get that right away," Dahlia added. "It's urgent. We can't go to the Town Council telling them that this is what we've heard. We have to be able to show them the documentation."

At some point in the meeting, Hal Walker slipped out to use the men's room. It didn't occur to anyone that he had never returned. It wasn't until Burt Payne made the phone call over to town hall that someone mentioned his absence.

"What happened to Hal anyway?" Maggie asked innocently.

"I think I know the answer to that," Burt replied stonily as he reentered the room. "I'd bet you about a hundred dollars he's been calling his friend Murton." Jillian frowned her confusion. "Just got off the phone with Palmer's office," Burt went on, "seems they know all about us wanting to schedule a hearing."

"How could they know that?" Jillian asked.

"Well I don't know, but they do," Burt said.

"Hal Walker, another snake in Wetherton," Duke said quietly. Burt shook his head.

"Hal's doing what he thinks is right, just like we're doing what we think is right." Burt paused. "The goods news is, we can have our meeting. The bad news is, because of the Thanksgiving holiday and the Council's Christmas schedule, the only time they can squeeze us in is the day after tomorrow."

"No way," Jillian choked. "How can they do that? It's not fair."

"Why can't we wait until after Thanksgiving," Maggie asked.

"Because the demolition delay will expire by then," Jillian answered. Anger and frustration rose up in their voices. What could they do? How could this happen?

"It's Murton," Duke nearly shouted. "Don't you see? He got to Palmer first. He's big money here in town. Don't forget folks, the historic district is a tiny little chunk of Wetherton. This guy's bringing big money into this town. Palmer listens to big money."

"Jillian, do you think you can get those documents faxed or overnight air or something? Anything?" Burt pleaded. "We'll pay the extra charges!"

"I'll try," she said, worry lines crossing her forehead. "I'll call you later," she said, rising to leave and grabbing her jacket. She ran out the door, intending to run all the way back to her house. Well, maybe not all the way back because it was clear she would pass out from hyperventilation. She made a mental note to start running again, and performed a funny race-walk that kept her moving as fast as she could. A few people enjoying a stroll on the green couldn't help but turn to stare at her. She hardly cared. Once again, the ability to laugh at herself was coming in handy.

She flew down the street, waving at the man at number 75, but never breaking stride. He stared as she walked by, offering his customary head nod. Fumbling with the gate lock she ran up the steps and in through the front door. Patriot meowed her surprise and raced off into the kitchen.

The computer was on. That was good. Sometimes it would just shut off for no apparent reason and no one, not even the guys from the Dork Squad could explain it. They would just shake their heads and say "you seriously need to upgrade this, it's like an antique." Jillian's fingers twittered away at the keyboard, her right hand grabbing at the mouse and steering her cursor through the cyber world of international communication.

Was there a message from Lady Rochester? Please oh please oh please, Jillian drummed through her head. Looking, looking, was it there, where ...... yes! She clicked on read.

Dear Jillian,
I am pleased to let you know that I will be meeting with my nephew later today to secure the copies you have requested. He should have them in the post to you shortly. Please confirm your address. This is all very exciting. I hope you are happy with your success.
Sincerely,
Jane Rochester

"Aaargh," Jillian shouted, like a character from the Peanuts cartoons. It was horrible! What could she do? This sweet, wonderful old woman had been so helpful and that wasn't good enough? Jillian had no choice. She quickly composed an e-mail back.

Dear Mrs. Rochester,
I can't thank you enough for all your help. I am very excited about our prospects for success. Unfortunately our meeting is scheduled for the day after tomorrow. Therefore, I need to receive those documents no later than tomorrow. Would it be possible for your nephew to send them overnight or by fax? Our address and fax numbers are attached. I'm so sorry to keep asking you for more information. I simply have no other options. As always, I am grateful for your help.
Regards,
Jillian Garrett

She clicked send. And then, it happened. It hadn't happened in months, but today it happened again. Her computer just flat out shut off and died.

CHAPTER TWENTY THREE

"It is not easy to be a woman in these times. One must be determined and strong, yet gentle and feminine. And one never knows which to be on which occasions." C.W.B. 1780

Lady Jane Alexandra Wentworth Rochester fidgeted with her necklace. It was a simple gold chain that rested perfectly on her weathered collarbone. James would arrive any minute, she imagined, and she still had not decided what she would say to him. Her pride had softened greatly since their last encounter, and while she was still angry, insulted and hurt, she was also able to see the view from James' side of the argument.

"Excuse me, Mum," Liza said, entering the drawing room where Jane sat waiting. "Your nephew just rang to say he'll be here in a few minutes time."

"Thank you Liza," Jane said softly.

"Would you like some tea, Mum?"

"Yes, please," Jane answered. "That would be very nice." Her old fingers drummed nervously on the arm of her wingchair. The thin delicate skin draped the blue veins on the back of her hand like a veil. These were hands that had known decades, whether they were planting in a garden, dancing at a party or typing away on a computer. These hands were full of life.

"Hello Aunt Jane," James said quietly appearing at the door. Jane looked up with a start and felt a tear glaze over her eye. She sniffed and blinked hard.

"Well, look what the cat dragged in," Jane offered with her patent brand of Janiness. James smiled a crooked, left-sided smile. He crossed the room to come over and sit in the chair next to her, but not before he pulled it from its place by the window over close to the arm of her own chair.

"I'm so very sorry," he offered quietly, and put his own hand upon hers, closing it with a squeeze. "I would rather die than disappoint you." Jane did not speak for a long moment. Finally, she cleared her throat.

"I accept your apology," she said proudly.

"You understand," James began, but Jane raised her free hand to stop him. She did not want to discuss the matter any further. There was no need. She did understand. Of course she did. Consumed with pride and anger, she had not seen it clearly, but now she did. If anyone understood the meaning of duty and responsibility it was Jane. She had lived a lifetime of duty and responsibility, and had served the legacy of her family well.

"I need you to help me with something," she began.

"Anything, of course," James answered.

"Good," she answered, looking over at him with a smile. "You're a fine young man James. It makes me very happy to know that some day you'll inherit Broadhurst Hall."

"Aunt Jane, let's not talk of such things."

"Well, I don't suppose I'll live forever. Although I might," she winked. "Let's go into the library," she said. "I'll need to show you something on my computer."

Chapter Twenty Four

"I will always listen to two sides of an argument, but submit that only one side will suit my liking." C.W.B. 1778

The meeting room at Wetherton Town Hall was a large open space. Mismatched folding chairs from every era of government were set out in makeshift rows. At the head of the room were two large oak tables and nine places, arching across the back and around the edges to create a semi-circle for council members. Each place had a microphone, not only to project their voices across the vast space but also to record the proceedings, along with a notepad of lined paper, a glass of water and a neatly sharpened pencil.

Jillian fidgeted in her seat. The last message she had received from Lady Jane was that the documents would arrive overnight and should be delivered to Jillian no later than 10:00 am. The time was now 9:32 am and no documents had yet arrived. Jillian gulped hard. Duke leaned over and whispered into her ear.

"Relax, will you?" he implored. "Everything's going to be fine." Arnold Murton glared at their group from the opposing side of the aisle. He had brought with him, as predicted, a team of engineers, attorneys and supporters. Hal Walker sat directly behind him, but looked down at the floor and kept his eyes averted from the Foundation's collective gaze.

"Turncoat," Duke whispered as he stared at Hal. "I'll never buy a nut or a bolt or anything from that guy again."

"Will you be quiet," Jillian strained. "I'm barely keeping it together here and you're talking about hardware."

"Not a washer or a ball of twine," Duke went on. Jillian turned to glare at him, but he was so deadpan serious that when the words "ball of twine" escaped his lips she couldn't help but laugh.

"Would you please be quiet," she begged. "You're killing me. Is Dahlia going to call?"

"As soon as that package arrives."

"If it arrives," Jillian added. "If." Movement at the front of the room suggested that the council members were ready to take their seats. Jillian glanced at her watch and silently mouthed a four-letter word that rarely escaped from her lips as the hearing began. First Selectman, Brian Palmer, was the first to speak.

"Thank you ladies and gentlemen for being here today," he began. "I can see by the turnout that we have a lot of interest in this issue and we will do our best to listen to what everyone has to say before we arrive at any decision." Palmer nodded to Murton who nodded back. Glancing to his right, he also nodded to the Historical Foundation who collectively nodded back.

"What we have on the table today is a demolition delay that has been imposed on the Beckwith house."

"Murton house," Arnold Murton interrupted. "It's the Murton house now." Palmer shrugged his apology.

"Of course, forgive me," he went on, "a demolition delay on the property at 426 Main Street." Palmer shuffled his papers and peered back up at the crowd from over the top of his reading glasses. "The debate, as I understand it, is an argument of historical significance of note."

"That's correct, sir," Burt Payne answered. Murton guffawed something under his breath that sounded like "historical significance my ass". Duke glared at him through tiny squinting eyes.

"Alright then," Palmer went on. "We'll hear the argument."

"Thank you Brian," Burt Payne said, raising his thin frame and scratching at the wispy gray hair that crossed his forehead. "I'd just like to take a moment to thank the council for being here on such short notice. Al, I know your daughter's just home from college and I sure do appreciate you spending the time with us this morning." Al nodded his consent.

"For cryin' out loud," Murton muttered to his entourage. "Is this a town council meeting or a ladies' luncheon?" Some chuckles spattered the room. Burt frowned.

"I think I speak for all Wetherton when I say that the issue at hand today has a profound impact on our history and our legacy for the future." Murton rolled his eyes. Jillian fidgeted with a piece of paper in front of her. She twisted it into a miniature scroll, until it unraveled and twirled off the table landing at her feet. Glancing at the floor for a long moment, she decided it was best not to retrieve it and started work on another scroll.

"Everyone in Wetherton knows this house. This house has been standing on this property on this spot for over 250 years," Burt said. Several council members nodded their heads in agreement. "Historical significance of note is a remarkably difficult standard to prove." Murton cocked his head to the left and whispered to the enormous man next to him.

"I knew it," he whispered loudly. "They're bluffing. They don't have anything," he smiled with satisfaction.

"Still," Burt went on, "we just knew we'd find the needle in the haystack. And we did." Murton nearly spit on the elderly woman in front of him. He glared at the Historical Foundation. Brian Palmer nodded.

"Alright Burt," Palmer said. "Let's hear it." At this Jillian stopped twirling her next scroll, cast a sideways glance at the door, shook her head and mouthed another four-letter word before looking up with a smile.

"Ladies and gentlemen," Burt said, "many of you know Jillian Garrett our Director of Marketing and Special Promotions down at the Historical Foundation. She's only been in Wetherton about ten years now, but we like her anyway." The room collectively chuckled. Jillian smiled with a good-natured shrug. "She's been working 'round the clock with so many other folks trying to solve this one," Burton went on. "I think you're going to be very interested in what she has to say." The entire room silently stared at Jillian. The young, the old, the politicians and the citizens, the friendly and the hostile all looked to her for words of enlightenment. She cleared her throat for strength.

"Thank you Burt," she said, rising to her feet, "and thank you ladies and gentlemen of the council. It's a privilege and an honor to be here." She glanced again at the door and then at Duke, who offered his encouragement with a single strong nod of the head. She exhaled loudly and pressed on.

"I have worked here in Wetherton for nearly ten years. In that time, I have applied my knowledge of history, of archaeology, of detecting and researching to every home, every story and every aspect of colonial life in this place to the best of my ability." Maggie Paul nodded emphatically, along with several others, who knew this to be true and who truly appreciated Jillian's dedication. "And I have never worked on a greater puzzle than the Beckwith family legacy. Except, perhaps," she paused, "for the mysterious disappearance of the wife of Erastus Robbins." Chuckling was again heard throughout the room, with only the Murton team showing no understanding of the inside joke. Murton frowned.

"This was a tough one," she went on, "no one was more relieved than I was when we finally cracked it." The council members looked up in anticipation. Brian Palmer pulled the reading glasses from his nose.

"And what did you find?" he asked with true interest. Jillian smiled.

"We found out that Horatio Beckwith was married to a woman named Margaret Woodsmith. Margaret Woodsmith was the sister of Anne Woodsmith Wentworth." A low, but audible gasp could be heard throughout the room. Murton turned to the man on his right and whispered something in his ear.

"Anne Woodsmith Wentworth was the mother of Catherine Wentworth Brownley," Jillian said, a deafening shout of marvel and dispute filling the room around her. Brian Palmer banged his gavel to calm the crowd.

"Ladies and gentlemen, please, let us hear what this young woman has to say." Murton's attorney, a stocky man with thick black hair streaked with gray, leaned over to whisper to Murton.

"It is true," Jillian went on, "confirmed by documentation found at Broadhurst Hall in England." More astonishment passed throughout the room. Imagine that! Documents concerning their little town all the way over in England! The room was positively buzzing. Jillian glanced at the clock. It was now 10:14.

"I assume," began Murton's attorney, rising to his feet in his dark blue suit, "that Ms. Garrett has authenticated this documentation." The council turned back to Jillian.

"Well," she began, "we know that it comes to us directly from the personal library of Lady Jane Wentworth Rochester." Murton's attorney glanced sideways with a smile.

"Really?" he interrupted. "And how do we know that?" Jillian bit hard on the insides of her cheeks.

"Because she told us that it did and we have no reason not to believe that." Murton's attorney scowled.

"Young lady," he condescended, "I'm afraid a court of law is going to require a little more proof than that." Jillian again glanced at the door. "Maybe you'd like to share this documentation with us so that we can all have a look for ourselves." Jillian exhaled loudly, while Duke sprang to his feet.

"Not a chance," Duke smirked. The attorney frowned. "If you think you're going to bully us you're wrong. We don't dig your scene, baby. This isn't a courtroom, this is a town council meeting." Brian Palmer cast a look of confusion to the council member on his left. Murton's attorney smiled a look of disbelief and Maggie Paul muttered a few "oh dears" in the next row behind.

"I think we've heard enough of this," Murton's attorney began cautiously. "Unless the Historical Foundation has legally authenticated documentation as proof of this claim that we can examine for ourselves, I'll have to contend that this is mere speculation if not utter hogwash." More gasping filled the air. Jillian swallowed hard and glanced again at the door. Duke smiled his crazy, maniacal smile and glanced around the room happily. Brian Palmer banged his gavel again to quiet the room.

"Ms Garrett," he began, "what proof can you provide to this council to support your allegations?" Jillian exhaled loudly.

"Well," she began softly, "the thing is …."

"Dahlia, guiding light of my life, what took you so long?" Duke interrupted. Jillian turned to see Dahlia pushing her way through the door. She was panting and red in the face, her arms were full of packages and an eco-friendly bag stuffed with paperwork dangled from her shoulder.

"I'm sorry to be arriving late Brian," Dahlia began, addressing the council and kissing Duke on the cheek, "but I was waiting for a very important package to arrive. She turned to the door and gestured with an outstretched arm. "Wethertonians, may I present James Wentworth Cavington, all the way from England to present on our behalf." A stunned Jillian Garrett turned to stare at the doorway along with everyone else in the room. In walked James, nephew of Lady Jane Alexandra Wentworth Rochester, heir to the Broadhurst estate and the Wentworth family fortune. He smiled obligingly to the crowd, his curly brown hair swirled in a mop at his brow, his bow-tie a brilliant kelly green flecked with spots of navy. The room dropped silent.

"Hello," James nodded pleasantly, "sorry to be late." He walked forward to take a place next to Dahlia who gestured encouragement. "I am the nephew of Lady Jane Rochester," he offered to everyone, "and I bring with me the documentation I presume you have been discussing." Now the room again erupted. Murton shouted at his attorney. The attorney shouted to the council. Maggie nodded emphatically to folks on her right and on her left, speaking with highly animated eyebrows and frenzied hand waving. Hal Walker stared glumly at the Historical Foundation. Jillian Garrett gaped with a vacant stare at James who leaned over to her and shouted over the crowd.

"You must be Ms. Garrett," he said, rising with perfect manners to extend his hand. "I'm James. I know you. It's a pleasure to finally meet you."

"And you," Jillian offered quietly shaking hands.

"My Aunt Jane insisted that I should come and help you. I hope I'm not too late."

"No," Jillian answered, shaking her head, "I think you got here just in time."

Brian Palmer banged his gavel and cried for attention. Slowly the room settled to a murmur, then a hush, then silence. Palmer rubbed his face hard with his left hand and pushed his reading glasses back onto his nose. He sipped his water and glared over his microphone.

"All right now," he blustered, scanning the room for signs of anyone who would defy his authority. "Burt, who is presenting your argument today?" Burt looked around at the expectant and dedicated faces of every Historical Foundation member. Duke pointed, only somewhat inconspicuously, at James.

"Uh, well, I guess it's this young fella from England," Burt said with a smile.

"All right, young fellow from England," Brian Palmer answered, "please proceed." James smiled and nodded.

"Right," he said rising again, "thank you very much." He surveyed the room, quickly making out the hostile construction conglomerate he had been warned to expect. He nodded agreeably in their direction. "I am here today to present documentation, found in our family library at Broadhurst Hall, confirming the names and marriages of Anne Woodsmith Wentworth, Margaret Woodsmith Beckwith and Catherine Wentworth Brownley." A little rumble ensued, but Brian Palmer quickly squelched the noise with a nasty glare in the direction of the offenders.

"Before leaving England I took the liberty of having an affidavit signed by our family attorney authenticating the content and provenance of these documents." He smiled specifically at the Murton team before returning his attention to the council. "I understand that further evaluation may be required. However, I can assure you that these are genuine 18th-century documents that are entirely unaltered in any way, and they do, indeed confirm that Margaret Woodsmith Beckwith resided here in the colony of Wetherton, Connecticut with her husband Horatio from 1769 until her death in 1783." James glanced at Jillian who smiled her gratitude, before approaching Brian Palmer with copies of everything required to render his ruling.

The council passed the papers between them, marveling at the secrets they revealed. Murton glared silently at the council members before him. Several members nodded, while Palmer shrugged his shoulders in agreement.

"Ladies and gentlemen," First Selectman Palmer began, "while this matter will clearly require further investigation and debate, this council believes there is adequate proof as to the assertion of historical significance of note for the property at 426 Main Street. Until further notice, the demolition delay is upheld indefinitely until such time that this claim is proved or disproved in a court of law." He surveyed the room quickly. "Meeting adjourned." He banged his gavel for the last time.

Every member of this Historical Foundation, all 121 in attendance, jumped to their feet in celebration. One could only compare it to the day when Wetherton, 500 miles to the north of Yorktown, finally learned of the decisive battle that ended the Revolution and earned the colonies their freedom. How odd that it should be an Englishman who would deliver their victory on this day.

Arnold Murton approached them with controlled rage. "I guess you people think you're pretty damned smart don't you?" Jillian stared at him and shrugged her shoulders. "Well let me tell you something," he went on, "first of all, this isn't over. I'll appeal. You'll lose." Duke snorted and everyone turned to look directly at him.

"What?" he said defensively. Murton squinted his eyes into slits and shook his head.

"Second of all, don't think for a minute that what you did here was a good thing. You saved a rotten, broken-down piece of crap house for what? For nothing." He leaned forward for full effect. Getting in their face, some might say. Jillian stepped forward to meet him, looking Mr. Murton straight in the eye, or rather the chin, as he was really quite tall.

"We're sorry Mr. Murton, but," she paused, "we just don't see it that way." Then she smiled. A crooked half-smile. Maybe it was a smirk, but it felt like a smile. Elation filled her soul. "Come on everybody," she said turning to the Foundation members standing all around her, "let's go to the tavern. Drinks are on me." Deafening hoots and hollers filled the room.

"Jillian dear," Maggie whispered, "it's only 11:45 in the morning." Jillian frowned.

"In England, it's cocktail hour," she replied with a wink.

Chapter Twenty Five

"Never miss a moment to rejoice." C.W.B. 1780

It was long past three when the last of the Foundation members departed the tavern. Drinks had turned into lunch, and before anyone knew it, the late autumn sky was beginning to turn dim.

She was tired. More tired than any woman in her early thirties should feel, she believed. The kind of bone-tired, drop-dead exhausted that made her think once again of Barbados and a week or two on the beach with Archibald Mack.

"It would never work out," she said, turning to the portrait of Catherine Wentworth Brownley that hung before her. "I mean really, what kind of relationship would that be?" Catherine didn't answer. She just smiled. Clearly, this was a woman who knew how to make the best of any situation. What could a 21st-century woman possibly know of hardship? Jillian stared up with respect and reverence.

"Ms. Garrett," James announced from the door, "I've forgotten to give you something." Jillian looked up, drowsy with fatigue and ale.

"What's that?" she replied with a sleepy smile.

"May I?" James asked, gesturing to the chair next to her. Jillian nodded. He settled in, fumbled through the leather briefcase he carried with him and produced a manila file folder with her name on it in large black letters. She frowned her curiosity and opened the folder before her.

It was a photocopy of a letter, a beautifully handwritten letter with a date of 30 November, 1784 at the top. Jillian glanced up at James, who shrugged encouragement to read on.

Dearest Mother,

I have learned that our father, God rest his soul, has passed on to greater glory. I am heartbroken for you and your grief. I have ached for so long to reach out to you, only too painfully aware of the notion that our father would not allow any communication between us. Even now, I know not whether these words will reach you, or find their home burning in your fires.

I am a mother of eight lovely, remarkable children, three sons and five daughters. My littlest two, Judith and Deborah, both bear a striking resemblance to you. So much so that it is difficult not to think of you when I stare into their beautiful faces.

By now you know that our colonies are free from England and the King. I do not doubt that you find no joy in this news, but I am filled with hope for our future now that our future is in our own hands.

You will hear, no doubt, that I foiled an assassination attempt on the lives of our General Washington and his French ally Lt. General Rochambeau. I am proud to have served our new country, as a woman, in such a way.

I miss you dear mother, and pray for you daily. I hope that you will pray for me as well, and my husband of all these thirteen years, and our children, your grandchildren. If you can find it in your heart to respond, I would be most grateful for any word, harsh or gentle, from your loving hand.

Your obedient and loving daughter,
Catherine

Jillian touched the paper gently with her fingertips and peered up at James with misty tired eyes. She smiled appreciatively.

"Where did you get this?" she asked. James shrugged.

"In the library," he answered. "We were doing research, Aunt Jane and I, and looking through dozens of old volumes. I found this, actually, in the pages of an old book of Houbraken engravings." He smiled. "It was likely hidden, I should think, or maybe just thoughtlessly tucked in the pages. Don't know." Jillian looked again at the hand of Catherine Wentworth Brownley and smiled.

"You probably think we're all a bunch of idiots, don't you?" she asked. James frowned.

"No," he replied. "Should I?" Jillian chuckled.

"No," she retorted, scratching her head. "But Jane, your Aunt, told me she thought I was "away with the fairies" so I think she thinks I'm a fool." Jillian laughed in a self-deprecating way.

"Not at all," James assured. "She wouldn't send me across the Atlantic on a moment's notice for a fool. At least, I don't think she would." They both laughed.

Jillian caught herself staring at James' bright bow-tie, and quickly turned away. He was nothing like what she imagined he would be. She had pictured a chubby, spoiled aristocratic brat, but she found him to be quite different. The man sitting next to her was tall and thin, with wildly curly brown hair, a strong, prominent jaw and the manners and air of a perfect gentleman. He seemed very much at ease in this strange American town and fell in instantly with the locals. Of course, he stood out like a sore thumb with that bow tie, but it seemed to reveal a refreshing sense of self-confidence. Jillian fumbled with the photocopies he had given her.

"Thank you for this," Jillian said finally. "There's a certain History Professor from North Carolina who would find this very interesting. Can I send him a copy?" James shrugged.

"Of course," he said. And so she did. And when Jillian finally tucked herself into bed that night, with Patriot on her lap, she picked up the phone and dialed Archibald Mack to inform him of the day's events.

CHAPTER TWENTY SIX

"I suffer so greatly from terrible headaches. It is a pity. For now is spring and I truly love spring. It is the time for rebirth, for all things new and for great celebration." C.W.B. 1791

Maggie Paul pursed her lips into the mirror of the costume room examining her reflection. Her hair was twisted into gentle curls, her cheeks were bright and rosy and her gown a beautiful buttercream yellow with tiny pink, purple and green ribbon roses. Today Maggie would play the role of Elizabeth Becker, a woman renowned for her great beauty in 18th-century Wetherton. Maggie could scarcely contain her pleasure .

"How do I look?" she asked Jillian who sat next to her, once again dressed as Catherine Wentworth Brownley. Jillian beamed.

"Maggie, you are absolutely breathtaking." Maggie gulped.

"I'm so nervous," she said. "I never get nervous, but today, I don't know. I feel like today people will really be looking at me. Like I'm really going to stand out as someone special."

"You are," Jillian answered, "and everybody will want to have their picture taken with you." Maggie burst into giggles.

"Heavens," she glowed. "My, my."

"Check me out," Duke roared, entering the room without invitation. He wore a militia man's jacket and carried a reproduction musket. "Imagine me with a gun," he said, rolling his eyes. "I am The Duke," he winked.

"Didn't I see you on the news last night?" Maggie asked. Duke smiled and nodded.

"Can you believe it? People still remember me." It was true. Duke had been rediscovered by the media after the demolition hearing. The Duke Parker of the seventies, fighter for women's rights, had become Duke Parker of the new millennium, fighter for historic preservation.

"I'm going to be interviewed by one of the networks this afternoon," he added.

Jillian smiled.

"That's wonderful, Mr. Big Shot. But remember, this morning you're just a regular old member of the Connecticut Militia. No divas or media darlings." He saluted his understanding.

Today was a day worth celebrating and everyone in town was full of excitement and anticipation. Today would mark the groundbreaking ceremony of the Wetherton Vistor's Center. Part museum, part reception hall, part exhibition of the past and part anticipation of the future, the center would be a focal point of the town's history and a celebration of the lives of everyone who ever lived or worked or touched the town of Wetherton.

No individual or accomplishment would be singled out as the centerpiece, but rather, it would showcase the collective accomplishments of generation upon generation. Wetherton was a wonderful town with a remarkable history and a citizenry of myriad talent and ability. In their final estimation, the Wetherton Historical Foundation unanimously agreed that it was in the very ordinariness of this place and its people that the extraordinary could be found. Jillian could not be more proud of this day and this achievement. It was an entirely perfect tribute to an entire town.

"Are we ready darling?" came the slurry, southern drawl of Archibald Mack from the doorway. He was dressed in the suit of an 18th-century gentleman, probably Samuel Weston who was a prominent attorney of the day, and he too was eager to begin the ceremony.

"Mr. Mack. You look very handsome," Jillian answered.

"Thank you my dear. I do feel this suit flatters me. My compliments to the tailor." He leaned his arm

236

forward to Maggie. "You look lovely ladies. Now, my darling, are we ready?" Maggie giggled and wound her hand through his arm.

"Yes sir," she answered demurely, and they walked out together into the waiting crowds.

"Where's your date Diabolita?" Duke asked with a sinister smile. Jillian shook her head.

"You're really starting to bug me, you know that," she said. Duke snarled.

"Sorry I'm late," was the reply. It was James crashing through the door. He was dressed as a British regimental officer including a sword that dangled from his belt. He swaggered toward Jillian for full effect and it certainly worked. "I think it suits me, don't you?"

"I love it," Jillian said with a smile, rising to her feet. "I can't think of a better man for the part."

"Yes, well, I couldn't help but notice I seem to be the only Englishman within town limits. Will I be tarred and feathered or hung if effigy?" Jillian smirked.

"While that is not the plan, if I were you, I wouldn't hang around in that outfit once the punch starts flowing," she answered.

"Point well taken." He leaned over and kissed her gently on the cheek. "Shall we go?"

"We shall," Jillian answered. She was positively glowing. Was it the day, the costume or the escort? No one could be certain, but Duke strongly suspected all three. He watched them walk out, hardly able to control his patent snarl.

At Broadhurst Hall, Lady Jane Alexandra Wentworth Rochester finished typing her congratulatory e-mail to Jillian and copied it to James. She beamed her own wise, crooked smile toward her computer screen.

"There aren't many things you can get past a wise old cow," she said to no one in particular. "No one will be pulling the wool over these eyes when it comes to love," she smiled, looking up at the black and white photo of a newly-wedded Lord Arthur and his Lady Jane. She sniffed away a tear and exhaled loudly.

"Now, let's see what "THECOLONEL" is up to today." She typed away at her computer, hoping for a post from him. Ah, yes, here he was, punctual as always. He was such a delight.

On a computer, nearly 6,000 miles away, a young boy of thirteen sat typing at his keyboard. His mother called out to him in Japanese.

"Get off that computer right now and do your homework," she said.

"Yes, yes, I will," he answered her while typing his final post.

I must go now for much business awaits my attention and I have a great many obligations. I will speak with you tomorrow good friends.
THECOLONEL.

THE END

BROWNLEY PUNCH

(Adapted from colonial recipes of New England and Virginia)

1 gallon apple cider
1 liter ginger ale
3 cups orange juice
3 cinnamon sticks broken
6 cloves
1 tsp grated nutmeg
5th dark rum
Fresh orange and lemon slices

Combine ingredients into large punch bowl. May be served warm, room temperature or chilled. Serves 24.